MURDER
IN
MIDWINTER

MURDER IN MIDWINTER

TEN CLASSIC CRIME STORIES FOR CHRISTMAS

Edited by Cecily Gayford

Dorothy L. Sayers · Cyril Hare
Nicholas Olde · Ruth Rendell
Margery Allingham · Arthur Conan Doyle
Edward D. Hoch · Anthony Berkeley
Ellis Peters · John Mortimer

P

PROFILE BOOKS

First published in Great Britain in 2020 by
PROFILE BOOKS LTD
29 Cloth Fair
London EC1A 7JQ
www.profilebooks.com

1 3 5 7 9 10 8 6 4 2

Typeset in Fournier by MacGuru Ltd
Printed and bound in Great Britain by
CPI Group (UK) Ltd, Croydon CR0 4YY

A CIP catalogue record for this book is available from the British Library.

ISBN 978 1 78816 614 0
eISBN 978 1 78816 615 7

Contents

The Queen's Square

Dorothy L. Sayers

'You Jack o' Di'monds, you Jack o' Di'monds,' said Mark
Sambourne, shaking a reproachful head, 'I know you of old.'
He rummaged beneath the white satin of his costume, pan-
elled with gigantic oblongs and spotted to represent a set of
dominoes. 'Hang this fancy rig! Where the blazes has the
fellow put my pockets? You rob my pocket, yes, you rob-a
my pocket, you rob my pocket of silver and go-ho-hold.
How much do you make it?' He extracted a fountain pen
and a chequebook.

'Five-seventeen-six,' said Lord Peter Wimsey. 'That's
right, isn't it, partner?' His huge blue-and-scarlet sleeves
rustled as he turned to Lady Hermione Creethorpe, who,
in her Queen of Clubs costume, looked a very redoubtable
virgin, as, indeed, she was.

'Quite right,' said the old lady, 'and I consider that very
cheap.'

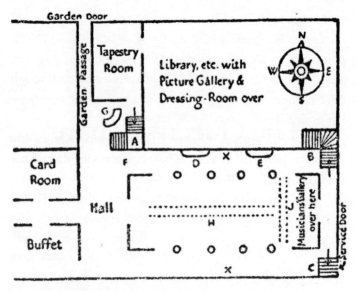

PLAN OF THE BALLROOM *A*, Stair to Dressing-room and Gallery; *B*, Stair to Gallery; *C*, Stair to Musicians' Gallery only; *D*, Settee where Joan Carstairs sat; *E*, Settee where Jim Playfair sat; *F*, Where Waits stood; *G*, Where Ephraim Dodd sat; *H*, Guests' 'Sir Roger'; *J*, Servants' 'Sir Roger'; *XX*, Hanging Lanterns; *O O O O*, Arcading.

'We haven't been playing long,' said Wimsey apologetically.

'It would have been more, Auntie,' observed Mrs Wrayburn, 'if you hadn't been greedy. You shouldn't have doubled those four spades of mine.'

Lady Hermione snorted, and Wimsey hastily cut in:

'It's a pity we've got to stop, but Deverill will never forgive us if we're not there to dance Sir Roger. He feels strongly about it. What's the time? Twenty past one. Sir Roger is timed to start sharp at half past. I suppose we'd better tootle back to the ballroom.'

'I suppose we had,' agreed Mrs Wrayburn. She stood up, displaying her dress, boldly patterned with the red and black points of a backgammon board. 'It's very good of you,' she added, as Lady Hermione's voluminous skirts swept through the hall ahead of them, 'to chuck your dancing to give Auntie her bridge. She does so hate to miss it.'

'Not at all,' replied Wimsey. 'It's a pleasure. And in any case I was jolly glad of a rest. These costumes are dashed hot for dancing in.'

'You make a splendid Jack of Diamonds, though. Such a good idea of Lady Deverill's, to make everybody come as a game. It cuts out all those wearisome pierrots and columbines.' They skirted the south-west angle of the ballroom and emerged into the south corridor, lit by a great hanging lantern in four lurid colours. Under the arcading they paused and stood watching the floor, where Sir Charles Deverill's guests were fox-trotting to a lively tune discoursed by the band in the musicians' gallery at the far end. 'Hullo, Giles!' added Mrs Wrayburn, 'you look hot.'

'I am hot,' said Giles Pomfret. 'I wish to goodness I hadn't been so clever about this infernal costume. It's a beautiful billiard table, but I can't sit down in it.' He mopped his heated brow, crowned with an elegant green lamp shade. 'The only rest I can get is to hitch my behind on a radiator, and as they're all in full blast, it's not very cooling. Thank goodness, I can always make these damned sandwich boards an excuse to get out of dancing.' He propped himself against the nearest column, looking martyred.

'Nina Hartford comes off best,' said Mrs Wrayburn. 'Water polo – so sensible – just a bathing dress and a ball;

3

though I must say it would look better on a less *Restoration* figure. Your playing cards are much the prettiest, and I think the chess pieces run you close. There goes Gerda Bellingham, dancing with her husband – isn't she *too* marvellous in that red wig? And the bustle and everything – my dear, so attractive. I'm glad they didn't make themselves too Lewis Carroll; Charmian Grayle is the sweetest White Queen – where is she, by the way?'

'I don't like that young woman,' said Lady Hermione; 'she's fast.'

'Dear lady!'

'I've no doubt you think me old-fashioned. Well, I'm glad I am. I say she's fast, and, what's more, heartless. I was watching her before supper, and I'm sorry for Tony Lee. She's been flirting as hard as she can go with Harry Vibart – not to give it a worse name – and she's got Jim Playfair on a string, too. She can't even leave Frank Bellingham alone, though she's staying in his house.'

'Oh, I say, Lady H!' protested Sambourne, 'you're a bit hard on Miss Grayle. I mean, she's an awfully sporting kid and all that.'

'I detest that word "sporting",' snapped Lady Hermione. 'Nowadays it merely means drunk and disorderly. And she's not such a kid either, young man. In three years' time she'll be a hag, if she goes on at this rate.'

'Dear Lady Hermione,' said Wimsey, 'we can't all be untouched by time, like you.'

'You could,' retorted the old lady, 'if you looked after your stomachs and your morals. Here comes Frank Bellingham

— looking for a drink, no doubt. Young people today seem to be positively pickled in gin.'

The foxtrot had come to an end, and the Red King was threading his way towards them through a group of applauding couples.

'Hullo, Bellingham!' said Wimsey. 'Your crown's crooked. Allow me.' He set wig and headdress to rights with skilful fingers. 'Not that I blame you. What crown is safe in these Bolshevik days?'

'Thanks,' said Bellingham. 'I say, I want a drink.'

'What did I tell you?' said Lady Hermione.

'Buzz along, then, old man,' said Wimsey. 'You've got four minutes. Mind you turn up in time for Sir Roger.'

'Right you are. Oh, I'm dancing it with Gerda, by the way. If you see her, you might tell her where I've gone to.'

'We will. Lady Hermione, you're honouring me, of course?'

'Nonsense! You're not expecting me to dance at my age? The Old Maid ought to be a wallflower.'

'Nothing of the sort. If only I'd had the luck to be born earlier, you and I should have appeared side by side, as Matrimony. Of course you're going to dance it with me — unless you mean to throw me over for one of these youngsters.'

'I've no use for youngsters,' said Lady Hermione. 'No guts. Spindle-shanks.' She darted a swift glance at Wimsey's scarlet hose. 'You at least have some suggestion of calves. I can stand up with you without blushing for you.'

Wimsey bowed his scarlet cap and curled wig in deep reverence over the gnarled knuckles extended to him.

'You make me the happiest of men. We'll show them all

how to do it. Right hand, left hand, both hands across, back to back, round you go and up the middle. There's Deverill going down to tell the band to begin. Punctual old bird, isn't he? Just two minutes to go ... What's the matter, Miss Carstairs? Lost your partner?'

'Yes – have you seen Tony Lee anywhere?'

'The White King? Not a sign. Nor the White Queen either. I expect they're together somewhere.'

'Probably. Poor old Jimmie Playfair is sitting patiently in the north corridor, looking like Casabianca.'

'You'd better go along and console him,' said Wimsey, laughing.

Joan Carstairs made a face and disappeared in the direction of the buffet, just as Sir Charles Deverill, giver of the party, bustled up to Wimsey and his companions, resplendent in a Chinese costume patterned with red and green dragons, bamboos, circles and characters, and carrying on his shoulder a stuffed bird with an enormous tail.

'Now, now,' he exclaimed, 'come along, come along, come along! All ready for Sir Roger. Got your partner, Wimsey? Ah, yes, Lady Hermione – splendid. You must come and stand next to your dear mother and me, Wimsey. Don't be late, don't be late. We want to dance it right through. The waits will begin at two o'clock – I hope they will arrive in good time. Dear me, dear me! Why aren't the servants in yet? I told Watson – I must go and speak to him.'

He darted away, and Wimsey, laughing, led his partner up to the top of the room, where his mother, the Dowager Duchess of Denver, stood waiting, magnificent as the Queen of Spades.

'Ah! here you are,' said the Duchess placidly. 'Dear Sir Charles – he was getting quite flustered. Such a man for punctuality – he ought to have been a Royalty. A delightful party, Hermione, isn't it? Sir Roger and the waits – quite medieval – and a Yule-log in the hall, with the steam-radiators and everything – so oppressive!'

'Tumty, tumty, tiddledy, tumty, tumty, tiddledy,' sang Lord Peter, as the band broke into the old tune. 'I do adore this music. Foot it featly here and there – oh! there's Gerda Bellingham. Just a moment! Mrs Bellingham – hi! your royal spouse awaits your Red Majesty's pleasure in the buffet. Do hurry him up. He's only got half a minute.'

The Red Queen smiled at him, her pale face and black eyes startlingly brilliant beneath her scarlet wig and crown.

'I'll bring him up to scratch all right,' she said, and passed on, laughing.

'So she will,' said the Dowager. 'You'll see that young man in the Cabinet before very long. Such a handsome couple on a public platform, and very sound, I'm told, about pigs, and that's so important, the British breakfast table being what it is.'

Sir Charles Deverill, looking a trifle heated, came hurrying back and took his place at the head of the double line of guests, which now extended three-quarters of the way down the ballroom. At the lower end, just in front of the musicians' gallery, the staff had filed in, to form a second Sir Roger, at right angles to the main set. The clock chimed the half-hour. Sir Charles, craning an anxious neck, counted the dancers.

'Eighteen couples. We're two couples short. How vexatious! Who are missing?'

'The Bellinghams?' said Wimsey. 'No, they're here. It's the White King and Queen, Badminton and Diabolo.'

'There's Badminton!' cried Mrs Wrayburn, signalling frantically across the room. 'Jim! Jim! Bother! He's gone back again. He's waiting for Charmian Grayle.'

'Well, we can't wait any longer,' said Sir Charles peevishly. 'Duchess, will you lead off?'

The Dowager obediently threw her black velvet train over her arm and skipped away down the centre, displaying an uncommonly neat pair of scarlet ankles. The two lines of dancers, breaking into the hop-and-skip step of the country dance, jigged sympathetically. Below them, the cross lines of black and white and livery coats followed their example with respect. Sir Charles Deverill, dancing solemnly down after the Duchess, joined hands with Nina Hartford from the far end of the line. Tumty, tumty, tiddledy, tumty, tumty, tiddledy ... the first couple turned outward and led the dancers down. Wimsey, catching the hand of Lady Hermione, stooped with her beneath the arch and came triumphantly up to the top of the room, in a magnificent rustle of silk and satin. 'My love,' sighed Wimsey, 'was clad in the black velvet, and I myself in cramoisie.' The old lady, well pleased, rapped him over the knuckles with her gilt sceptre. Hands clapped merrily.

'Down we go again,' said Wimsey, and the Queen of Clubs and Emperor of the great Mahjongg dynasty twirled and capered in the centre. The Queen of Spades danced up to meet her Jack of Diamonds. 'Bézique,' said Wimsey; 'double Bézique,' as he gave both his hands to the Dowager. Tumty, tumty, tiddledy. He again gave his hand to the Queen of

8

Clubs and led her down. Under their lifted arms the other seventeen couples passed. Then Lady Deverill and her partner followed them down – then five more couples.

'We're working nicely to time,' said Sir Charles, with his eye on the clock. 'I worked it out at two minutes per couple. Ah! here's one of the missing pairs.' He waved an agitated arm. 'Come into the centre – come along – in here.'

A man whose head was decorated with a huge shuttlecock, and Joan Carstairs, dressed as a Diabolo, had emerged from the north corridor. Sir Charles, like a fussy rooster with two frightened hens, guided and pushed them into place between two couples who had not yet done their 'hands across', and heaved a sigh of relief. It would have worried him to see them miss their turn. The clock chimed a quarter to two.

'I say, Playfair, have you seen Charmian Grayle or Tony Lee anywhere about?' asked Giles Pomfret of the Badminton costume. 'Sir Charles is quite upset because we aren't complete.'

'Not a sign of 'em. I was supposed to be dancing this with Charmian, but she vanished upstairs and hasn't come down again. Then Joan came barging along looking for Tony, and we thought we'd better see it through together.'

'Here are the waits coming in,' broke in Joan Carstairs. 'Aren't they sweet? Too-too-truly-rural!'

Between the columns on the north side of the ballroom the waits could be seen filing into place in the corridor, under the command of the Vicar. Sir Roger jigged on his exhausting way. Hands across. Down the centre and up again. Giles Pomfret, groaning, scrambled in his sandwich boards beneath the lengthening arch of hands for the fifteenth time. Tumty, tiddledy. The nineteenth couple wove their way through the dance. Once again, Sir Charles and the Dowager Duchess, both as fresh as paint, stood at the top of the room. The clapping was loudly renewed; the orchestra fell silent; the guests broke up into groups; the servants arranged themselves in a neat line at the lower end of the room; the clock struck two; and the Vicar, receiving a signal from Sir Charles, held his tuning-fork to his ear and gave forth a sonorous A. The waits burst shrilly into the opening bars of 'Good King Wenceslas'.

It was just as the night was growing darker and the wind blowing stronger that a figure came thrusting its way through the ranks of the singers, and hurried across to where Sir Charles stood; Tony Lee, with his face as white as his costume.

'Charmian … in the tapestry room … dead … strangled.'

Superintendent Johnson sat in the library, taking down the evidence of the haggard revellers, who were ushered in upon him one by one. First, Tony Lee, his haunted eyes like dark hollows in a mask of grey paper.

'Miss Grayle had promised to dance with me the last dance before Sir Roger; it was a foxtrot. I waited for her in the passage under the musicians' gallery. She never came. I did not search for her. I did not see her dancing with anyone else. When the dance was nearly over, I went out into the garden, by way of the service door under the musicians' stair. I stayed in the garden till Sir Roger de Coverley was over …'

'Was anybody with you, sir?'

'No, nobody.'

'You stayed alone in the garden from – yes, from 1.20 to past 2 o'clock. Rather disagreeable, was it not, sir, with the snow on the ground?' The Superintendent glanced keenly from Tony's stained and sodden white shoes to his strained face.

'I didn't notice. The room was hot – I wanted air. I saw the waits arrive at about 1.40 – I daresay they saw me. I came in a little after 2 o'clock ...'

'By the service door again, sir?'

'No; by the garden door on the other side of the house, at the end of the passage which runs along beside the tapestry room. I heard singing going on in the ballroom and saw two men sitting in the little recess at the foot of the staircase on the left-hand side of the passage. I think one of them was the gardener. I went into the tapestry room ...'

'With any particular purpose in mind, sir?'

'No – except that I wasn't keen on rejoining the party. I wanted to be quiet.' He paused; the Superintendent said nothing. 'Then I went into the tapestry room. The light was out. I switched it on and saw – Miss Grayle. She was lying close against the radiator. I thought she had fainted. I went over to her and found she was – dead. I only waited long enough to be sure, and then I went into the ballroom and gave the alarm.'

'Thank you, sir. Now, may I ask, what were your relations with Miss Grayle?'

'I – I admired her very much.'

'Engaged to her, sir?'

'No, not exactly.'

11

'No quarrel – misunderstanding – anything of that sort?'

'Oh, no!'

Superintendent Johnson looked at him again, and again said nothing, but his experienced mind informed him:

'He's lying.'

Aloud he only thanked and dismissed Tony. The White King stumbled drearily out, and the Red King took his place.

'Miss Grayle,' said Frank Bellingham, 'is a friend of my wife and myself; she was staying at our house. Mr Lee is also our guest. We all came in one party. I believe there was some kind of understanding between Miss Grayle and Mr Lee – no actual engagement. She was a very bright, lively, popular girl. I have known her for about six years, and my wife has known her since our marriage. I know of no one who could have borne a grudge against Miss Grayle. I danced with her the last dance but two – it was a waltz. After that came a foxtrot and then Sir Roger. She left me at the end of the waltz; I think she said she was going upstairs to tidy. I think she went out by the door at the upper end of the ballroom. I never saw her again. The ladies' dressing-room is on the second floor, next door to the picture-gallery. You reach it by the staircase that goes up from the garden passage. You have to pass the door of the tapestry room to get there. The only other way to the dressing-room is by the stair at the east end of the ballroom, which goes up to the picture-gallery. You would then have to pass through the picture-gallery to get to the dressing-room. I know the house well; my wife and I have often stayed here.'

Next came Lady Hermione, whose evidence, delivered at great length, amounted to this:

'Charmian Grayle was a minx and no loss to anybody. I am not surprised that someone has strangled her. Women like that ought to be strangled. I would cheerfully have strangled her myself. She has been making Tony Lee's life a burden to him for the last six weeks. I saw her flirting with Mr Vibart tonight on purpose to make Mr Lee jealous. She made eyes at Mr Bellingham and Mr Playfair. She made eyes at everybody. I should think at least half a dozen people had very good reason to wish her dead.'

Mr Vibart, who arrived dressed in a gaudy Polo costume, and still ludicrously clutching a hobby-horse, said that he had danced several times that evening with Miss Grayle. She was a damn sportin' girl, rattlin' good fun. Well, a bit hot, perhaps, but, dash it all, the poor kid was dead. He might have kissed her once or twice, perhaps, but no harm in that. Well, perhaps poor old Lee did take it a bit hard. Miss Grayle liked pulling Tony's leg. He himself had liked Miss Grayle and was dashed cut-up about the whole beastly business.

Mrs Bellingham confirmed her husband's evidence. Miss Grayle had been their guest, and they were all on the very best of terms. She felt sure that Mr Lee and Miss Grayle had been very fond of one another. She had not seen Miss Grayle during the last three dances, but had attached no importance to that. If she had thought about it at all, she would have supposed Miss Grayle was sitting out with somebody. She herself had not been up to the dressing-room since about midnight, and had not seen Miss Grayle go upstairs. She had first missed Miss Grayle when they all stood up for Sir Roger.

Mrs Wrayburn mentioned that she had seen Miss Carstairs in the ballroom looking for Mr Lee, just as Sir

Charles Deverill went down to speak to the band. Miss Carstairs had then mentioned that Mr Playfair was in the north corridor, waiting for Miss Grayle. She could say for certain that the time was then 1.28. She had seen Mr Playfair himself at 1.30. He had looked in from the corridor and gone out again. The whole party had then been standing up together, except Miss Grayle, Miss Carstairs, Mr Lee and Mr Playfair. She knew that, because Sir Charles had counted the couples.

Then came Jim Playfair, with a most valuable piece of evidence.

'Miss Grayle was engaged to me for Sir Roger de Coverley. I went to wait for her in the north corridor as soon as the previous dance was over. That was at 1.25. I sat on the settee in the eastern half of the corridor. I saw Sir Charles go down to speak to the band. Almost immediately afterwards, I saw Miss Grayle come out of the passage under the musicians' gallery and go up the stairs at the end of the corridor. I called out: "Hurry up! they're just going to begin." I do not think she heard me; she did not reply. I am quite sure I saw her. The staircase has open banisters. There is no light in that corner except from the swinging lantern in the corridor, but that is very powerful. I could not be mistaken in the costume. I waited for Miss Grayle till the dance was half over; then I gave it up and joined forces with Miss Carstairs, who had also mislaid her partner.'

The maid in attendance on the dressing-room was next examined. She and the gardener were the only two servants who had not danced Sir Roger. She had not quitted the dressing-room at any time since supper, except that she might

14

have gone as far as the door. Miss Grayle had certainly not entered the dressing-room during the last hour of the dance.

The Vicar, much worried and distressed, said that his party had arrived by the garden door at 1.40. He had noticed a man in a white costume smoking a cigarette in the garden. The waits had removed their outer clothing in the garden passage and then gone out to take up their position in the north corridor. Nobody had passed them till Mr Lee had come in with his sad news.

Mr Ephraim Dodd, the sexton, made an important addition to this evidence. This aged gentleman was, as he confessed, no singer, but was accustomed to go round with the waits to carry the lantern and collecting box. He had taken a seat in the garden passage 'to rest me pore feet'. He had seen the gentleman come in from the garden 'all in white with a crown on 'is 'ead'. The choir were then singing 'Bring me flesh and bring me wine'. The gentleman had looked about a bit, 'made a face, like', and gone into the room at the foot of the stairs. He hadn't been absent 'more nor a minute', when he 'come out faster than he gone in', and had rushed immediately into the ballroom.

In addition to all this, there was, of course, the evidence of Dr Pattison. He was a guest at the dance, and had hastened to view the body of Miss Grayle as soon as the alarm was given. He was of opinion that she had been brutally strangled by someone standing in front of her. She was a tall, strong girl, and he thought it would have needed a man's strength to overpower her. When he saw her at five minutes past two he concluded that she must have been killed within the last hour, but not within the last five minutes or so. The body was still quite warm, but, since it had fallen close to the hot radiator, they could not rely very much upon that indication.

Superintendent Johnson rubbed a thoughtful ear and turned to Lord Peter Wimsey, who had been able to confirm much of the previous evidence and, in particular, the exact times at which various incidents had occurred. The Superintendent knew Wimsey well, and made no bones about taking him into his confidence.

'You see how it stands, my lord. If the poor young lady was killed when Dr Pattison says, it narrows it down a good bit. She was last seen dancing with Mr Bellingham at – call it 1.20. At 2 o'clock she was dead. That gives us forty minutes. But if we're to believe Mr Playfair, it narrows it down still further. He says he saw her alive just after Sir Charles went down to speak to the band, which you put at 1.28. That means that there's only five people who could possibly have done it, because all the rest were in the ballroom after that, dancing Sir Roger. There's the maid in the dressing-room; between you and me, sir, I think we can leave her out. She's a little slip of a thing, and it's not clear what motive she could have had. Besides, I've known her from a child, and she isn't the sort to do it. Then there's the gardener; I haven't seen him yet, but there again, he's a man I know well, and I'd as soon suspect myself. Well now, there's this Mr Tony Lee, Miss Carstairs, and Mr Playfair himself. The girl's the least probable, for physical reasons, and besides, strangling isn't a woman's crime – not as a rule. But Mr Lee – that's a queer story, if you like. What was he doing all that time out in the garden by himself?'

'It sounds to me,' said Wimsey, 'as if Miss Grayle had

16

given him the push and he had gone into the garden to eat worms.'

'Exactly, my lord; and that's where his motive might come in.'

'So it might,' said Wimsey, 'but look here. There's a couple of inches of snow on the ground. If you can confirm the time at which he went out, you ought to be able to see, from his tracks, whether he came in again before Ephraim Dodd saw him. Also, where he went in the interval and whether he was alone.'

'That's a good idea, my lord. I'll send my sergeant to make inquiries.'

'Then there's Mr Bellingham. Suppose he killed her after the end of his waltz with her. Did anyone see him in the interval between that and the foxtrot?'

'Quite, my lord. I've thought of that. But you see where *that* leads. It means that Mr Playfair must have been in a conspiracy with him to do it. And from all we hear, that doesn't seem likely.'

'No more it does. In fact, I happen to know that Mr Bellingham and Mr Playfair were not on the best of terms. You can wash that out.'

'I think so, my lord. And that brings us to Mr Playfair. It's him we're relying on for the time. We haven't found anyone who saw Miss Grayle during the dance before his – that was the foxtrot. What was to prevent him doing it then? Wait a bit. What does he say himself? Says he danced the foxtrot with the Duchess of Denver.' The Superintendent's face fell, and he hunted through his notes again. 'She confirms that. Says she was with him during the interval and danced the whole dance with him. Well, my lord, I suppose we can take Her Grace's word for it.'

'I think you can,' said Wimsey, smiling. 'I've known my mother practically since my birth, and have always found her very reliable.'

'Yes, my lord. Well, that brings us to the end of the foxtrot. After that, Miss Carstairs saw Mr Playfair waiting in the north corridor. She says she noticed him several times during the interval and spoke to him. And Mrs Wrayburn saw him there at 1.30 or thereabouts. Then at 1.45 he and Miss Carstairs came and joined the company. Now, is there anyone who can check all these points? That's the next thing we've got to see to.'

Within a very few minutes, abundant confirmation was forthcoming. Mervyn Bunter, Lord Peter's personal man, said that he had been helping to take refreshments along to the buffet. Throughout the interval between the waltz and the foxtrot, Mr Lee had been standing by the service door beneath the musicians' stair, and halfway through the foxtrot he had been seen to go out into the garden by way of the servants' hall. The police sergeant had examined the tracks in the snow and found that Mr Lee had not been joined by any other person, and that there was only the one set of his footprints, leaving the house by the servants' hall and returning by the garden door near the tapestry room. Several persons were also found who had seen Mr Bellingham in the interval between the waltz and the foxtrot, and who were able to say that he had danced the foxtrot through with Mrs Bellingham. Joan Carstairs had also been seen continuously throughout the waltz and the foxtrot, and during the following interval and the beginning of Sir Roger. Moreover, the servants who had danced at the lower end of the room were positive that from 1.29 to 1.45 Mr Playfair had sat continuously on the settee in the north corridor, except for the few seconds during which he had glanced into the ballroom. They were also certain that during that time no one had gone up the staircase at the lower end of the corridor, while Mr Dodd was equally positive that, after 1.40, nobody except Mr Lee had entered the garden passage or the tapestry room.

Finally, the circle was closed by William Hoggarty, the gardener. He asserted with the most obvious sincerity that from 1.30 to 1.40 he had been stationed in the garden passage to receive the waits and marshal them to their places. During that time, no one had come down the stair from the picture-gallery or entered the tapestry room. From 1.40 onwards, he had sat beside Mr Dodd in the passage and nobody had passed him except Mr Lee.

These points being settled, there was no further reason to doubt Jim Playfair's evidence, since his partners were able to prove his whereabouts during the waltz, the foxtrot and the intervening interval. At 1.28 or just after, he had seen Charmian Grayle alive. At 2.02 she had been found dead in the tapestry room. During that interval, no one had been seen to enter the room, and every person had been accounted for.

At 6 o'clock, the exhausted guests had been allowed to go to their rooms, accommodation being provided in the house for those who, like the Bellinghams, had come from a distance, since the Superintendent had announced his intention of interrogating them all afresh later in the day.

This new inquiry produced no result. Lord Peter Wimsey did not take part in it. He and Bunter (who was an expert photographer) occupied themselves in photographing the ballroom and adjacent rooms and corridors from every imaginable point of view, for, as Lord Peter said, 'You never know what may turn out to be relevant.' Late in the afternoon they retired together to the cellar, where with dishes, chemicals and safelight hastily procured from the local chemist, they proceeded to develop the plates.

'That's the lot, my lord,' observed Bunter at length, sloshing the final plate in the water and tipping it into the hypo. 'You can switch the light on now, my lord.'

Wimsey did so, blinking in the sudden white glare.

'A very hefty bit of work,' said he. 'Hullo! What's that plateful of blood you've got there?'

'That's the red backing they put on these plates, my lord, to obviate halation. You may have observed me washing it off before inserting the plate in the developing-dish. Halation, my lord, is a phenomenon …'

Wimsey was not attending.

'But why didn't I notice it before?' he demanded. 'That stuff looked to me exactly like clear water.'

'So it would, my lord, in the red safelight. The appearance of whiteness is produced,' added Bunter sententiously, 'by the reflection of *all* the available light. When all the available light is red, red and white are, naturally, indistinguishable. Similarly, in a green light …'

'Good God!' said Wimsey. 'Wait a moment, Bunter, I must think this out … Here! damn those plates – let them be. I want you upstairs.'

He led the way at a canter to the ballroom, dark now, with the windows in the south corridor already curtained and only the dimness of the December evening filtering through the high windows of the clerestory above the arcading. He first turned on the three great chandeliers in the ballroom itself. Owing to the heavy oak panelling that rose to the roof at both ends and all four angles of the room, these threw no light at all upon the staircase at the lower end of the north corridor. Next, he turned on the light in the four-sided hanging lantern, which hung in the north corridor above and between the two settees. A vivid shaft of green light immediately flooded the lower half of the corridor and the staircase; the upper half was bathed in strong amber, while the remaining sides of the lantern showed red towards the ballroom and blue towards the corridor wall.

Wimsey shook his head.

'Not much room for error there. Unless – I know! Run, Bunter, and ask Miss Carstairs and Mr Playfair to come here a moment.'

While Bunter was gone, Wimsey borrowed a stepladder from the kitchen and carefully examined the fixing of the lantern. It was a temporary affair, the lantern being supported by a hook screwed into a beam and lit by means of a flex run from the socket of a permanent fixture at a little distance.

'Now, you two,' said Wimsey, when the two guests arrived, 'I want to make a little experiment. Will you sit down on this settee, Playfair, as you did last night. And you, Miss Carstairs – I picked you out to help because you're wearing a white dress. Will you go up the stairs at the end of the corridor as Miss Grayle did last night. I want to know whether it looks the same to Playfair as it did then – bar all the other people, of course.'

He watched them as they carried out this manoeuvre. Jim Playfair looked puzzled.

'It doesn't seem quite the same, somehow. I don't know what the difference is, but there is a difference.'

Joan, returning, agreed with him.

'I was sitting on that other settee part of the time,' she said, 'and it looks different to me. I think it's darker.'

'Lighter,' said Jim.

'Good!' said Wimsey. 'That's what I wanted you to say. Now, Bunter, swing that lantern through a quarter-turn to the left.'

The moment this was done, Joan gave a little cry.

'That's it! That's it! The blue light! I remember thinking how frosty-faced those poor waits looked as they came in.'

'And you, Playfair?'

'That's right,' said Jim, satisfied. 'The light was red last night. *I* remember thinking how warm and cosy it looked.'

Wimsey laughed.

'We're on to it, Bunter. What's the chessboard rule? *The Queen stands on a square of her own colour.* Find the maid who looked after the dressing-room, and ask her whether Mrs Bellingham was there last night between the foxtrot and Sir Roger.'

In five minutes Bunter was back with his report.

'The maid says, my lord, that Mrs Bellingham did not come into the dressing-room at that time. But she saw her come out of the picture-gallery and run downstairs towards the tapestry room just as the band struck up Sir Roger.'

'And that,' said Wimsey, 'was at 1.29.'

'Mrs Bellingham?' said Jim. 'But you said you saw her yourself in the ballroom before 1.30. She couldn't have had time to commit the murder.'

'No, she couldn't,' said Wimsey. 'But Charmian Grayle was dead long before that. It was the Red Queen, not the White, you saw upon the staircase. Find out why Mrs Bellingham lied about her movements, and then we shall know the truth.'

'A very sad affair, my lord,' said Superintendent Johnson, some hours later. 'Mr Bellingham came across with it like a gentleman as soon as we told him we had evidence against his wife. It appears that Miss Grayle knew certain facts about him which would have been very damaging to his political career. She'd been getting money out of him for years. Earlier in the evening she surprised him by making fresh demands. During the last waltz they had together, they went into the tapestry room and a quarrel took place. He lost his temper and laid hands on her. He says he never meant to hurt her seriously, but she started to scream and he took hold of her throat to silence her and – sort of accidentally – throttled her. When he found what he'd done, he left her there and came away, feeling, as he says, all of a daze. He had the next dance with his wife. He told her what had happened, and then discovered that he'd left the little sceptre affair he was carrying in the room with the body. Mrs Bellingham – she's a brave woman – undertook to fetch it back. She slipped through the dark passage under the musicians' gallery – which was empty – and up the stair to the picture-gallery. She did not hear Mr Playfair speak to her. She ran through the gallery and down the other stair, secured the sceptre and hid it under her own dress. Later, she heard from Mr Playfair about what he saw, and realised that in the red light he had mistaken her for the White Queen. In the early hours of this morning, she slipped downstairs and managed to get the lantern shifted round. Of course, she's an accessory after the fact, but she's the kind of wife a man would like to have. I hope they let her off light.'

'Amen!' said Lord Peter Wimsey.

Sister Bessie

Cyril Hare

At Christmas-time we gladly greet
    Each old familiar face.
At Christmas time we hope to meet
    At th' old familiar place.
Five hundred loving greetings, dear,
    From you to me
To welcome in the glad New Year
    I look to see!

Hilda Trent turned the Christmas card over with her carefully manicured fingers as she read the idiotic lines aloud.

'Did you ever hear anything so completely palsied?' she asked her husband. 'I wonder who on earth they can get to write the stuff. Timothy, do you know anybody called Leech?'

'Leech?'

'Yes – that's what it says: "From your old Leech." Must be a friend of yours. The only Leech I ever knew spelt her name with an a and this one has two e's.' She looked at the envelope. 'Yes, it was addressed to you. Who is the old Leech?' She flicked the card across the breakfast table.

Timothy stared hard at the rhyme and the scrawled message beneath it.

'I haven't the least idea,' he said slowly.

As he spoke he was taking in, with a sense of cold misery, the fact that the printed message on the card had been neatly altered by hand. The word 'Five' was in ink. The original, poet no doubt, had been content with 'A hundred loving greetings'.

'Put it on the mantelpiece with the others,' said his wife. 'There's a nice paunchy robin on the outside.'

'Damn it, no!' In a sudden access of rage he tore the card in two and flung the pieces into the fire.

It was silly of him, he reflected as he travelled up to the City half an hour later, to break out in that way in front of Hilda; but she would put it down to the nervous strain about which she was always pestering him to take medical advice. Not for all the gold in the Bank of England could he have stood the sight of that damnable jingle on his dining-room mantelpiece. The insolence of it! The cool, calculated devilry! All the way to London the train wheels beat out the maddening rhythm:

'At Christmas-time we gladly greet …'

And he had thought that the last payment had seen the end of it. He had returned from James's funeral triumphant in the certain belief that he had attended the burial of the blood-sucker who called himself 'Leech'. But he was wrong, it seemed.

'Five hundred loving greetings, dear ... '

Five hundred! Last year it had been three, and that had been bad enough. It had meant selling out some holdings at an awkward moment. And now five hundred, with the market in its present state! How in the name of all that was horrible was he going to raise the money?

He would raise it, of course. He would have to. The sickening, familiar routine would be gone through again. The cash in Treasury notes would be packed in an unobtrusive parcel and left in the cloakroom at Waterloo. Next day he would park his car as usual in the railway yard at his local station. Beneath the windscreen wiper – 'the old familiar place' – would be tucked the cloakroom ticket. When he came down again from work in the evening the ticket would be gone. And that would be that – till next time. It was the way that Leech preferred it and he had no option but to comply.

The one certain thing that Trent knew about the identity of his blackmailer was that he – or could it be she? – was a member of his family. His family! Thank heaven, they were no true kindred of his. So far as he knew he had no blood relation alive. But 'his' family they had been, ever since, when he was a tiny, ailing boy, his father had married the gentle, ineffective Mary Grigson, with her long trail of soft, useless children. And when the influenza epidemic of 1919 carried off John Trent he had been left to be brought up as one of that clinging, grasping clan. He had got on in the world, made money, married money, but he had never got away from the 'Grigsons'. Save for his stepmother, to whom he grudgingly acknowledged that he owed his start in life, how he loathed them all! But 'his' family they remained, expecting to be treated with brotherly affection, demanding his presence at family reunions, especially at Christmas-time.

'At Christmas-time we hope to meet …'

He put down his paper unread and stared forlornly out of the carriage window. It was at Christmas-time, four years before, that the whole thing started – at his stepmother's Christmas Eve party, just such a boring family function as the one he would have to attend in a few days' time. There had been some silly games to amuse the children – Blind Man's Buff and Musical Chairs – and in the course of them his wallet must have slipped from his pocket. He discovered the loss next morning, went round to the house and retrieved it. But when it came into his hands again there was one item missing from its contents. Just one. A letter, quite short and explicit, signed in a name that had about then become fairly notorious in connection with an unsavoury enquiry into certain large-scale dealings in government securities. How he could have been fool enough to keep it a moment longer than was necessary! … but it was no good going back on that.

And then the messages from Leech had begun. Leech had the letter. Leech considered it his duty to send it to the principal of Trent's firm, who was also Trent's father-in-law. But, meanwhile, Leech was a trifle short of money, and for a small consideration ... So it had begun, and so, year in and year out, it had gone on.

He had been so sure that it was James! That seedy, unsuccessful stock-jobber, with his gambling debts and his inordinate thirst for whisky, had seemed the very stuff of which blackmailers are made. But he had got rid of James last February, and here was Leech again, hungrier than ever. Trent shifted uneasily in his seat. 'Got rid of him' was hardly the right way to put it. One must be fair to oneself. He had merely assisted James to get rid of his worthless self. He had done no more than ask James to dinner at his club, fill him up with whisky and leave him to drive home on a foggy night with the roads treacherous with frost. There had been an unfortunate incident on the Kingston bypass, and that was the end of James – and, incidentally, of two perfect strangers who had happened to be on the road at the same time. Forget it! The point was that the dinner – and the whisky – had been a dead loss. He would not make the same mistake again. This Christmas Eve he intended to make sure who his persecutor was. Once he knew, there would be no half measures.

Revelation came to him midway through Mrs John Trent's party – at the very moment, in fact, when the presents were being distributed from the Christmas tree, when the room was bathed in the soft radiance of coloured candles and noisy with the 'Oohs!' and 'Ahs!' of excited children and with the rustle of hastily unfolded paper parcels. It was so simple, and so unexpected, that he could have laughed aloud. Appropriately enough, it was his own contribution to the party that was responsible. For some time past it had been his unwritten duty, as the prosperous member of the family, to present his stepmother with some delicacy to help out the straitened resources of her house in providing a feast worthy of the occasion. This year, his gift had taken the form of half a dozen bottles of champagne – part of a consignment which he suspected of being corked. That champagne, acting on a head unused to anything stronger than lemonade, was enough to loosen Bessie's tongue for one fatal instant.

Bessie! Of all people, faded, spinsterish Bessie! Bessie, with her woolwork and her charities – Bessie with her large, stupid, appealing eyes and her air of frustration, that put you in mind of a bud frosted just before it could come into flower! And yet, when you came to think of it, it was natural enough. Probably, of all the Grigson tribe, he disliked her the most. He felt for her all the loathing one must naturally feel for a person one has treated badly; and he had been simple enough to believe that she did not resent it.

She was just his own age, and from the moment that he had been introduced into the family had constituted herself his protector against the unkindness of his elder stepbrother. She had been, in her revoltingly sentimental phrase, his 'own special sister'. As they grew up, the roles were reversed, and she became his protégée, the admiring spectator of his early struggles. Then it had become pretty clear that she and everybody else expected him to marry her. He had considered the idea quite seriously for some time. She was pretty enough in those days, and, as the phrase went, worshipped the ground he trod on. But he had had the good sense to see in time that he must look elsewhere if he wanted to make his way in the world. His engagement to Hilda had been a blow to Bessie. Her old-maidish look and her absorption in good works dated from then. But she had been sweetly forgiving – to all appearances. Now, as he stood there under the mistletoe, with a ridiculous paper cap on his head, he marvelled how he could have been so easily deceived. As though, after all, anyone could have written that Christmas card but a woman!

Bessie was smiling at him still – smiling with the confidential air of the mildly tipsy, her upturned shiny nose glowing pink in the candle-light. She had assumed a slightly puzzled expression, as though trying to recollect what she had said. Timothy smiled back and raised his glass to her. He was stone-cold sober, and he could remind her of her words when the occasion arose.

'My present for you, Timothy, is in the post. You'll get it tomorrow, I expect. I thought you'd like a change from those horrid Christmas cards!'

And the words had been accompanied with an unmistakable wink.

'Uncle Timothy!' One of James's bouncing girls jumped up at him and gave him a smacking kiss. He put her down with a grin and tickled her ribs as he did so. He suddenly felt light-hearted and on good terms with all the world – one woman excepted. He moved away from the mistletoe and strolled round the room, exchanging pleasantries with all the family. He could look them in the face now without a qualm. He clicked glasses with Roger, the prematurely aged, overworked GP. No need to worry now whether his money was going in that direction! He slapped Peter on the back and endured patiently five minutes' confidential chat on the difficulties of the motor-car business in these days. To Marjorie, James's widow, looking wan and ever so brave in her made-over black frock, he spoke just the right words of blended sympathy and cheer. He even found in his pockets some half-crowns for his great, hulking step-nephews. Then he was standing by his stepmother near the fireplace, whence she presided quietly over the noisy, cheerful scene, beaming gentle good nature from her faded blue eyes.

'A delightful evening,' he said, and meant it.

'Thanks to you, Timothy, in great part,' she replied. 'You have always been so good to us.'

Wonderful what a little doubtful champagne would do! He would have given a lot to see her face if he were to say: 'I suppose you are not aware that your youngest daughter, who is just now pulling a cracker with that ugly little boy of Peter's, is blackmailing me and that I shortly intend to stop her mouth for good?'

He turned away. What a gang they all were! What a shabby, out-at-elbows gang! Not a decently cut suit or a well-turned-out woman among the lot of them! And he had imagined that his money had been going to support some of them! Why, they all simply reeked of honest poverty! He could see it now. Bessie explained everything. It was typical of her twisted mind to wring cash from him by threats and give it all away in charities.

'You have always been so good to us.' Come to think of it, his stepmother was worth the whole of the rest put together. She must be hard put to it, keeping up Father's old house, with precious little coming in from her children. Perhaps one day, when his money was really his own again, he might see his way to do something for her … But there was a lot to do before he could indulge in extravagant fancies like that.

Hilda was coming across the room towards him. Her elegance made an agreeable contrast to the get-up of the Grigson women. She looked tired and rather bored, which was not unusual for her at parties at this house.

'Timothy,' she murmured, 'can't we get out of here? My head feels like a ton of bricks, and if I'm going to be fit for anything tomorrow morning …'

Timothy cut her short.

'You go home straight away, darling,' he said. 'I can see that it's high time you were in bed. Take the car. I can walk – it's a fine evening. Don't wait up for me.'

'You're not coming? I thought you said …'

'No. I shall have to stay and see the party through. There's a little matter of family business I'd better dispose of while I have the chance.'

Hilda looked at him in slightly amused surprise.

'Well, if you feel that way,' she said. 'You seem to be very devoted to your family all of a sudden. You'd better keep an eye on Bessie while you are about it. She's had about as much as she can carry.'

Hilda was right. Bessie was decidedly merry. And Timothy continued to keep an eye on her. Thanks to his attentions, by the end of the evening, when Christmas Day had been seen in and the guests were fumbling for their wraps, she had reached a stage when she could barely stand. 'Another glass,' thought Timothy from the depths of his experience, 'and she'll pass right out.'

'I'll give you a lift home, Bessie,' said Roger, looking at her with a professional eye. 'We can just squeeze you in.'

'Oh, nonsense, Roger!' Bessie giggled. 'I can manage perfectly well. As if I couldn't walk as far as the end of the drive!'

'I'll look after her,' said Timothy heartily. 'I'm walking myself, and we can guide each other's wandering footsteps home. Where's your coat, Bessie? Are you sure you've got all your precious presents?'

He prolonged his leave-taking until all the rest had gone, then helped Bessie into her worn fur coat and stepped out of the house, supporting her with an affectionate right arm. It was all going to be too deliciously simple.

Bessie lived in the lodge of the old house. She preferred to be independent, and the arrangement suited everyone, especially since James after one of his reverses on the turf had brought his family to live with his mother to save expense. It suited Timothy admirably now. Tenderly he escorted her to the end of the drive, tenderly he assisted her to insert her latchkey in the door, tenderly he supported her into the little sitting-room that gave out of the hall.

There Bessie considerately saved him an enormous amount of trouble and a possibly unpleasant scene. As he put her down upon the sofa she finally succumbed to the champagne. Her eyes closed, her mouth opened and she lay like a log where he had placed her.

Timothy was genuinely relieved. He was prepared to go to any lengths to rid himself from the menace of blackmail, but if he could lay his hands on the damning letter without physical violence he would be well satisfied. It would be open to him to take it out of Bessie in other ways later on. He looked quickly round the room. He knew its contents by heart. It had hardly changed at all since the day when Bessie first furnished her own room when she left school. The same old battered desk stood in the corner, where from the earliest days she had kept her treasures. He flung it open, and a flood of bills, receipts, charitable appeals and yet more charitable appeals came cascading out. One after another, he went through the drawers with ever-increasing urgency, but still failed to find what he sought. Finally he came upon a small inner drawer which resisted his attempts to open it. He tugged at it in vain, and then seized the poker from the fireplace and burst the flimsy lock by main force. Then he dragged the drawer from its place and settled himself to examine its contents.

It was crammed as full as it could hold with papers. At the very top was the programme of a May Week Ball for his last year at Cambridge. Then there were snapshots, press-cuttings – an account of his own wedding among them – and, for the rest, piles of letters, all in his handwriting. The wretched woman seemed to have hoarded every scrap he had ever written to her. As he turned them over, some of the phrases he had used in them floated into his mind, and he began to apprehend for the first time what the depth of her resentment must have been when he threw her over.

But where the devil did she keep the only letter that mattered?

As he straightened himself from the desk he heard close behind him a hideous, choking sound. He spun round quickly. Bessie was standing behind him, her face a mask of horror. Her mouth was wide open in dismay. She drew a long shuddering breath. In another moment she was going to scream at the top of her voice …

Timothy's pent-up fury could be contained no longer. With all his force he drove his fist full into that gaping, foolish face. Bessie went down as though she had been shot and her head struck the leg of a table with the crack of a dry stick broken in two. She did not move again.

Although it was quiet enough in the room after that, he never heard his stepmother come in. Perhaps it was the sound of his own pulses drumming in his ears that had deafened him. He did not even know how long she had been there. Certainly it was long enough for her to take in everything that was to be seen there, for her voice, when she spoke, was perfectly under control.

'You have killed Bessie,' she said. It was a calm statement of fact rather than an accusation.

He nodded, speechless.

'But you have not found the letter.'

He shook his head.

'Didn't you understand what she told you this evening? The letter is in the post. It was her Christmas present to you. Poor, simple, loving Bessie!'

He stared at her, aghast.

'It was only just now that I found that it was missing from my jewel-case,' she went on, still in the same flat, quiet voice. 'I don't know how she found out about it, but love – even a crazy love like hers – gives people a strange insight sometimes.'

He licked his dry lips.

'Then you were Leech?' he faltered.

'Of course. Who else? How otherwise do you think I could have kept the house open and my children out of debt on my income? No, Timothy, don't come any nearer. You are not going to commit two murders tonight. I don't think you have the nerve in any case, but to be on the safe side I have brought the little pistol your father gave me when he came out of the army in 1918. Sit down.'

He found himself crouching on the sofa, looking helplessly up into her pitiless old face. The body that had been Bessie lay between them.

'Bessie's heart was very weak,' she said reflectively. 'Roger had been worried about it for some time. If I have a word with him, I daresay he will see his way to issue a death certificate. It will, of course, be a little expensive. Shall we say a thousand pounds this year instead of five hundred? You would prefer that, Timothy, I dare say, to – the alternative?'

Once more Timothy nodded in silence.

'Very well. I shall speak to Roger in the morning – after you have returned me Bessie's Christmas present. I shall require that for future use. You can go now, Timothy.'

The Invisible Weapon

Nicholas Olde

Before the snow had time to melt the great frost was upon us; and, in a few days, every pond and dyke was covered with half a foot of ice.

Hern and I were spending a week in a village in Lincolnshire, and, at the sight of the frozen fen, we sent to Peterborough for skates in keen anticipation of some happy days upon the ice.

'And now,' said Hern, 'as our skates will not be here until tomorrow, we had better take this opportunity of going to see Grumby Castle. I had not intended to go until later in the week, but, as neither of us wants to lose a day's skating, let us take advantage of Lord Grumby's permission immediately. The castle, as I told you, is being thoroughly overhauled to be ready for his occupation in the spring.'

Thus it was that, that same morning, we turned our backs upon the fen and trudged through the powdery snow into the undulating country towards the west until at last we came within sight of that historic pile and passed through the lodge gates and up the stately avenue. When we reached the great entrance door Hern took out Lord Grumby's letter to show to the caretaker – but it was not a caretaker that opened to our knock. It was a policeman.

The policeman looked at the letter and shook his head.

'I'll ask the inspector anyhow,' he said, and disappeared with the letter in his hand.

The inspector arrived on the doorstep a minute later.

'You are not Mr Rowland Hern, the detective, are you?' he asked.

'The same, inspector,' said Hern. 'I didn't know that I was known so far afield.'

'Good gracious, yes!' said the inspector. 'We've all heard of you. There's nothing strange in that. But that you should be here this morning is a very strange coincidence indeed.'

'Why so?' asked Hern.

'Because,' said the inspector, 'there is a problem to be solved in this castle that is just after your own heart. A most mysterious thing has happened here. Please come inside.'

We followed him through a vestibule littered with builders' paraphernalia and he led us up the wide stairway.

'A murder has been committed in this castle – not two hours since,' said the inspector. 'There is only one man who could have done it – and he could not have done it.'

'It certainly does seem to be a bit of a puzzle when put like that,' said Hern. 'Are you sure that it is not a riddle, like "When is a door not a door?"'

We had reached the top of the stairs.

'I will tell you the whole story from start to – well, to the present moment,' said the inspector. 'You see this door on the left? It is the door of the ante-room to the great ballroom; and the ante-room is vital to this mystery for two reasons. In the first place, it is, for the time being, absolutely the only way by which the ballroom can be entered. The door at the other end has been bricked up in accordance with his lordship's scheme of reconstruction, and the proposed new doorway has not yet been knocked through the wall: (that is one occasion when a door is not a door),' he added with a smile; 'and even the fireplaces have been removed and the chimneys blocked since a new heating system has rendered them superfluous. In the second place,' he continued, 'the work in the ballroom itself being practically finished, this ante-room has been, for the time being, appropriated as an office by the contractors. Consequently it is occupied all day by draughtsmen and clerks and others, and no one can enter or leave the ballroom during office hours unseen.

'Among other alterations and improvements that have been carried out is, as I have said, the installation of a heating apparatus; and there appears to have been a good deal of trouble over this.

'It has been installed by a local engineer named Henry Whelk, and the working of it under tests has been so unsatis-factory that his lordship insisted, some time since, on calling in a consulting engineer, a man named Blanco Persimmon.

'Henry Whelk has, from the first, very much resented the "interference", as he calls it, of this man; and the relations between the two have been, for some weeks, strained almost to the breaking-point.

'A few days ago the contractor received a letter from Mr Persimmon saying that he would be here this morning and would make a further test of the apparatus. He asked them to inform Whelk and to see to the firing of the boiler.

'Persimmon arrived first and went into the ballroom to inspect the radiators. He was there, talking to one of the clerks, when Whelk arrived and the clerk returned at once to the ante-room and shut the ballroom door behind him.

'Five minutes later Whelk came out and told the clerks to have the cock turned on that allows the hot water to circulate in that branch of the system, and to see that the ballroom door was not opened until Mr Persimmon came out, as he was going to test the temperature. He spoke with his usual resentment of the consultant and told the clerks that the latter had imagined that he could see a crack in one of the radiators which he thought would leak under pressure, and that that was his real reason for having the ballroom branch of the heating system connected up.

'In the meantime he took a seat in the ante-room with the intention of waiting there to hear Persimmon's report when he came out. Mr Hern,' said the inspector gravely, 'Persimmon never did come out.'

'Do you mean that he is still there?' asked Hern.

'He is still there,' said the inspector. 'He will be there until the ambulance comes to take him to the mortuary.'

'Has a doctor seen the body?' asked Hern.

'Yes,' said the inspector. 'He left five minutes before you came. He went by a field path, so you did not meet him in the avenue.

'Persimmon died of a fracture at the base of the skull

caused by a violent blow delivered with some very heavy weapon. But we cannot find any weapon at all.

'Of course the clerks detained Whelk when, Persimmon failing to appear, they discovered the body. They kept Whelk here until our arrival, and he is now detained at the police station. We have searched him, at his own suggestion; but nothing heavier than a cigarette-holder was found upon his person.'

'What about his boots?' asked Hern.

'Well, he has shoes on,' said the inspector, 'and very light shoes too – unusually light for snowy weather. They could not possibly have struck the terrible blow that broke poor Persimmon's skull and smashed the flesh to a pulp. Whelk had an attaché-case too. I have it here still, and it contains nothing but papers.'

'I suppose,' said Hern, 'that you have made sure that there is no weapon concealed about the body of Persimmon?'

'Yes,' said the inspector. 'I considered that possibility and have made quite sure.'

'Could not a weapon have been thrown out of one of the windows?' asked Hern.

'It could have been,' answered the inspector, 'but it wasn't. That is certain because no one could open them without leaving finger-marks. The insides of the sashes have only just been painted, and the paint is still wet; while the hooks for lifting them have not yet been fixed.

'I have examined every inch of every sash systematically and thoroughly, and no finger has touched them. They are very heavy sashes too, and it would require considerable force to raise them without the hooks. No. It is a puzzle. And, although I feel that I must detain him, I cannot believe that Whelk can be the culprit. Would a guilty man wait there, actually abusing his victim before witnesses, until his crime was discovered? Impossible! Again, could he have inflicted that ghastly wound with a cigarette-holder? Quite impossible! But then the whole thing is quite impossible from beginning to end.'

'May I go into the ballroom?' said Hern.

'Certainly,' said the inspector.

He led the way through the ante-room, where three or four scared clerks were simulating industry at desks and drawing-boards, and we entered the great ballroom.

'Here is poor Persimmon's body,' said the inspector; and we saw the sprawling corpse, with its terribly battered skull, face down, upon the floor near one of the radiators.

'So the radiator did leak after all,' said Hern, pointing to a pool of water beside it.

'Yes,' said the inspector. 'But it does not seem to have leaked since I had the apparatus disconnected. The room was like an oven when I came in.'

Hern went all round the great bare hall examining everything – floor, walls and windows. Then he looked closely at the radiators.

'There is no part of these that he could detach?' he asked. 'No pipes or valves?'

'Certainly not, unless he had a wrench,' said the inspector; 'and he hadn't got a wrench.'

'Could anyone have come through the windows from outside?' asked Hern.

'They could be reached by a ladder,' said the inspector;

'but the snow beneath them is untrodden.'

'Well,' said Hern; 'there doesn't seem to be anything here to help us. May I have a look at Whelk's case and papers?'

'Certainly,' said the inspector. 'Come into the ante-room. I've locked them in a cupboard.'

We followed him and he fetched a fair-sized attaché-case, laid it on a table and opened it.

Hern took out the papers and examined the inside of the case.

'A botanical specimen!' he exclaimed, picking up a tiny blade of grass. 'Did he carry botanical specimens about in his case? It seems a bit damp inside,' he added; 'especially at the side furthest from the handle. But let's have a look at the papers. Hullo! What's this?'

'It seems to be nothing but some notes for his business diary,' said the inspector.

Feb. 12. Letter from Jones. Mr Filbert called *re* estimate.
Feb. 13. Office closed.
Feb. 14. Letter from Perkins & Fisher *re* Grumby Castle.
Feb. 15. Letter from Smith & Co. Wrote Messrs. Caraway *re* repairs to boiler. Visit Grumby Castle and meet Persimmon 10.30 A.M.

'February the 15th is today.'

'Yes,' said Hern. 'The ink seems to have run a bit, doesn't it? Whereabouts does Whelk live?'

'He lives in Market Grumby,' said the inspector. His house is not far from where he is now – the police-station. Market Grumby lies over there – north of the castle. That footpath that goes off at right angles from the avenue leads to the Market Grumby road.'

Hern put everything back carefully into the case – even the blade of grass – and handed it back to the inspector.

'When do you expect the ambulance?' he asked.

'It should be here in a few minutes,' said the inspector. 'I must wait, of course, until it comes.'

'Well,' said Hern. 'I suppose, when the body has gone, there will be no harm in mopping up that mess in there? There is a certain amount of blood as well as that pool of water.'

'No harm at all,' said the inspector.

'Well then,' said Hern. 'Please have it done. And, if it is not asking too much, could you oblige me by having the hot water turned on once more and waiting until I come back. I shall not be away for long; and I think that it may help in the solution of your problem.'

'Certainly,' said the inspector.

Hern and I went out again into the snowy drive and found, without difficulty, the path that led towards Market Grumby, for, in spite of the covering snow, it was clearly marked by footprints.

We walked along until we saw the opening into the road. A cottage stood on one side of the path, close to the road; and on the other side was a pond.

This was covered, like every pond, with a thick covering of ice, but in one spot, opposite the cottage, the ice had been broken with a pick and here an old man was dipping a bucket.

The water in the hole looked black against the gleaming ice and the sun glinted on the edges of the fragments loosened and thrown aside by the pick.

'Took a bit of trouble to break it, I expect,' said Hern to the old man.

'Took me half an hour,' grumbled the old fellow; 'it's that thick.'

'Is that the way to Market Grumby?' asked Hern, pointing to the road.

'That's it,' said the other, and went into the cottage with his bucket.

The snow in the few yards between the cottage and the hole in the ice was trodden hard by the hobnailed boots of the old man, but Hern pointed out to me that another set of footprints, of a much less bucolic type, could be seen beside them.

'Let us go back,' he said, 'and see how the inspector is getting on with the heating apparatus.'

'I've had it on for half an hour now,' said the inspector when we got back to the ante-room. 'The ambulance came soon after you went out.'

'Well,' said Hern. 'Let us see how that leak is going on'; and he opened the door of the ballroom.

'Good heavens,' cried the inspector. 'It's not leaking now.'

'It never did leak,' said Hern.

'What is the meaning of it all?' asked the inspector.

'You remember,' said Hern, 'that you came to the conclusion that if Whelk had been guilty he would have got away before his crime had been discovered.

'Well, my conclusion is different. In fact, I think that, if he had been innocent, he would not have waited.'

'Why so?' asked the inspector.

'I will tell you,' said Hern. 'Whelk had to stay or he would certainly have been hanged. He hated Persimmon and had every reason for *taking* his life. If he had gone away you would have said that he had hidden the weapon that killed Persimmon.

'Don't you see that his only chance was to stay until you had searched him and found that he had no weapon? Was not that a clear proof of his innocence?'

'But there must have been some weapon,' exclaimed the worried inspector. 'Where is the weapon?'

'There was a weapon,' said Hern, 'and you and I saw it lying beside the corpse.'

'I saw no weapon,' said the inspector.

'Do you remember,' said Hern, 'that your first account of the problem made me think of a certain old riddle? Well, the answer to this problem is the answer to a new riddle: "When is a weapon not a weapon?"'

'I give it up,' said the inspector promptly.

'The answer to that riddle,' said Hern, 'is "when it melts".'

The inspector gasped.

'I will tell you,' said Hern, 'what happened. There is a pond close to the Market Grumby road, and Whelk passed this as he was coming here this morning to meet his enemy. The thick ice on that pond has been broken so that a bucket may be dipped, and chunks of broken ice lie all around the hole. Whelk saw these, and a terrible thought came into his wicked head. Everything fitted perfectly. He had found a weapon that would do its foul work and disappear. He picked up the biggest block of ice that would go inside his case. I dare say that it weighed twenty pounds. He waited until his enemy stooped to examine a radiator, and then he opened his case and brought down his twenty-pound sledge-hammer on the victim's skull.

'Then he put his weapon against the radiator, had the heat turned on, told his story about a leak, and waited calmly until a search should prove his innocence.

'But by the very quality for which he chose his weapon, that weapon has betrayed him in the end. For that jagged chunk of ice began to melt before its time – very slightly, it is true, but just enough to damp the side of the case on which it rested, to make the ink run on his papers and to set loose one tiny blade of grass that had frozen on to it as it lay beside the pond. A very tiny blade but big enough to slay the murderer.

'If you will go to the pond, inspector, you will find footsteps leading to it which are not the cottager's footsteps; and, if you compare them with the shoes that Henry Whelk is wearing, you will find that they tally.

'And, if they do not tally, then you may ask your friends a new riddle.'

'What is that?' asked the officer.

'"When is a detective not a detective?"' replied my friend; 'and the answer will be "When he is Rowland Hern."'

Paintbox Place

Ruth Rendell

Elderly ladies as detectives are not unknown in fiction. Avice Julian could think of two or three, the creations of celebrated authors, and no doubt there were more. It would seem that the quiet routine of an old woman's life, her penchant for gossip and knitting and her curiosity, born of boredom, provide a suitable climate for the consideration of motive and the assessment of clues. In fiction, that is. Would it, Mrs Julian sometimes wondered, also be true in reality?

She took a personal interest. She was eighty-four years old, thin, sharp-witted, arthritic, cantankerous and intolerant. Most of her time she spent sitting in an upright chair in the bay window of her drawing room in her very large house, observing what her neighbours got up to. From the elderly ladies of mystery fiction, though, she differed in one important respect. They were spinsters, she was a widow. In fact, she had been twice married and twice widowed. Could that, she asked herself after reading a particularly apposite detective novel, be of significance? Could it affect the deductive powers and it be her spinsterhood which made Miss Marple, say, a detective of genius? Perhaps. Anthropologists say (Mrs Julian was an erudite person) that in ancient societies maidenhood was revered as having awesome and unique powers. It might be that this was true and that prolonged virginity, though in many respects disagreeable, only serves to enhance them. Possibly, one day, she would have an opportunity to put to the test the Aged Female Sleuth Theory. She saw enough from her window, sitting there knitting herself a twinset in dark blue two-ply. Mostly she eyed the block of houses opposite, on the other side of broad, tree-lined Abelard Avenue.

There were six of them, all joined together, all exactly the same. They all had three storeys, plate-glass windows, a bit of concrete to put the car on, a flowerbed, an outside cupboard to put parcels in and an outside cupboard to put the rubbish sack in. Mrs Julian thought that unhygienic. She had an old-fashioned dustbin, though she had to keep a black plastic bag inside it if she wanted Northway Borough Council to collect her rubbish.

The houses had been built on the site of an old mansion. There had been several such in Abelard Avenue, as well as big houses like Mrs Julian's which were not quite mansions. Most of these had been pulled down and those which remained converted into flats. They would do that to hers when she was gone, thought Mrs Julian, those nephews and nieces and great-nephews and great-nieces of hers would do that. She had watched the houses opposite being built.

About ten years ago it had been. She called them the paint-box houses because there was something about them that reminded her of a child's drawing and because each had its front door painted a different colour, yellow, red, blue, lime, orange and chocolate.

'It's called Paragon Place,' said Mrs Upton, her cleaner and general help, when the building was completed.

'What a ridiculous name! Paintbox Place would be far more suitable.'

Mrs Upton ignored this as she ignored all of Avice Julian's remarks which she regarded as 'showing off', affected or just plain senile. 'They do say,' she said, 'that the next thing'll be they'll start building on that bit of waste ground next door.'

'Waste ground?' said Mrs Julian distantly. 'Can you possibly mean the wood?'

'Waste ground' had certainly been a misnomer, though 'wood' was an exaggeration. It was a couple of rustic acres, more or less covered with trees of which part of one side bordered Mrs Julian's garden, part the Great North Road, and which had its narrow frontage on Abelard Avenue. People used the path through it as a short cut from the station. At Mrs Upton's unwelcome forebodings, Avice Julian had got up and gone to the right-hand side of the bay window which overlooked the 'wood' and thought how disagreeable it would be to have another Paintbox Place on her back door-step. In these days when society seemed to have gone mad, when the cost of living was frightening, when there were endless strikes and she was asked to pay 98 per cent income tax on the interest on some of her investments, it was quite possible, anything could happen.

However, no houses were built next door to Mrs Julian. It appeared that the 'wood', though hardly National Trust or an Area of Outstanding Natural Beauty, was nevertheless scheduled as 'not for residential development'. For her lifetime, it seemed, she would look out on birch trees and green turf and small hawthorn bushes – when she was not, that is, looking out on the inhabitants of Paintbox Place, on Mr and Mrs Arnold and Mr Laindon and the Nicholsons, all young people, none of them much over forty. Their activities were of absorbing interest to Mrs Julian as she knitted away in dark blue two-ply, and a source too of disapproval and sometimes outright condemnation.

After Christmas, in the depths of the winter, when Mrs Julian was in the kitchen watching Mrs Upton peeling potatoes for lunch, Mrs Upton said: 'You're lucky I'm private, have you thought of that?'

This was beyond Mrs Julian's understanding. 'I beg your pardon?'

'I mean it's lucky for you I'm not one of those council home helps. They're all coming out on strike, the lot of them coming out. They're NUPE, see? Don't you read your paper?'

Mrs Julian certainly did read her paper, the *Daily Telegraph*, which was delivered to her door each morning. She read it from cover to cover after she had had her breakfast, and she was well aware that the National Union of Public Employees was making rumbling noises and threatening to bring its members out over a pay increase. It was typical, in her view, of the age in which she found herself living. Someone or other was always on strike. But she had very little idea of how to identify the Public Employee and had hoped the threatened action would not affect her. To Mrs Upton she said as much.

'Not affect you?' said Mrs Upton, furiously scalping brussels sprouts. She seemed to find Mrs Julian's innocence uproariously funny. 'Well, there'll be no gritters on the roads for a start and maybe you've noticed it's snowing again. Gritters are NUPE. They'll have to close the schools so there'll be kids all over the streets. School caretakers are NUPE. No ambulances if you fall on the ice and break your leg, no hospital porters, and what's more, no dustmen. We won't none of us get our rubbish collected on account of dustmen are NUPE. So how about that for not affecting you?'

Mrs Julian's dustbin, kept just inside the front gate on a concrete slab and concealed from view by a laurel bush and a cotoneaster, was not emptied that week. On the following Monday she looked out of the right-hand side of the bay window and saw under the birch trees, on the frosty ground, a dozen or so black plastic sacks, apparently filled with rubbish, their tops secured with wire fasteners. There was no end to the propensities of some people for making disgusting litter, thought Mrs Julian, give them half a chance. She would telephone Northway Council, she would telephone the police. But first she would put on her squirrel coat and take her stick and go out and have a good look.

The snow had melted, the pavement was wet. A car had pulled up and a young woman in jeans and a pair of those silly boots that came up to the thighs like in a pantomime was taking two more black plastic sacks out of the back of it. Mrs Julian was on the point of telling her in no uncertain terms to remove her rubbish at once, when she caught sight of a notice stuck up under the trees. The notice was of plywood with printing on it in red chalk: *Northway Council Refuse Tip. Bags This Way.*

Mrs Julian went back into her house. She told Mrs Upton about the refuse tip and Mrs Upton said she already knew but hadn't told Mrs Julian because it would only upset her.

'You don't know what the world's coming to, do you?' said Mrs Upton, opening a tin of peaches for lunch.

'I most certainly do know,' said Mrs Julian. 'Anarchy. Anarchy is what it is coming to.'

Throughout the week the refuse on the tip mounted. Fortunately, the weather was very cold; as yet there was no smell. In Paintbox Place black plastic sacks of rubbish began to appear outside the cupboard doors, on the steps beside the coloured front doors, overflowing into the narrow flower-beds. Mrs Upton came five days a week but not on Saturdays or Sundays. When the doorbell rang at ten on Saturday morning Mrs Julian answered it herself and there outside was Mr Arnold from the house with the red front door, behind him on the gravel drive a wheelbarrow containing five black plastic sacks of rubbish.

He was a good-looking, cheerful, polite man was Mr Arnold. Forty-two or three, she supposed. Sometimes she fancied she had seen a melancholy look in his eyes. No wonder, she could well understand if he was melancholic. He said good morning, and he was on his way to the tip with his rubbish and Mr Laindon's and could he take hers too?

'That's very kind and thoughtful of you, Mr Arnold,' said

Mrs Julian. 'You'll find my bag inside the dustbin at the gate. I do appreciate it.'

'No trouble,' said Mr Arnold. 'I'll make a point of collecting your bag, shall I, while the strike lasts?'

Mrs Julian thought. A plan was forming in her mind. 'That won't be necessary, Mr Arnold. I shall be disposing of my waste by other means. Composting, burning,' she said, 'beating tins flat, that kind of thing. Now if everyone were to do the same ...'

'Ah, life's too short for that, Mrs Julian,' said Mr Arnold and he smiled and went off with his wheelbarrow before she could say what was on the tip of her tongue, that it was shorter for her than for most people.

She watched him take her sack out of the dustbin and trundle his barrow up the slope and along the path between the wet black mounds. Poor man. Many an evening, when Mr Arnold was working late, she had seen the chocolate front door open and young Mr Laindon, divorced, they said, just before he came there, emerge and tap at the red front door and be admitted. Once she had seen Mrs Arnold and Mr Laindon coming back from the station together, taking the short cut through the 'wood'. They had been enjoying each other's company and laughing, though it had been cold and quite late, all of ten at night. And here was Mr Arnold performing kindly little services for Mr Laindon, all innocent of how he was deceived. Or perhaps he was not quite innocent, not ignorant and that accounted for his sad eyes. Perhaps he was like Othello who doted yet doubted, suspected yet strongly loved. It was all very disagreeable, thought Avice Julian, employing one of her favourite words.

She went back into the kitchen and examined the boiler, a small coke-burning furnace disused since 1963 when the late Alexander Julian had installed central heating. The chimney, she was sure, was swept, the boiler could be used again. Tins could be hammered flat and stacked temporarily in the garden shed. And – why not? – she would start a compost heap. No one should be without a compost heap at the best of times, any alternative was most wasteful.

Her neighbours might contribute to the squalor; she would not. Presently she wrapped herself up in her late husband's Burberry and made her way down to the end of the garden. On the 'wood' side, in the far corner, that would be the place. Up against the fence, thought Mrs Julian. She found a bundle of stout sticks in the shed – Alexander had once grown runner beans up them – and selecting four of these, managed to drive them into the soft earth, one at each of the angles of a roughly conceived square. Next, a strip of chicken wire went round the posts to form an enclosure. She would get Mrs Upton to buy her some garotta next time she went shopping. Avice Julian knew all about making compost heaps, she and her first husband had been experts during the war.

In the afternoon, refreshed by a nap, she emptied the vegetable cupboard and found some strange potatoes growing stems and leaves and some carrots covered in blue fur. Mrs Upton was not a hygienic housekeeper. The potatoes and carrots formed the foundation of the new compost heap. Mrs Julian pulled up a handful of weeds and scattered them on the top.

'I shall have my work cut out, I can see that,' said Mrs

Upton on Monday morning. She laughed unpleasantly. 'I'm sure I don't know when the cleaning'll get done if I'm traipsing up and down the garden path all day long.'

Between them they got the boiler alight and fed it Saturday's *Daily Telegraph* and Sunday's *Observer*. Mrs Upton hammered out a can that had contained baked beans and banged her thumb. She made a tremendous fuss about it which Mrs Julian tried to ignore. Mrs Julian went back to her window, cast on for the second sleeve of the dark blue two-ply jumper, and watched women coming in cars with their rubbish sacks for the tip. Some of them hardly bothered to set foot on the pavement but opened the boots of their cars and hurled the sacks from where they stood. With extreme distaste, Mrs Julian watched one of these sacks strike the trunk of a tree and burst open, scattering tins and glass and peelings and leavings and dregs and grounds in all directions.

During the last week of January, Mrs Julian always made her marmalade. She saw no reason to discontinue this custom because she was eighty-four. Grumbling and moaning about her back and varicose veins, Mrs Upton went out to buy preserving sugar and Seville oranges. Mrs Julian peeled potatoes and prepared a cabbage for lunch, carrying the peelings and the outer leaves down the garden to the compost heap herself. Most of the orange peel would go on there in due course. Mrs Julian's marmalade was the clear jelly kind with only strands of rind in it, pared hair-thin.

They made the first batch in the afternoon. Mr Arnold called on the following morning with his barrow. 'Your private refuse operative, Mrs Julian, at your service.'

'Ah, but I've done what I told you I should do,' she said

and insisted on his coming down the garden with her to see the compost heap.

'You eat a lot of oranges,' said Mr Arnold.

Then she told him about the marmalade and Mr Arnold said he had never tasted home-made marmalade, he didn't know people made it any more. This shocked Mrs Julian and rather confirmed her opinion of Mrs Arnold. She gave him a jar of marmalade and he was profuse in his thanks.

She was glad to get indoors again. The meteorological people had been right when they said there was another cold spell coming. Mrs Julian knitted and looked out of the window and saw Mrs Arnold brought back from somewhere or other by Mr Laindon in his car. By lunchtime it had begun to snow. The heavy, grey, louring sky looked full of snow.

This did not deter Mrs Julian's great-niece from dropping in unexpectedly with her boyfriend. They said frankly that they had come to look at the rubbish tip which was said to be the biggest in London apart from the one which filled the whole of Leicester Square. They stood in the window staring at it and giggling each time anyone arrived with fresh offerings.

'It's surrealistic!' shrieked the great-niece as a sack, weighted down with snow, rolled slowly out of the branches of a tree where it had been suspended for some days. 'It's fantastic! I could stand here all day just watching it.'

Mrs Julian was very glad that she did not but departed after about an hour (with a jar of marmalade) to something called the Screen on the Hill which turned out to be a cinema in Hampstead. After they had gone it snowed harder than ever. There was a heavy frost that night and the next.

'You don't want to set foot outside,' said Mrs Upton on Monday morning. 'The pavements are like glass.' And she went off into a long tale about her son Stewart who was a police constable finding an old lady who had slipped over and was lying helpless on the ice.

Mrs Julian nodded impatiently. 'I have no intention whatsoever of going outside. And you must be very careful when you go down that path to the compost heap.'

They made a second batch of marmalade. The boiler refused to light so Mrs Julian said to leave it but try it again tomorrow, for there was quite an accumulation of newspapers to be burnt. Mrs Julian sat in the window, sewing together the sections of the dark blue two-ply jumper and watching the people coming through the snow to the refuse tip. Capped with snow, the mounds on the tip resembled a mountain range. In the Arctic perhaps, thought Mrs Julian fancifully, or on some planet where the temperature was always sub-zero.

All the week it snowed and froze and snowed and melted and froze again. Mrs Julian stayed indoors. Her nephew, the one who wrote science fiction, phoned to ask if she was all right, and her other nephew, the one who was a commercial photographer, came round to sweep her drive clear of snow. By the time he arrived Mr Laindon had already done it, but Mrs Julian gave him a jar of marmalade just the same. She had resisted giving one to Mr Laindon because of the way he carried on with Mrs Arnold.

It started thawing on Saturday. Mrs Julian sat in the window, casting on for the left front of her cardigan and watching the snow and ice drip away and flow down the gutters. She left the curtains undrawn, as she often did, when it got dark.

At about eight Mrs Arnold came out of the red front door and Mr Laindon came out of the chocolate front door and they stood chatting and laughing together until Mr Arnold came out. Mr Arnold unlocked the doors of his car and said something to Mr Laindon. How Mrs Julian wished she could have heard what it was! Mr Laindon only shook his head. She saw Mrs Arnold get quickly into the car and shut the door. Very cowardly, not wanting to get involved, thought Mrs Julian. Mr Arnold was arguing now with Mr Laindon, trying to persuade him to something, apparently. Perhaps to leave Mrs Arnold alone. But all Mr Laindon did was give a silly sort of laugh and retreat into the house with the chocolate door. The Arnolds went off, Mr Arnold driving quite recklessly fast in this sort of weather, as if he were fearfully late for wherever they were going or, more likely, in a great rage.

Mrs Julian saw nothing of Mr Laindon on the following day, the Sunday, but in the afternoon she saw Mrs Arnold go out on her own. She crossed the road from Paintbox Place and took the path, still mercifully clear of rubbish sacks, through the 'wood' towards the station. Off to a secret assignation, Mrs Julian supposed. The weather was drier and less cold but she felt no inclination to go out. She sat in the window, doing the ribbing part of the left front of her cardigan and noting that the rubbish sacks were mounting again in Paintbox Place. For some reason, laziness perhaps, Mr Arnold had failed to clear them away on Saturday morning. Mrs Julian had a nap and a cup of tea and read the *Observer*.

It pleased her that Mrs Upton had burnt up all the old newspapers. At any rate, there were none to be seen. But what had she done with the empty tins? Mrs Julian looked everywhere for the hammered-out, empty tins. She looked in the kitchen cupboards and the cupboards under the stairs and even in the dining room and the morning room. You never knew with people like Mrs Upton. Perhaps she had put them in the shed, perhaps she had actually done what her employer suggested and put them in the shed.

Mrs Julian went back to the living room, back to her window, and got there just in time to see Mr Arnold letting himself into his house. Time tended to pass slowly for her at weekends and she was surprised to find it was as late as nine o'clock. It had begun to rain. She could see the slanting rain shining gold in the light from the lamps in Paintbox Place.

She sat in the window and picked up her knitting. After a little while the red front door opened and Mr Arnold came out. He had changed out of his wet clothes, changed grey trousers for dark brown, blue jacket for sweater and anorak. He took hold of the nearest rubbish sack and dragged it just inside the door. Within a minute or two he had come out again, carrying the sack, which he loaded onto the barrow he fetched from the parking area.

It was at this point that Mrs Julian's telephone rang. The phone was at the other end of the room. Her caller was the elder of her nephews, the commercial photographer, wanting to know if he might borrow pieces from her Second Empire bedroom furniture for some set or background. They had all enjoyed the marmalade, it was nearly gone. Mrs Julian said he should have another jar of marmalade next year but he certainly could not borrow her furniture. She didn't want pictures of her wardrobe and dressing table all over those vulgar magazines, thank you very much. When she returned to her point of vantage at the window Mr Arnold had disappeared.

Disappeared, that is, from the forecourt of Paintbox Place. Mrs Julian crossed to the right-hand side of the bay to draw the curtains and shut out the rain, and there he was scaling the wet slippery black mountains, clutching a rubbish sack in his hand. The sack looked none too secure, for its side had been punctured by the neck of a bottle and its top was fastened not with a wire fastener but wound round and round with blue string. Finally, he dropped it at the side of one of the high mounds round the birch tree. Mrs Julian drew the curtains.

Mrs Upton arrived punctually in the morning, agog with her news. It was a blessing she had such a strong constitution, Mrs Julian thought. Many a woman of her advanced years would have been made ill – or worse – by hearing a thing like that.

'How can you possibly know?' she said. 'There's nothing in this morning's paper.'

Stewart, of course. Stewart, the policeman.

'She was coming home from the station,' said Mrs Upton, 'through that bit of waste ground.' She cocked a thumb in the direction of the 'wood'. 'Asking for trouble, wasn't she? Nasty dark lonely place. This chap, whoever he was, he clouted her over the head with what they call a blunt instrument. That was about half past eight, though they never found her till ten. Stewart says there was blood all over, turned him up proper it did, and him used to it.'

'What a shocking thing,' said Mrs Julian. 'What a dreadful thing. Poor Mrs Arnold.'

'Murdered for the cash in her handbag, though there wasn't all that much. No one's safe these days.'

When such an event takes place it is almost impossible for some hours to deflect one's thoughts onto any other subject. Her knitting lying in her lap, Mrs Julian sat in the window, contemplating the paintbox houses. A vehicle that was certainly a police car, though it had no blue lamp, arrived in the course of the morning and two policemen in plain clothes were admitted to the house with the red front door. Presumably by Mr Arnold who was not, however, visible to Mrs Julian.

What must it be like to lose, in so violent a manner, one's marriage partner? Even so unsatisfactory a marriage partner as poor Mrs Arnold had been. Did Mr Laindon know? Mrs Julian wondered. She found herself incapable of imagining what his feelings must be. No one came out of or went into any of the houses in Paintbox Place and at one o'clock Mrs Julian had to leave her window and go into the dining room for lunch.

'Of course you know what the police always say, don't you?' said Mrs Upton, sticking a rather underdone lamb chop down in front of her. 'The husband's always the first to be suspected. Shows marriage up in a shocking light, don't you reckon?'

Mrs Julian made no reply but merely lifted her shoulders. Both her husbands had been devoted to her and she told herself that she had no personal experience of the kind of uncivilised relationship Mrs Upton was talking about. But could she say the same for Mrs Arnold? Had she not, in fact, for weeks, for months, now been deploring the state of the Arnolds' marriage and even awaiting some fearful climax?

It was at this point, or soon after when she was back in her window, that Avice Julian began to see herself as a possible Miss Marple or Miss Silver, though she had not recently been reading the works of either of those ladies' creators. Rather it was that she saw the sound common sense which lay behind the notion of elderly women as detectives. Who else has the leisure to be so observant? Who else had behind them a lifetime of knowledge of human nature? Who else has suffered sufficient disillusionment to be able to face so squarely such unpalatable facts?

Beyond a doubt, the facts Mrs Julian was facing were unpalatable. Nevertheless, she marshalled them. Mrs Arnold had been an unfaithful wife. She had been conducting some sort of love affair with Mr Laindon. That Mr Arnold had not known of it was evident from her conduct of this extramarital adventure in his absence. That he was beginning to be aware of it was apparent from his behaviour of Saturday evening. What more probable than that he had set off to meet his wife at the station on Sunday evening, had quarrelled with her about this very matter, and had struck her down in a jealous rage? When Mrs Julian had seen him first he had been running home from the scene of the crime, clutching to him under his jacket the weapon for which Mrs Upton said the police were now searching.

The morning had been dull and damp but after lunch it had dried up and a weak, watery sun came out. Mrs Julian put on her squirrel coat and went out into the garden, the first time she had been out for nine days.

The compost heap had not increased much in size. Perhaps the weight of snow had flattened it down or, more likely, Mrs Upton had failed in her duty. Displeased, Mrs Julian went back into the front garden and down to the gate where she lifted the lid of her dustbin, confident of what she would find inside. But, no, she had done Mrs Upton an injustice. The dustbin was empty and quite clean. She stood by the fence and viewed the tip.

What an eyesore it was! A considerable amount of leakage, due to careless packing and fastening, had taken place, and the wet, fetid, black hillocks were strewn all over with torn and soggy paper, cartons and packages, while in the valleys between clustered, like some evil growth, a conglomeration of decaying fruit and vegetable parings, mildewed bread, tea leaves, coffee grounds and broken glass. In one hollow there was movement. Maggots or the twitching nose of a rat? Mrs Julian shuddered and looked hastily away. She raised her eyes to take in the continued presence under the birch tree of the sack Mr Arnold had deposited there on the previous evening, the sack that was punctured by the neck of a bottle and bound with blue string.

She returned to the house. Was she justified in keeping this knowledge of hers to herself? There was by then no doubt in her mind as to what Mr Arnold had done. After killing his wife he had run home, changed his bloodstained clothes for clean ones and, fetching in the rubbish sack from outside, inserted into it the garments he had just removed and the blunt instrument, so-called, he had used. An iron bar perhaps or a length of metal piping he had picked up in the 'wood'. In so doing he had mislaid the wire fastener and could find no other, so he had been obliged to fasten the sack with the nearest thing to hand, a piece of string. Then across the road with it as he had been on several previous occasions, this time to deposit there a sack containing evidence that would incriminate him if found on his property. But what could be more anonymous than a black plastic sack on a council refuse tip? There it would be only one among a thousand and, he must have supposed, impossible to identify.

Mrs Julian disliked the idea of harming her kind and thoughtful neighbour. But justice must be done. If she was in possession of knowledge the police could not otherwise acquire, it was plainly her duty to reveal it. And the more she thought of it the more convinced she was that there was the correct solution to the crime against Mrs Arnold. Would not Miss Seaton have thought so? Would not Miss Marple, having found parallels between Mr Arnold's behaviour and that of some St Mary Mead husband, having considered and weighed the awful significance of the quarrel on Saturday night and the extraordinary circumstance of taking rubbish to a tip at nine thirty on a wet Sunday evening, would she not have laid the whole matter before the CID?

She hesitated for only a few minutes before fetching the telephone directory and looking up the number. By three o'clock in the afternoon she was making a call to her local police station.

The detective sergeant and constable who came to see Mrs Julian half an hour later showed no surprise at being supplied with information by such as she. Perhaps they too read the works of the inventors of elderly lady sleuths. They treated Mrs Julian with great courtesy and after she had told them what she suspected they suggested she accompany them to the vicinity of the tip and point out the incriminating sack.

However, it was quite possible for her to do this from the right-hand side of the bay window. The detectives nodded and wrote things in notebooks and thanked her and went away, and after a little while a van arrived and a policeman in uniform got out and removed the sack. Mrs Julian sat in the window, working away at the lacy pattern on the front of her dark blue cardigan and watching for the arrest of Mr Arnold. She watched with trepidation and fear for him and a reluctant sympathy. There were policemen about the area all day, tramping around among the rubbish sacks, investigating gardens and ringing doorbells, but none of them went to arrest Mr Arnold.

Nothing happened at all apart from Mr Laindon calling at eight in the evening. He seemed very upset and his face looked white and drawn. He had come, he said, to ask Mrs Julian if she would care to contribute to the cost of a wreath for Mrs Arnold or would she be sending flowers personally?

'I should prefer to see to my own little floral tribute,' said Mrs Julian rather frostily.

'Just as you like, of course. I'm really going round asking people to give myself something to do. I feel absolutely bowled over by this business. They were wonderful to me, the Arnolds, you know. You couldn't have better friends. I was feeling pretty grim when I first came here – my divorce and all that – and the Arnolds, well, they looked after me like a brother, never let me be on my own, even insisted I go out with them. And now a terrible thing like this has to happen and to a wonderful person like that ...'

Mrs Julian had no wish to listen to this sort of thing. No doubt, there were some gullible enough to believe it. She went to bed wondering if the arrest would take place during the night, discreetly, so that the neighbours should not witness it.

The paintbox houses looked just the same in the morning. But of course they would. The arrest of Mr Arnold would hardly affect their appearance. The phone rang at 9.30 and Mrs Upton took the call. She came into the morning room where Mrs Julian was finishing her breakfast.

'The police want to come round and see you again. I said I'd ask. I said you mightn't be up to it, not being so young as you used to be.'

'Neither are you or they,' said Mrs Julian and then she spoke to the police herself and told them to come whenever it suited them.

During the next half hour some not disagreeable fantasies went round in Mrs Julian's head. Such is often the outcome of identifying with characters in fiction. She imagined herself congratulated on her acumen and even, on a future occasion when some other baffling crime had taken place, consulted by policemen of high rank. Mrs Upton had served her well on the whole, as well as could be expected in these trying times. Perhaps one day, when it came to the question of Stewart's promotion, a word from her in the right place ...

The doorbell rang. It was the same detective sergeant and detective constable. Mrs Julian was a little disappointed, she thought she rated an inspector now. They greeted her with jovial smiles and invited her into her own kitchen where they said they had something to show her. Between them they were lugging a large canvas bag.

The sergeant asked Mrs Upton if she could find them a sheet of newspaper, and before Mrs Julian could say that they had burnt all the newspapers, Saturday's *Daily Telegraph* was produced from where it had been secreted. Then, to Mrs Julian's amazement, he pulled out of the canvas bag the black plastic rubbish sack, punctured on one side and secured at the top with blue string, which she had seen Mr Arnold deposit on the tip on Sunday evening.

'I hope you won't find it too distasteful, madam,' he said, 'just to cast your eyes over some of the contents of this bag.'

Mrs Julian was astounded that he should ask such a thing of someone of her age. But she indicated with a faint nod and wave of her hand that she would comply, while inwardly she braced herself for the sight of some hideous bludgeon, perhaps encrusted with blood and hair, and for the emergence from the depths of the sack of a bloodstained jacket and pair of trousers. She would not faint or cry out, she was determined on that, whatever she might see.

It was the constable who untied the string and spread open the neck of the sack. With care, the sergeant began to remove its contents and to drop them on the newspaper Mrs Upton had laid on the floor. He dropped them, in so far as he could, in small separate heaps: a quantity of orange peel, a few lengths of dark blue two-ply knitting wool, innumerable Earl Grey tea bags, potato peelings, cabbage leaves, a lamb chop bone, the sherry bottle whose neck had pierced the side of the sack, and seven copies of the *Daily Telegraph* with one of the *Observer*, all with 'Julian, 1 Abelard Avenue' scrawled above the masthead …

Mrs Julian surveyed her kitchen floor. She looked at the sergeant and the constable and at the yard or so of dark blue two-ply knitting wool which he still held in his hand and which he had unwound from the neck of the sack. 'I fail to understand,' she said.

'I'm afraid this sack would appear to contain waste from your own household, Mrs Julian,' said the sergeant. 'In other words to have been yours and been disposed of from your premises.'

Mrs Julian sat down. She sat down rather heavily on one of the bentwood chairs and fixed her eyes on the opposite wall and felt a strange tingling hot sensation in her face that she hadn't experienced for some sixty years. She was blushing.

'I see,' she said.

The constable began stuffing the garbage back into the sack. Mrs Upton watched him, giggling.

'If you haven't consumed all our stock of sherry, Mrs Upton,' said Mrs Julian, 'perhaps we might offer these two gentlemen a glass.'

The policemen, though on duty – which Mrs Julian had formerly supposed put the consumption of alcohol out of the question – took two glasses apiece. They were not at a loss for words and chatted away with Mrs Upton, possibly on the subject of the past and future exploits of Stewart. Mrs Julian scarcely listened and said nothing. She understood perfectly what had happened, Mr Arnold changing his clothes because they were wet, deciding to empty his rubbish that night because he had forgotten or failed to do so on the

Saturday morning, gathering up his own and very likely Mr Laindon's too. At that point she had left the window to go to the telephone. In the few minutes during which she had been talking to her nephew, Mr Arnold had passed her gate with his barrow, lifted the lid of her dustbin and, finding a full sack within, taken it with him. It was this sack, her own, that she had seen him disposing of on the tip when she had next looked out.

No wonder the boiler had hardly ever been alight, no wonder the compost heap had scarcely grown. Once the snow and frost began and she knew her employer meant to remain indoors, Mrs Upton had abandoned the hygiene regimen and reverted to sack and dustbin. And this was what it had led to.

The two policemen left, obligingly discarding the sack on to the tip as they passed it. Mrs Upton looked at Mrs Julian and Mrs Julian looked at Mrs Upton and Mrs Upton said very brightly: 'Well, I wonder what all that was about then?'

Mrs Julian longed and longed for the old days when she would have given her notice on the spot, but that was impossible now. Where would she find a replacement? So all she said was, knowing it to be incomprehensible: 'A faux pas, Mrs Upton, that's what it was,' and walked slowly off and into the living room where she picked up her knitting from the chair by the window and carried it into the furthest corner of the room.

As a detective she was a failure. Yet, ironically, it was directly due to her efforts that Mrs Arnold's murderer was brought to justice. Mrs Julian could not long keep away from her window and when she returned to it the next day it was to see the council men dismantling the tip and removing the sacks to some distant disposal unit or incinerator. As her newspaper had told her, the strike was over. But the hunt for the murder weapon was not. There was more room to manoeuvre and investigate now the rubbish was gone. By nightfall the weapon had been found and twenty-four hours later the young out-of-work mechanic who had struck Mrs Arnold down for the contents of her handbag had been arrested and charged.

They traced him through the spanner with which he had killed her and which, passing Mrs Julian's garden fence, he had thrust into the depths of her compost heap.

The Pro and the Con

Margery Allingham

Mr Campion, stepping out of the cold sunlight of the Monte Carlo square into the dim warmth of the Casino vestibule, saw a plain good-tempered female face which reminded him, for some reason he could not instantly trace, of beautiful food.

He glanced at the woman curiously. She was square and respectable and would have been a natural part of the landscape at any country church fête, but here, among a cosmopolitan crowd on a late afternoon in the height of the Côte d'Azur season, she was as out of place as a real dandelion in a bouquet of wax orchids.

She did not see him and he moved on, completed the usual formalities, and wandered into the Grande Salle. He did not cross to the tables but stood watching for a moment, his long thin figure hidden in the shadow of the columns. It was a scene he knew well but one which never failed to thrill him. Apart from the usual large percentage of tourists and wealthy regular visitors there were the professional gamblers, earnest folk with systems, and, of course, the strange and rather terrible old ladies, avid behind their make-up.

However, it was not at these that Mr Campion gazed with such benevolent interest. Here and there among the throng he saw a face he recognised. A woman with grey hair and the carriage of a duchess caught his attention and he raised his eyebrows. He had not known that Mrs Marie Peeler, alias Edna Marie James, alias the Comtesse de Richechamps Lisieux, was out of Holloway already.

There were others to interest him also. At one of the *chemin* tables he noticed a large man with very blue eyes and the stamp of the Navy about him sitting beside a very pretty girl and her father. Mr Campion eyed father and daughter sympathetically and hoped they could afford so expensive an acquaintance.

He had been playing his private game of 'spot the crook' for some minutes before he saw Digby Sellers. The man came lounging across the room, his hands in his pockets, his sharp bright eyes peering inquisitively from beneath carefully lowered lids. Considered dispassionately, Mr Campion decided, even for a third-rate con man his technique was bad. In spite of his unobtrusive clothes he looked at first glance exactly what he was, a fishy little person, completely untrustworthy. Campion marvelled at his success in an overcrowded profession and glanced round for the other figure who should have accompanied him.

Tubby Bream had been Digby Sellers' partner in crime for so many years that the police of two continents had come to regard them as inseparable. Bream, Mr Campion knew, was generally considered to have the brains of the act. At the moment he was nowhere to be seen and Campion missed that solid, respectable figure with the unctuous manner and the fatherly smile.

Mr Campion suddenly succumbed to an urge to observe Mr Sellers more closely. Moving quietly from his position in the shadow he followed the man out into the vestibule and arrived through the double doors just in time to see him snubbed by the female with the plain sensible face. Campion came upon the scene at the moment when the woman's plump countenance was burning with maidenly resentment and Mr Sellers was hurrying away abashed.

'I don't know you and I don't want to,' the lady observed to his retreating figure.

The voice and the blush recalled her to Mr Campion's bewildered mind. On their previous meeting, however, the colour in her face had been occasioned by the heat rather than by embarrassment.

'Why, it's Rose, isn't it?' he said.

She turned and stared at him.

'Oh, good afternoon, sir.' There was relief in her tone. 'It's very foreign here, sir, isn't it?'

'Very,' he agreed and hesitated, remembering just in time that while he might find the presence of Margaret Bunting-worth's invaluable Suffolk cook alone in the Casino at Monte Carlo unexpected, he could hardly say so without the risk of giving offence.

Rose was disposed to chat.

'Alice is coming for me in five minutes,' she remarked

confidentially. 'I didn't go right inside because you have to pay, but I thought I'd come into the building because then I can say I have when we get home.'

Mr Campion's astonishment increased.

'Alice? That's the housemaid, isn't it?' he said. 'Dear me, is she here too?'

'Oh yes, sir. We're all here.' Rose spoke placidly. 'Me, Alice, the Missus and Miss Jane. We're all staying at the Hotel Mimosita, sir. I'm sure the Missus would be very pleased to see you if you cared to call.'

His curiosity thoroughly aroused, Mr Campion went down to the Hotel Mimosita without more ado.

Margaret Buntingworth met him with open arms in the literal as well as figurative sense of the term. Rising from her basket chair on the terrace, which imperilled both the vermouth-cassis at her plump elbow and the American seated directly behind her, she welcomed him like a mother.

'Oh, my dear boy!' Her words tumbled over one another as they always did. 'Oh, Albert! Oh, my dear! Do sit down. Do have a drink. What a fantastic place! How on earth did you get here? Isn't it all too absurd? Come into the lounge. It's cooler, the flies aren't so filthy and there aren't such hordes of people.'

The solid American, the only person in sight at this siesta hour, glanced up in mild reproach, but Mr Campion was whisked away.

Margaret was forty-five, natural blonde, plump, vivacious and essentially a countrywoman. As he glanced at her across the small table in the Mimosita's florid lounge Mr Campion wondered if she had ever grown up. Her china-blue eyes danced with childlike excitement and the ruffles on her ample bosom were fastened with one of the little coral trinkets which are sold to the tourists all along the coast.

'It's exciting,' she said. 'I've always wanted to come here but I've never had enough money. Morty and I used to talk about Monte Carlo years ago.' She paused and frowned. 'I wish Morty were here now,' she added as the thought occurred to her. 'He'd tell me what to do in an instant. Still, here we are and the bills are paid till the end of the week so I expect it's all right. It's marvellous seeing you.'

Mr Campion blinked. He had always thought that the defunct Buntingworth had been christened 'George', but he knew Margaret well enough to realise that she might easily have renamed him in her own mind, or on the other hand might equally well be speaking of the hero of the last novel to take her fancy. The reference to some sort of predicament disturbed him, however. Margaret was not the sort of person to be trusted with a predicament.

'What happened?' he inquired. 'Come into a fortune?'

'Oh no, not so exciting as that.' The blue eyes saddened momentarily before they began to twinkle again. 'I've let the house, my dear – let it really well.'

Mr Campion tried not to look bewildered.

'Not Swallows Hall?' he asked involuntarily.

She laughed. 'It's the only house I've got, my pet. It's a dear old place but awfully cold in the winter, and of course it is miles from anywhere. It wants doing up too just now. Modernising, you know. Re-wiring and central heating and that sort of thing. So I was delighted when these people took it. They gave me three hundred down and promised me another three hundred at the end of the week. I jumped at it. Wouldn't you?'

The man in the horn-rimmed spectacles gaped at her.

'Six hundred pounds?' he said faintly. 'You've sold the place ...'

'No, just let it.' Margaret was beaming. 'Let it for three months at fifty pounds a week. Isn't it good?'

'Unbelievable,' said her visitor bluntly. 'You ought to be head of the Board of Trade. Any catch in it?'

'Well, I'm wondering.' Mrs Buntingworth's still pretty face was grave. 'The rest of the money hasn't turned up yet and it's a week overdue. I wish Morty were here. He'd tell me just the sort of wire to send.'

Mr Campion was still mystified.

'I say,' he said, 'don't think me unkind, but in your part of Suffolk rents are inclined to be cheap, aren't they?'

'I know.' Mrs Buntingworth was smiling. 'That's the lovely part. These people just came out of the blue and put down the money. They insisted that I took a holiday and they said they didn't want any of the servants, and when I was hesitating, wondering where I'd go, they suddenly suggested that I took the suite they had booked and couldn't use. It was rather a wild idea, but Rose and Alice have worked for me for years and years and have never had a decent holiday in their lives, and I suddenly said to myself "Well, why not?" So here we all are.'

'Stop,' murmured Mr Campion who was becoming confused. 'Who booked the suite? Who couldn't use it?'

'The people who've taken the house, of course,' said Mrs Buntingworth calmly. 'A Mrs Sacret and her husband. I didn't see him. She and I fixed up everything between us.'

There was a long pause before she looked up. Her natural featherbrained expression had given way to unexpected shrewdness.

'I say,' she said, 'do you think it all sounds a bit fishy? I do now I'm here. Frankly, I've been trying not to think about it. Mrs Sacret seemed such a nice woman, so rich and friendly. I was fed up. Keeping the place eats up my income and I never have any fun. It was terribly cold, too, and unbelievably dull. So I fell for the scheme and got so excited that I didn't really have time to think things out until I got here. We arrived within a week of her seeing the house. Now I'm beginning to wonder. It seems so funny, doesn't it, anyone wanting to bury themselves at Swallows Hall in the winter? I do wish I had Morty with me.'

Mr Campion endeavoured to be cheerful.

'You've got the three hundred pounds, anyway,' he said.

Margaret met his eyes.

'If you ask me, that's the fishiest part about it,' she remarked, echoing his own private opinion. 'I can't tell you how worried I've been. There's nothing of value in the house, of course, nothing they could steal that would be worth their while, and there can't be anything hidden there, buried treasure or that sort of thing. Albert, you're all mixed up with the police. You ought to be able to help me if anyone can. Supposing these people weren't straight, what could they be up to down at Swallows Hall?'

Mr Campion was silent. In his mind's eye he saw again the big rambling Tudor house standing in a belt of trees six miles from the nearest village. He imagined it in winter, cold, draughty and damp. He looked at Margaret blankly.

'Heaven only knows,' he said.

Margaret frowned. 'I ought not to have let it,' she said. 'But they would have it. I refused point-blank at first, but I couldn't get rid of them. The woman had just set her heart on it, she said, and her offers got better and better until I just had to take it. What shall I do? I'm so far away.'

Mr Campion grinned at her. 'I'm on my way home,' he said at last. 'I've been on a cruise with some people. I left the yacht at San Remo. I'm catching a morning plane from Nice. I'll reconnoitre a bit for you, shall I?'

Mrs Buntingworth's relief was childlike.

'Oh, my dear,' she said, 'if only you would! You're so frightfully clever, Albert. Apart from Morty you're the only person I know who can really deal with difficult situations. Do you remember how wonderful you were the night when the roof leaked?'

Mr Campion modestly ignored the tribute.

'Look here,' he said, 'about this Mrs Sacret, what does she look like?'

Margaret considered. 'Oh, rather nice,' she said. 'About my age, small and dark and soignée, with quite a broad forehead.'

Her visitor's face grew blank.

'She hadn't a very faint, not unattractive cast in one eye, I suppose?' he inquired quietly.

Mrs Buntingworth gaped. 'How did you know?'

Campion was silent. So Dorothy Dawson, of all people, was at Swallows Hall, he reflected. Dorothy Dawson had passed as Mrs Tubby Bream before now, and Tubby Bream's partner, Digby Sellers, was keeping an eye on Margaret

Buntingworth's maid here in Monte Carlo. It was all rather significant.

Margaret escorted him to the door of the hotel.

'The odd thing is what on earth these Sacret people can be doing at Swallows Hall if they're not honest,' she said as they parted. 'After all, what can they possibly hope to gain?'

'What indeed?' echoed Mr Campion and it was with a view to elucidating that very point that he wandered into Scotland Yard on the morning after his return home.

Superintendent Stanislaus Oates welcomed him with heavy humour and underlying affection.

'Sellers and Bream?' he said, leaning back in his hard chair behind his scrupulously tidy desk. 'Con men, aren't they? Baker's the man you want. We'll have him in.'

He spoke into the house phone and returned to his visitor with a smile.

'You're quite the little busy these days, aren't you?' he observed. 'All your pals seem to get into trouble some time or other. Do you pick 'em, or just attract suckers naturally?'

'Neither. I am obliging.' Mr Campion put forward the explanation modestly. 'Crooks come to the crook conscious; you know that.'

'Ah, but I get paid for it,' said the Superintendent. 'Hallo, Baker, this is Mr Campion. He does it for the thrill.'

Inspector Baker, who had just entered, was a square, sober-looking young man who regarded Campion severely but was anxious to assist.

'Those two have split, I think,' he said, glancing at a type-written sheet in his hand. 'Sellers came back from Canada a fortnight ago and left the country three days later. Bream has been in London for the last six months living in a flat in Maida Vale. The Dawson woman was with them. We kept an eye on them in the usual way, of course, and one of our men thought there was something brewing a month or so ago. But the punter got wise and nothing transpired. Now they've disappeared and I'm afraid we've lost them. If you ask me, they were getting anxious. Bream likes his comforts and usually needs a bit of capital behind him for his little flutters. Funds were rather low, I should think.'

Mr Campion contributed his own small store of information concerning the partnership and the two Yard men listened to him attentively.

'A lonely house?' inquired the Superintendent at last. 'Lonely and biggish?'

'It's certainly lonely and fairly big, but not attractive in winter.' Mr Campion spoke feelingly.

'Still, it's been a good home in its time?' suggested Inspector Baker. 'Worth a bit some years ago?'

Campion was still mystified.

'Yes,' he admitted. 'Property out there has gone right down, of course, but in its heyday it might have fetched fifteen or twenty thousand pounds. Still, I don't see ...'

The Inspector met the eyes of his superior officer.

'Sounds like "the old home" again,' he said.

'It does, doesn't it?' Oates was thoughtful. 'Sellers!' he ejaculated suddenly. 'That's it. Sellers met the sucker on the boat coming home from Canada, of course. He, Bream and the woman must have been going to team up in Monte for the season, but when he arrived home he had this scheme all set, having picked it up on the boat. Bream and Dorothy dealt with Mrs Buntingworth and bundled her off to the suite they'd already booked, not being certain of getting her right out of the way by any other method. Sellers followed her to watch things that end, because, of course, he couldn't appear at the house, while Bream and Dorothy are down there now, I suppose, in the thick of it.'

Mr Campion leant back in the visitor's chair and stretched his long thin legs in front of him.

'This is all very interesting,' he said mildly, 'but I don't follow it. What exactly do you mean by "the old home"?'

'Good heavens, something he doesn't know at last,' said the Superintendent, his lugubrious face brightening. 'You tell him, Baker. I like to see him learn.'

The Inspector fixed his visitor with a chilly eye.

'Well, you see, Mr Campion,' he began, 'every now and again a man who has made good overseas returns to this country with the intention of purchasing his old home at all costs. Sometimes he's foolish enough to talk about it on the boat and a clever crook can get details out of him. During the voyage the crook can usually size up his man and decide if the game is worth the candle. If it is, he arranges for an accomplice to get hold of the house. Sometimes they go so far as to buy it very cheaply, sometimes they just rent it. Anyway they get possession, and then, since they've always been careful to pick a really rich man, they run him up over the deal and clear a packet. If they buy the place it's not criminal, of course, but in this case, if they've merely rented it, they'll be letting themselves in for false title deeds and heaven knows what.'

Mr Campion remained silent for some time and the Superintendent laughed.

'He's thinking of the wickedness and ingenuity of man,' he said. 'It surprises me myself sometimes. You'd better go along to the county police, my boy. They can't do anything until the fellow actually pays over cash, of course, but either they or we will pick up Bream and Dorothy in the end. Well, well, we aim to please. Anything else you'd like to know?'

'Yes,' said Campion slowly. 'Yes, there is, rather. You're obviously right, of course, but there is one point I don't see at all. I'll tell you some time. Thank you kindly for the lecture. Most instructive. See you when I get back.'

'Oh, Campion,' Oates called him when he reached the door, and when he spoke he was not joking. 'Look out for Bream. He's nasty when he's cornered. Got a dirty streak in him.'

'My dear fellow' – Campion was grinning – 'there's nothing I'm so careful of as my valuable skin.'

Oates grunted. 'I'm not so sure,' he said. 'Still, never say I didn't warn you. So long.'

Mr Campion returned to his flat where he was detained by an unexpected visitor. The following day brought unavoidable delays also, so that it was not until the afternoon of the third day of his return that he turned the nose of his big four-litre Lagonda into the overgrown drive of Swallows Hall.

The long, low, half-timbered house, which was so prettily rose-entwined in summer, had an untidy and dilapidated aspect in mid-January. The miniature park was desolate, the iron railings flattened in many places and the grass long and yellow through lack of grazing.

As he came slowly up the moss-grown way he fancied he saw a curtain drop back into place across one of the lower windows. His ring, too, was answered with suspicious promptness and he found himself looking down at Dorothy Dawson herself as soon as the door opened.

She had dressed the part, he noticed. Her country tweeds were good but shabby and her make-up was restrained almost to the point of absence. She looked up into his face and he saw her eyes flicker.

It was evident that he was not the person she had expected but there was no way of telling if she had recognised him. Her expression remained polite and questioning.

'Mr Sacret?' he inquired.

'Yes. Will you come in here? I'll tell my husband.'

Her voice was very soft and she led him swiftly into Margaret's shabby drawing room. Mr Campion found himself a little surprised. Although she had shown no sign of actual haste the whole incident had passed with most unusual speed, and it occurred to him that he had never before entered any house with such little delay. He glanced at his watch. It was a minute to three.

He heard the quick step on the stones of the hall outside a second before the door swung open with a subdued rattle of *portière* rings and Tubby Bream came hurrying into the room.

His round white face shone smug and benevolent above the neatest of dark suits, and his grey hair, which was longer than is customary, was sleeked down on either side of a centre parting which added considerably to the general lay-reader effect.

In the doorway he paused with theatrical astonishment.

'Why, if it isn't Mr Campion,' he said. 'Inquisitive, friendly

Mr Campion. My dear wife said she thought it was you but she couldn't be sure. Well, well, what a pity you should choose just this moment for a call.'

He had a thick, not unmelodious voice with a crack in it, and all the time he was speaking, his small bright eyes shot little darting glances about the room, now out of the window, now at his visitor's face. He was a shorter man than Campion but his shoulders were powerful and his neck square.

'It's a pity,' he repeated. 'Such a very inconvenient time. Let me see now, you're not actually connected with the police, are you, Mr Campion? Just a dilettante, if I may use the word?'

Mr Campion shrugged his shoulders.

'I'm an old friend of Mrs Buntingworth's,' he began. 'That's the only reason I'm here.'

'Oh dear!' Bream's small round eyes widened. 'Oh dear, isn't that interesting? Have you known her long, Mr Campion?'

'Since I was a child.'

'Thirty years or more?' Bream was rubbing his fat hands together. 'How unfortunate. Really it couldn't be more unfortunate. You're so untrustworthy and there's such a little time. In fact' – he tugged at the chain leading to his fob pocket – 'there really isn't any time at all. A minute to the hour, I see. *Put up your hands, Mr Campion.*'

It was a new trick and one that added considerably, Mr Campion felt, to his education. The wicked little snub-nosed Colt shot into the pudgy white hand with the speed and smoothness of a conjuring trick while the chain dangled harmlessly.

'You're making a great mistake, Bream,' he began but the other interrupted him.

'Put up your hands. It's a question of time. Put up your hands.'

There was nothing for it. Mr Campion raised his arms.

'Turn round, please.' The liquid voice with the unexpected harshness in it was complacent. 'I'm afraid I can't keep you in the drawing room. We're expecting an important visitor, you see. He's due at three o'clock. Dorothy, my dear …'

Mr Campion did not hear Dorothy Dawson come into the room, but with the nose of the Colt pressing dangerously into a spot between his shoulder-blades, he was forced to suffer her to bind his wrists behind him. The strands of soft cord cut viciously into his flesh and he knew at once that it was not the first time she had tied up a captive. He ventured to congratulate her.

'No talking, if you please.' Bream was breathing on his neck and the revolver muzzle pressed a little harder. 'This way. The cupboard where the baskets are, Dorothy. Such a damp little hole, I'm afraid, Mr Campion, but you weren't invited, you know. Walk quickly, please.'

Campion suffered himself to be driven into the disused butler's pantry across the hall where Margaret kept her gardening baskets. It was damp and smelt of mice.

The moment his foot touched the brick floor the man behind him sprang. The ferocity of the attack was wholly unwarranted and, unable to defend himself, Campion went down like a log in the darkness. He kicked out, only to receive a blow above the ear with the butt end of the gun which knocked him senseless.

When he came to himself a few minutes later his ankles were tied with the same paralysing tightness and there was a wad of paper in his mouth, kept in place by a strangling handkerchief.

'Tubby, he's here.'

The woman's whisper reached the young man through the open doorway into the hall and he heard Bream's voice replying.

'Let him in then, my dear. I'll straighten myself. What an inconvenient visit from the silly, silly fellow.'

The pantry door closed, the key turned softly in the lock and Campion heard the pattering of feet trotting towards the back of the house. He lay still. The effects of the blow he had received had by no means worn off and he dared not make an attempt to try the full strength of his bonds until he was sure he had all his wits about him.

Meanwhile there was plenty to interest him. Far off down the hall he heard the front door open. He listened intently but had no need to strain his ears. The newcomer had a voice which entirely defeated its owner's obvious efforts to soften it. His military, not to say parade-ground tones echoed round the old house, setting the glasses ringing.

'Mrs Sacret? Got my letter? Very obligin' of you. Just home, don't you know. Naturally anxious to see the old place again. Just the same, just the same. Not a stone altered, thank God.'

At this point the stranger evidently blew his nose and in spite of the acute discomfort which he suffered Mr Campion's eyes widened and he pricked up his ears. There is a type of Englishman which cannot be copied. Caricatured, they make an unconvincing spectacle. Mr Campion wished he could see Mr Digby Sellers' dupe, for he sounded genuine, and that brought up the one point which had puzzled him ever since he had visited the Superintendent, the same point which had brought him down to Swallows Hall and head first into his present predicament.

Meanwhile, a conducted tour of the house was evidentiy taking place. The visitor's stentorian tones, punctuated by soft murmurs from the woman and Bream's less frequent unctuous rumbles, sounded at intervals from all over the house. Always the newcomer's theme was the same.

'Hasn't changed; hasn't changed. Used to play in here, don't you know. Happy days … youth … childhood. Makin' a fool of myself, I'm afraid. But affectin', you know, very affectin'.'

In the basket cupboard Mr Campion wrestled with his bonds. His hands and feet were numb and the gag was choking him. The experience was both painful and infuriating. Even his attempts to make a noise were frustrated, for not only was it impossible for him to move but the effects of the blow, coupled with the lack of air, fast made him faint.

Meanwhile the party seemed to have gone into the garden. The visitor's voice, muffled but still quite audible, percolated through the lath and plaster walls. Campion caught a few disjointed phrases.

'Stayin' at Ipswich a couple of days … have to think it over, don't you know … lot of money … need repairin'. Who had the place before you, do you know? What? God bless my soul!'

There followed a long period of silence, broken only, for Mr Campion, by exquisitely distasteful scratchings in the panelling near his left ear. He cursed himself mildly and closed his eyes.

His next conscious moment came nearly an hour later when the door was thrust cautiously open and he saw the silhouette of a square head and shoulders against the faint light of the hall.

'I think we might now consider our other visitor, Dorothy my dear.' Bream's voice was ingratiating and somehow anticipatory. 'Well, Mr Campion, comfortable, I hope?'

He came soft-footed into the room, managing to tread on the edge of Campion's upper arm, driving his heel hard into the flesh. The young man forced himself to remain inert and was rewarded.

'Dorothy' – Bream's voice was sharp – 'come here. Bring a light.'

'Oh, what's happened? What's happened? You haven't killed him?'

'That would be awkward, my child, wouldn't it? He's such an old friend of the police.'

There was a laugh in the fat voice but it was not altogether one of amusement.

'Oh, don't –' The woman sounded genuinely frightened. 'You're so crazily cruel. There was no need to hit him as you did. If you've killed him …'

'Be quiet, my dear. Help me to get him out of here. He's alive all right.'

Together they dragged the young man out into the hall and Bream bent down and tore the gag out of his mouth. The woman brought a glass of water. Mr Campion drank and thanked her feebly.

At the sound of his voice Bream chuckled.

'That's better, that's better,' he said, smoothing his large moist hands down the sides of his coat. 'It's all most unfortunate. I don't like to have to inconvenience anyone like this, especially a guest. But it's entirely your own fault, you know, for choosing to come at such a very awkward moment. Believe me, my young friend, if you had called at any other time, any other time at all, it would have been very different. As it is, you've put me in a very uncomfortable position. I really don't see what to do with you. If you were only more dependable.'

He broke off with a sigh of regret and stood looking down at his victim, a sad smile on his round white face.

'How are the wrists?' he inquired presently. 'Sore? I feared so. Dear dear, this is very awkward. You may have to remain like that for some time. I don't see what else I can do, do you, Dorothy, my dear? Since he's precipitated himself into my – ah – my business affairs, I fear he may have to stay here until the project goes through. You see, Mr Campion, if I let you go you may so easily spoil all my beautiful work.'

Mr Campion stirred painfully.

'I hope your visitor liked his old home,' he said bitterly.

'Oh, he did.' The round eyes became shrewd and twinkling. 'You overheard him, did you? He had a rather loud voice, hadn't he? I was afraid you might. Ah well, that practically clinches the matter, doesn't it? You must certainly spend a day or two with us. I see no other way out.'

He was silent for a moment or so, lost in contemplation of the younger man's discomfort.

'Yes, he liked it very much indeed,' he went on at last, still in the bantering affected tone he had adopted throughout their entire interview. 'I think I can safely say that he is in love with it. Such a charming man, Mr Campion. You'd have been touched if you'd seen his eyes light up at each familiar scene. I was quite affected. I think we shall have an offer from him in the morning. Oh yes, I do indeed. When I told him I was thinking of cutting down the trees and refacing the house he seemed quite disturbed.'

Mr Campion opened his eyes.

'He didn't attempt to borrow a tenner, I suppose?' he murmured.

Bream raised his eyebrows.

'No,' he said. 'No, he did not. He was hardly the type. What a pity you couldn't meet.'

Mr Campion began to laugh. The exertion hurt him considerably but he was genuinely amused.

'Bream,' he said faintly, 'do you see any reason why I should give you a hand out of your filthy troubles? You always were pigheaded and now, damn it, you deserve what's coming to you.'

There was a long silence after he had spoken and he remained very still, his eyes closed. The other man pulled up a chair and sat down on it. He was not exactly shaken but the habitual crook has a suspicious mind.

'Mr Campion,' he began quietly, 'why exactly did you come down here?'

'On an errand of mercy.' Mr Campion's voice was faint but resentful. 'Like most acts of pure charity it was misunderstood. You can go and hang yourself, Bream, before I help you now!'

'Perhaps you'd care to explain a little more fully?' The soft voice was very gentle. 'My wife is in the back of the house now. I mention this because women are squeamish, as you know, and you might think I might hesitate to persuade you to talk a little if she were present.'

He began to beat a slow tattoo on Campion's shinbone with the heel of his broad shoe.

'Good God, what do you think I'm here for!' The righteous anger in Campion's voice was convincing. 'Do you think I would go scouring the country in an attempt to capture your scurvy little hide? That's a job for the police. I came here in a perfectly friendly spirit. I happen to have a useful piece of information which would save you time and money, and because you happen to be in the house of a friend of mine, and after the showdown I thought you might work off some of your natural resentment on the house itself, I dropped in to give you a brotherly tip. Instead of listening to me, as any sane man would, you started this kind of monkey-trick. Use your head, Bream.'

'But, Mr Campion, you gave me no option.' There was the beginning of doubt in the greasy voice and the man on the floor was quick to press his advantage.

'Option be damned,' he said cheerfully. 'You were so afraid that your bird would drop in and find me that you lost your nerve. If you'd only paused to consider the obvious it might have dawned on you that if I meant to be unfriendly, I had only to run round to the county police, who would have bided their time, waited until you'd done something they could pin on you, and walked in at the psychological moment to nab you in the decent and time-honoured manner.'

'But, Mr Campion, consider ...' Bream's voice was unhappy. 'Supposing you had dropped in here by chance ...'

Campion stirred. 'Is this the kind of place anyone would drop into by chance?' he demanded. 'Mrs Buntingworth is in the south of France. I left her there three days ago. When she gave me a description of your wife, I recognised it, and when I called in at the Yard the other morning they were kind enough to explain the game you were probably playing. And so, because I knew something you didn't, I came trotting down here in a positively brotherly spirit instead of going to the police. Now, believe me, I don't feel brotherly and you can sit here and wait for Nemesis.'

'Oh, Mr Campion.' Bream had lost his banter and his voice and manner were no longer carefully matched to his costume. He was still wary but his eyes were anxious. 'I'm beginning to be very interested.'

'Very likely, but I'm in pain,' suggested his victim. 'My wrists are raw and I'm feeling spiteful. If you have any sense at all, you'll untie them. After all, you've got the gun; I haven't.'

The reasonableness of the request seemed to appeal to the crook. He cut the cords carefully and stepped back.

'I think I'll leave your ankles, if you don't mind,' he said. 'I'm not so agile as I was and I can't trust you at all.'

Mr Campion wriggled into a sitting position and rubbed his bruised wrists. His yellow hair was dishevelled and his pale eyes were hard and angry.

'Now, what do you think you are going to do?' he inquired. 'It's a pretty heavy sentence for assault, you know, and quite a set-out for murder.'

Bream scowled. 'You may be lying,' he suggested softly.

'Oh, have a heart, man.' Campion sounded exasperated. 'Is there any other reasonable explanation for my coming down here at all? Haven't I told you the obvious truth? Haven't I behaved like any other sane man in similar circumstances? You're the fellow who's lost his head and jumped into trouble feet first. However, I'll do you one more courtesy just to prove how well I meant. I told you I had known Mrs Buntingworth all my life. What I haven't mentioned is that I knew her father and mother, who lived in this house until they died and it had to go up for sale. Mrs Buntingworth's husband bought it, I believe. Now do you see what I'm driving at?'

Tubby Bream sat forward in his chair, his plump face even more pallid than before.

'Yes, Mr Campion.'

'Margaret Buntingworth was the only child of her parents,' Mr Campion continued, still with the same weary exasperation. 'So any noisy, middle-aged gentleman who comes roaring round here, moaning about his old home, is bogus, my poor friend. He's just another practitioner like yourself, working up to a loan or a dud cheque or whatever piece of fancy work is his particular speciality. In fact, you've been done. Now are you grateful?'

Bream's jaw tightened. 'But Sellers ...' he began.

Mr Campion was derisive. 'I saw Sellers in Monte Carlo,' he said, 'and believe me he wouldn't deceive a nursemaid. No; your overseas pal saw Sellers on the boat, recognised a weak brother with capital, and played him for a sucker, trusting to match his wits against yours when the time came. Better face up to it.'

Bream rose to his feet and walked slowly down the room. He looked a dangerous little customer with his heavy shoulders and short, powerful arms. It was evident that he was going over Campion's arguments in his mind and was finding them unpleasantly convincing.

Suddenly, however, he swung round.

'No you don't, Campion!' he said sharply.

The young man withdrew his hands from the ankle bonds and looked unwaveringly into the muzzle of the little Colt.

'All right,' he said, shrugging his shoulders. 'But frankly, I don't see the point of all this. What are you going to do, exactly? In view of all the facts, I mean.'

'Find out if you're right.'

'And when you discover that I am?'

The man laughed.

'Then I shan't waste my time any longer, of course,' he said. 'We shall clear out. Unfortunately, I can't trust you to keep your fingers out of my affairs, so naturally you'll have to stay behind. It's a cold house, I know, but you're tough. I should think you'd be alive when they find you.'

Mr Campion looked incredulous.

'But that's suicide on your part,' he said. 'Scotland Yard know I came down here to look for you. They'll get you if I die, Bream.'

The man in the neat dark suit spread out his hands.

'It's a risk I shall have to take,' he said. 'I may leave word for a village woman to come and clear up on Monday. If she's conscientious – well, you'll only have had four days of it.'

Campion sat stiffly, staring up at him. His pale eyes looked furious and Bream was amused.

'My dear wife says that there are rats in the outer kitchen,' he began. 'Of course, they'll cling to you for the warmth. But they're companionable little creatures if they're not hungry.'

His voice changed again and for a moment he showed the anger which was consuming him.

'If you're right, I hope they start in on you,' he said. 'Hullo, the thought's too much for you, is it?'

Mr Campion's eyes had closed and now he swayed violently and slumped down upon the stones, his face pallid and his mouth loose. Bream advanced cautiously to kick the inert body in the ribs. It rolled lifelessly and the man laughed.

Slipping the gun into his pocket he stepped forward and bent down to raise his victim's eyelids. Because of his bulk he had to kneel to do so, and as his body swung down a hand as delicate as any pickpocket's moved quietly and Mr Campion's long fingers closed gratefully over the little gun.

'Get back. Shout and I'll plug you.'

The vigorous voice startled Bream quite as much as the sudden movement, which brought his adversary up on one elbow, the revolver levelled. He darted backwards and Campion grinned dangerously as the startled figure flattened against the panelling of the opposite wall.

'Of course, there's no earthly reason why I shouldn't kill you,' he observed affably. 'I've got a bona-fide self defence plea. That's where I'm one up on you. Stick your hands up and come away from that bell.'

Bream did not hesitate.

'I was getting at you, Mr Campion,' he said huskily. 'You brought me a bit of bad news and I dare say it made me angry.'

'Well, make up your mind.' The man on the floor was aggressively pleased. 'Is this your idea of humour or ill temper? Don't move!'

The final admonition was occasioned by a wholly unexpected development. The front door at the other end of the hall was moving furtively. Campion kept his gun turned on Bream.

'Now go over,' he whispered. 'I'll shoot, remember.'

Obediently the crook edged towards the widening door, his arms raised. From his place of vantage on the floor Mr Campion had an excellent view of the ensuing scene. Over the threshold, stepping gingerly to avoid making a sound, came a red-faced, white-haired stranger who stopped in his tracks, not unnaturally, when confronted by the spread-eagled Bream.

'Beg your pardon,' he ejaculated, his bright eyes widening and his face burning with embarrassment. 'Ought not to have come bargin' in again like this. Very foolish of me.' He cleared his throat noisily. 'Tell you what happened. Matter of fact was nearly in Ipswich when it came to me I wanted to clinch the deal. Came back, came up to the door, saw it wasn't latched and couldn't resist the impulse to come in like I used to thirty years ago. Good God, man, don't stand lookin' at me like that. What have you got your hands up for?'

'Oh, my hat. The colonial,' murmured Mr Campion wearily.

Bream was quick to seize the advantage.

'Look out!' he shouted and leapt behind the bewildered visitor for the open door.

Campion fired, but avoiding the newcomer the shot went wide and splintered the woodwork of the door frame.

'God bless my soul!' The stranger peered into the shadow of the hall and suddenly perceived Campion still sitting on the floor. 'Firin'?' he demanded. 'You can't do that here, man. Get up and fight like a Christian. Oh, I see, tied you up, has he? What are you doin'? Burglin'? Put that gun away.'

This matter-of-fact reaction to what must have seemed, to say the least of it, a remarkable situation had a profound effect upon the young man. The newcomer was such a perfect specimen of his type that to doubt his integrity seemed comparable with the suspicion that the Nelson Monument was built of plaster.

'I say, is this really your old home?' he heard himself saying stupidly.

'Certainly. Best years of my life were spent in this house and I hope to die in it. Don't see what the devil it's got to do with you, though. Got him, Sacret?'

He spoke a moment too soon. Bream, who had been creeping up behind Campion from the inner doorway, had not quite reached his goal. Campion swung over just as the man leapt. The gun shot out of his hand and slithered across the stones towards the stranger. Bream was after it instantly but Campion gripped him by the lapel and they rolled over together.

'Pick it up!' he shouted, trying to put authority into his voice. 'Pick it up, for the love of Mike! This chap's dangerous.'

The rest of his appeal was choked as Bream's hands found his throat. His blunt fingers dug into his neck and he found himself weaken.

'Look out, man, you'll kill him!' The stranger's vigorous voice echoed through the room. 'Stand up, sir! I've got you covered. What are you doin', damn you? The feller's tied.'

The shocked astonishment in the last phrase had its effect. The fingers relaxed their strangle-hold and Bream staggered to his feet, his puffy face twisted in a depreciatory grimace.

'I'm afraid I forgot myself,' he said. 'He frightened me. I'll take the gun, shall I?'

'No!'

Campion's croak was frantic in its appeal and the stranger stepped back.

'Wait a moment,' he said. 'Keep your distance, sir. Untie the feller's legs. Like to have this all made clear, if you don't mind.'

'Oh, come now, really.' Bream had gone back to his old ingratiating manner. 'This is my house, you know.'

'Lying,' whispered Campion again. 'Don't let him have the gun.'

'Not your house, eh?' The newcomer seized the suggestion with interest. 'Hang it, whose house is it? Must get that straight. Explain yourselves, both of you.'

'All in good time.' Bream was edging forward. 'I'll just take the gun first. They – they are such dangerous things.'

'The devil you do! Stand back.' The old man was showing remarkable spirit. 'This fellow here has made a serious allegation and I'd like it properly refuted. Frankly, Sacret, there were one or two things you said this afternoon which made me wonder. Do you know you pointed out the old walnut on the lower lawn and told me there were fine pears on it last year? At the time I thought it was a slip of the tongue, but now I'm beginnin' to look at it in a different light.'

Bream drew back from the revolver.

'This is an outrage,' he said feelingly. 'Holding up a man in his own house.'

The newcomer's bright blue eyes snapped suspiciously.

'Who's house is it?' he demanded, his voice raising. 'For the last time, sir, who owns this house?'

'I do, I'm afraid. Is anything wrong?'

The pleasant voice from the doorway behind them startled everybody. Margaret Buntingworth, followed by Jane, Rose and Alice, to say nothing of a taximan with the luggage, trooped into the hall. Margaret was weary, dishevelled and utterly charming, the complete mistress of any situation.

The stranger thrust the gun behind him and stepped back. Bream gaped helplessly and Mr Campion perforce remained where he was. Margaret caught sight of him and paused in the act of removing her travelling coat.

'Oh, Albert,' she said, 'how very nice of you to be here! I didn't see you at first down there. I got your telegram, my dear, and we packed up and came home just as soon as we could. What on earth are you doing? Your ankles ... Dear me, is something going on?'

She turned to face the others, passing over Bream, who evidently meant nothing to her, and came face to face with the stranger. The man stared at her for a moment, grew an even more virulent crimson, and finally uttered a single strangled word.

'Meggie!' he said.

Margaret Buntingworth dropped her coat, her gloves,

and the rolled travelling rug which contained the two half-litres of Eau de Cologne she had smuggled so successfully through the customs. Her little scream was an expression of pure delight.

'Morty!' she said. 'Oh, Morty, my dear boy, how you startled me!'

Mr Campion bent forward and began to untie his ankles. He looked up at Bream.

'Twenty-four hours,' he said meaningly. 'And it's a great deal more than you deserve.'

The man glanced at him and nodded. His face was blank. Without a look behind him he made for the inner door.

As Campion scrambled painfully to a chair Margaret came over to him, dragging the newcomer behind her.

'Isn't this all wonderful?' she said, her eyes dancing. 'Morty says you two haven't actually met yet. My dear, this is Morty himself. I haven't seen him for years and years and years. He used to live in a cottage down by the plantation and we used to play together up here when we were kids. He was the cleverest boy in the world. I cried my eyes out when he went away. He always promised to come back and buy the old house for me but, of course, I never believed him. Neither of us wrote, of course. You know how it is. And now here he is! Morty, you haven't changed a bit.'

'I've never forgotten you, Meggie.' The stranger seemed suddenly overcome with shyness. 'Matter of fact I came down here in the hope – in the hope – ' He coughed, blew his nose and steered away from a dangerous subject.

'Upset me to see that chap in possession,' he remarked. 'Where is he, by the way? Somethin' very funny was goin' on here just now, Meggie. We'll have to have an explanation from you, young feller. I'm completely in the dark. Where is that man Sacret?'

'Oh, the Sacrets!' Margaret remembered them with consternation. 'I forgot all about them. You put them clean out of my head, Morty. I've let the house. I ought not to be here if everything's all right. What has happened, Albert? Where are the Sacrets, dear?'

Campion ceased to massage his bruised ankles.

'If you listen,' he said, 'you'll just hear their car going off down the drive. I should forget 'em, if I were you. Something tells me that neither of us will hear of them for some considerable time.'

Margaret frowned and gave the subject up as being too difficult.

'Perhaps if we all had some food and something to drink?' she suggested. 'Food helps the brain so, don't you think? After we've eaten you two boys must tell me all about it. Morty, can you draw a cork?'

'Comin', me dear.' The stranger strode after her, regaining his youth at every step.

Mr Campion rose stiffly to his feet and practised walking.

Much later that evening the two men sat before the fire in the big shabby drawing room. Margaret had gone to bed after an orgy of remembrances. Morty glanced round the room affectionately.

'Just as I remember it,' he said. 'Foolish of me to confuse everybody by callin' it my old home. Had always thought of it that way, you see.'

Mr Campion looked into the fire.

'Thinking of buying it?' he inquired.

The elder man cocked a bright blue eye in his direction. 'Well,' he said evasively, 'I've found just exactly what I was lookin' for, don't you know.'

The Adventure of the Beryl Coronet

Arthur Conan Doyle

'Holmes,' said I, as I stood one morning in our bow-window looking down the street, 'here is a madman coming along. It seems rather sad that his relatives should allow him to come out alone.'

My friend rose lazily from his armchair and stood with his hands in the pockets of his dressing gown, looking over my shoulder. It was a bright, crisp February morning, and the snow of the day before still lay deep upon the ground, shimmering brightly in the wintry sun. Down the centre of Baker Street it had been ploughed into a brown crumbly band by the traffic, but at either side and on the heaped-up edges of the foot-paths it still lay as white as when it fell. The grey pavement had been cleaned and scraped, but was still dangerously slippery, so that there were fewer passengers than usual. Indeed, from the direction of the Metropolitan Station no one was coming save the single gentleman whose eccentric conduct had drawn my attention.

He was a man of about fifty, tall, portly, and imposing, with a massive, strongly marked face and a commanding figure. He was dressed in a sombre yet rich style, in black frock-coat, shining hat, neat brown gaiters, and well-cut pearl-grey trousers. Yet his actions were in absurd contrast to the dignity of his dress and features, for he was running hard, with occasional little springs, such as a weary man gives who is little accustomed to set any tax upon his legs. As he ran he jerked his hands up and down, waggled his head, and writhed his face into the most extraordinary contortions.

'What on earth can be the matter with him?' I asked. 'He is looking up at the numbers of the houses.'

'I believe that he is coming here,' said Holmes, rubbing his hands.

'Here?'

'Yes; I rather think he is coming to consult me professionally. I think that I recognise the symptoms. Ha! did I not tell you?' As he spoke, the man, puffing and blowing, rushed at our door and pulled at our bell until the whole house resounded with the clanging.

A few moments later he was in our room, still puffing, still gesticulating, but with so fixed a look of grief and despair in his eyes that our smiles were turned in an instant to horror and pity. For a while he could not get his words out, but swayed his body and plucked at his hair like one who has been driven to the extreme limits of his reason. Then, suddenly springing to his feet, he beat his head against the wall with such force that we both rushed upon him and tore him away to the centre of the room. Sherlock Holmes pushed him down into the easy-chair, and, sitting beside him, patted his hand, and chatted with him in the easy, soothing tones which he knew so well how to employ.

'You have come to me to tell your story, have you not?' said he. 'You are fatigued with your haste. Pray wait until you have recovered yourself, and then I shall be most happy to look into any little problem which you may submit to me.'

The man sat for a minute or more with a heaving chest, fighting against his emotion. Then he passed his handkerchief over his brow, set his lips tight, and turned his face towards us.

'No doubt you think me mad?' said he.

'I see that you have had some great trouble,' responded Holmes.

'God knows I have! – a trouble which is enough to unseat my reason, so sudden and so terrible is it. Public disgrace I might have faced, although I am a man whose character has never yet borne a stain. Private affliction also is the lot of every man; but the two coming together, and in so frightful a form, have been enough to shake my very soul. Besides, it is not I alone. The very noblest in the land may suffer, unless some way be found out of this horrible affair.'

'Pray compose yourself, sir,' said Holmes, 'and let me have a clear account of who you are, and what it is that has befallen you.'

'My name,' answered our visitor, 'is probably familiar to your ears. I am Alexander Holder, of the banking firm of Holder & Stevenson, of Threadneedle Street.'

The name was indeed well known to us as belonging to the

senior partner in the second-largest private banking concern in the City of London. What could have happened, then, to bring one of the foremost citizens of London to this most pitiable pass? We waited, all curiosity, until with another effort he braced himself to tell his story.

'I feel that time is of value,' said he; 'that is why I hastened here when the police inspector suggested that I should secure your co-operation. I came to Baker Street by the Underground, and hurried from there on foot, for the cabs go slowly through this snow. That is why I was so out of breath, for I am a man who takes very little exercise. I feel better now, and I will put the facts before you as shortly and yet as clearly as I can.

'It is, of course, well known to you that in a successful banking business as much depends upon our being able to find remunerative investments for our funds as upon our increasing our connection and the number of our depositors. One of our most lucrative means of laying out money is in the shape of loans, where the security is unimpeachable. We have done a good deal in this direction during the last few years, and there are many noble families to whom we have advanced large sums upon the security of their pictures, libraries, or plate.

'Yesterday morning I was seated in my office at the bank when a card was brought in to me by one of the clerks. I started when I saw the name, for it was that of none other than – well, perhaps even to you I had better say no more than that it was a name which is a household word all over the earth – one of the highest, noblest, most exalted names in England. I was overwhelmed by the honour, and attempted, when he entered, to say so, but he plunged at once into business with the air of a man who wishes to hurry quickly through a disagreeable task.

"'Mr Holder,' said he, 'I have been informed that you are in the habit of advancing money.'

"'The firm do so when the security is good,' I answered.

"'It is absolutely essential to me,' said he, 'that I should have fifty thousand pounds at once. I could of course borrow so trifling a sum ten times over from my friends, but I much prefer to make it a matter of business, and to carry out that business myself. In my position you can readily understand that it is unwise to place one's self under obligations.'

"'For how long, may I ask, do you want this sum?' I asked.

"'Next Monday I have a large sum due to me, and I shall then most certainly repay what you advance, with whatever interest you think it right to charge. But it is very essential to me that the money should be paid at once.'

"'I should be happy to advance it without further parley from my own private purse,' said I, 'were it not that the strain would be rather more than it could bear. If, on the other hand, I am to do it in the name of the firm, then in justice to my partner I must insist that, even in your case, every business-like precaution should be taken.'

"'I should much prefer to have it so,' said he, raising up a square, black morocco case which he had laid beside his chair. 'You have doubtless heard of the Beryl Coronet?'

"'One of the most precious public possessions of the empire,' said I.

"'Precisely.' He opened the case, and there, imbedded

in soft, flesh-coloured velvet, lay the magnificent piece of jewelry which he had named. "There are thirty-nine enormous beryls," said he, "and the price of the gold chasing is incalculable. The lowest estimate would put the worth of the coronet at double the sum which I have asked. I am prepared to leave it with you as my security."

'I took the precious case into my hands and looked in some perplexity from it to my illustrious client.

'"You doubt its value?" he asked.

'"Not at all. I only doubt ..."

'"The propriety of my leaving it. You may set your mind at rest about that. I should not dream of doing so were it not absolutely certain that I should be able in four days to reclaim it. It is a pure matter of form. Is the security sufficient?"

'"Ample."

'"You understand, Mr Holder, that I am giving you a strong proof of the confidence which I have in you, founded upon all that I have heard of you. I rely upon you not only to be discreet and to refrain from all gossip upon the matter, but, above all, to preserve this coronet with every possible precaution, because I need not say that a great public scandal would be caused if any harm were to befall it. Any injury to it would be almost as serious as its complete loss, for there are no beryls in the world to match these, and it would be impossible to replace them. I leave it with you, however, with every confidence, and I shall call for it in person on Monday morning."

'Seeing that my client was anxious to leave, I said no more; but, calling for my cashier, I ordered him to pay over fifty thousand-pound notes. When I was alone once more, however, with the precious case lying upon the table in front of me, I could not but think with some misgivings of the immense responsibility which it entailed upon me. There could be no doubt that, as it was a national possession, a horrible scandal would ensue if any misfortune should occur to it. I already regretted having ever consented to take charge of it. However, it was too late to alter the matter now, so I locked it up in my private safe, and turned once more to my work.

'When evening came I felt that it would be an imprudence to leave so precious a thing in the office behind me. Bankers' safes had been forced before now, and why should not mine be? If so, how terrible would be the position in which I should find myself! I determined, therefore, that for the next few days I would always carry the case backward and forward with me, so that it might never be really out of my reach. With this intention, I called a cab, and drove out to my house at Streatham, carrying the jewel with me. I did not breathe freely until I had taken it upstairs and locked it in the bureau of my dressing-room.

'And now a word as to my household, Mr Holmes, for I wish you to thoroughly understand the situation. My groom and my page sleep out of the house, and may be set aside altogether. I have three maid-servants who have been with me a number of years, and whose absolute reliability is quite above suspicion. Another, Lucy Parr, the second waiting-maid, has only been in my service a few months. She came with an excellent character, however, and has always given me satisfaction. She is a very pretty girl, and has attracted admirers who have occasionally hung about the place. That is the only drawback which we have found to her, but we believe her to be a thoroughly good girl in every way.

'So much for the servants. My family itself is so small that it will not take me long to describe it. I am a widower, and have an only son, Arthur. He has been a disappointment to me, Mr Holmes – a grievous disappointment. I have no doubt that I am myself to blame. People tell me that I have spoiled him. Very likely I have. When my dear wife died I felt that he was all I had to love. I could not bear to see the smile fade even for a moment from his face. I have never denied him a wish. Perhaps it would have been better for both of us had I been sterner, but I meant it for the best.

'It was naturally my intention that he should succeed me in my business, but he was not of a business turn. He was wild, wayward, and, to speak the truth, I could not trust him in the handling of large sums of money. When he was young he became a member of an aristocratic club, and there, having charming manners, he was soon the intimate of a number of men with long purses and expensive habits. He learned to play heavily at cards and to squander money on the turf, until he had again and again to come to me and implore me to give him an advance upon his allowance, that he might settle his debts of honour. He tried more than once to break away from the dangerous company which he was keeping, but each time the influence of his friend Sir George Burnwell was enough to draw him back again.

'And, indeed, I could not wonder that such a man as Sir George Burnwell should gain an influence over him, for he has frequently brought him to my house, and I have found myself that I could hardly resist the fascination of his manner.

He is older than Arthur, a man of the world to his fingertips, one who had been everywhere, seen everything, a brilliant talker, and a man of great personal beauty. Yet when I think of him in cold blood, far away from the glamour of his presence, I am convinced from his cynical speech, and the look which I have caught in his eyes, that he is one who should be deeply distrusted. So I think, and so, too, thinks my little Mary, who has a woman's quick insight into character.

'And now there is only she to be described. She is my niece; but when my brother died five years ago and left her alone in the world I adopted her, and have looked upon her ever since as my daughter. She is a sunbeam in my house – sweet, loving, beautiful, a wonderful manager and house-keeper, yet as tender and quiet and gentle as a woman could be. She is my right hand. I do not know what I could do without her. In only one matter has she ever gone against my wishes. Twice my boy has asked her to marry him, for he loves her devotedly, but each time she has refused him. I think that if anyone could have drawn him into the right path it would have been she, and that his marriage might have changed his whole life; but now, alas! it is too late – for ever too late!

'Now, Mr Holmes, you know the people who live under my roof, and I shall continue with my miserable story.

'When we were taking coffee in the drawing room that night, after dinner, I told Arthur and Mary my experience, and of the precious treasure which we had under our roof, suppressing only the name of my client. Lucy Parr, who had brought in the coffee, had, I am sure, left the room; but I cannot swear that the door was closed. Mary and Arthur were much interested, and wished to see the famous coronet, but I thought it better not to disturb it.

'"Where have you put it?" asked Arthur.

'"In my own bureau."

'"Well, I hope to goodness the house won't be burgled during the night," said he.

'"It is locked up," I answered.

'"Oh, any old key will fit that bureau. When I was a youngster I have opened it myself with the key of the box-room cupboard."

'He often had a wild way of talking, so that I thought little of what he said. He followed me to my room, however, that night with a very grave face.

'"Look here, dad," said he, with his eyes cast down, "can you let me have two hundred pounds?"

'"No, I cannot!" I answered, sharply. "I have been far too generous with you in money matters."

'"You have been very kind," said he: "but I must have this money, or else I can never show my face inside the club again."

'"And a very good thing, too!" I cried.

'"Yes, but you would not have me leave it a dishonoured man," said he. "I could not bear the disgrace. I must raise the money in some way, and if you will not let me have it, then I must try other means."

'I was very angry, for this was the third demand during the month. "You shall not have a farthing from me," I cried; on which he bowed and left the room without another word.

'When he was gone I unlocked my bureau, made sure that my treasure was safe, and locked it again. Then I started to go round the house to see that all was secure – a duty which I usually leave to Mary, but which I thought it well to perform myself that night. As I came down the stairs I saw Mary herself at the side window of the hall, which she closed and fastened as I approached.

'"Tell me, dad," said she, looking, I thought, a little disturbed, "did you give Lucy, the maid, leave to go out tonight?"

'"Certainly not."

'"She came in just now by the back door. I have no doubt that she has only been to the side gate to see someone; but I think that it is hardly safe, and should be stopped."

'"You must speak to her in the morning, or I will, if you prefer it. Are you sure that everything is fastened?"

'"Quite sure, dad."

'"Then, good-night." I kissed her, and went up to my bedroom again, where I was soon asleep.

'I am endeavouring to tell you everything, Mr Holmes, which may have any bearing upon the case, but I beg that you will question me upon any point which I do not make clear.'

'On the contrary, your statement is singularly lucid.'

'I come to a part of my story now in which I should wish to be particularly so. I am not a very heavy sleeper, and the anxiety in my mind tended, no doubt, to make me even less so than usual. About two in the morning, then, I was awakened by some sound in the house. It had ceased ere I was wide awake, but it had left an impression behind it as though a window had gently closed somewhere. I lay listening with all my ears. Suddenly, to my horror, there was a distinct sound of footsteps moving softly in the next room. I slipped out of bed, all palpitating with fear, and peeped round the corner of my dressing-room door.

'"Arthur!" I screamed, "you villain! you thief! How dare you touch that coronet?"

'The gas was half up, as I had left it, and my unhappy boy, dressed only in his shirt and trousers, was standing beside the light, holding the coronet in his hands. He appeared to be wrenching at it, or bending it with all his strength. At my cry he dropped it from his grasp, and turned as pale as death. I snatched it up and examined it. One of the gold corners, with three of the beryls in it, was missing.

'"You blackguard!" I shouted, beside myself with rage. "You have destroyed it! You have dishonoured me for ever! Where are the jewels which you have stolen?"

'"Stolen!" he cried.

'"Yes, you thief!" I roared, shaking him by the shoulder.

'"There are none missing. There cannot be any missing," said he.

'"There are three missing. And you know where they are. Must I call you a liar as well as a thief? Did I not see you trying to tear off another piece?"

'"You have called me names enough," said he; "I will not stand it any longer. I shall not say another word about this business since you have chosen to insult me. I will leave your house in the morning and make my own way in the world."

'"You shall leave it in the hands of the police!" I cried, half mad with grief and rage. "I shall have this matter probed to the bottom."

'"You shall learn nothing from me," said he, with a passion

such as I should not have thought was in his nature. "If you choose to call the police, let the police find what they can."

'By this time the whole house was astir, for I had raised my voice in my anger. Mary was the first to rush into my room, and, at the sight of the coronet and of Arthur's face, she read the whole story, and, with a scream, fell down senseless on the ground. I sent the housemaid for the police, and put the investigation into their hands at once. When the inspector and a constable entered the house, Arthur, who had stood sullenly with his arms folded, asked me whether it was my intention to charge him with theft. I answered that it had ceased to be a private matter, but had become a public one, since the ruined coronet was national property. I was determined that the law should have its way in everything.

'"At least," said he, "you will not have me arrested at once. It would be to your advantage as well as mine if I might leave the house for five minutes."

'"That you may get away, or perhaps that you may conceal what you have stolen," said I. And then realising the dreadful position in which I was placed, I implored him to remember that not only my honour, but that of one who was far greater than I was at stake; and that he threatened to raise a scandal which would convulse the nation. He might avert it all if he would but tell me what he had done with the three missing stones.

'"You may as well face the matter," said I; "you have been caught in the act, and no confession could make your guilt more heinous. If you but make such reparation as is in your power, by telling us where the beryls are, all shall be forgiven and forgotten."

'"Keep your forgiveness for those who ask for it," he answered, turning away from me, with a sneer. I saw that he was too hardened for any words of mine to influence him. There was but one way for it. I called in the inspector, and gave him into custody. A search was made at once, not only of his person, but of his room, and of every portion of the house where he could possibly have concealed the gems; but no trace of them could be found, nor would the wretched boy open his mouth for all our persuasions and our threats. This morning he was removed to a cell, and I, after going through all the police formalities, have hurried round to you, to implore you to use your skill in unravelling the matter. The police have openly confessed that they can at present make nothing of it. You may go to any expense which you think necessary. I have already offered a reward of a thousand pounds. My God, what shall I do! I have lost my honour, my gems, and my son in one night. Oh, what shall I do!'

He put a hand on either side of his head, and rocked himself to and fro, droning to himself like a child whose grief has got beyond words.

Sherlock Holmes sat silent for some few minutes, with his brows knitted and his eyes fixed upon the fire.

'Do you receive much company?' he asked.

'None, save my partner with his family, and an occasional friend of Arthur's. Sir George Burnwell has been several times lately. No one else, I think.'

'Do you go out much in society?'

'Arthur does. Mary and I stay at home. We neither of us care for it.'

'That is unusual in a young girl.'

'She is of a quiet nature. Besides, she is not so very young. She is four-and-twenty.'

'This matter, from what you say, seems to have been a shock to her also.'

'Terrible! She is even more affected than I.'

'You have neither of you any doubt as to your son's guilt?'

'How can we have, when I saw him with my own eyes with the coronet in his hands.'

'I hardly consider that a conclusive proof. Was the remainder of the coronet at all injured?'

'Yes, it was twisted.'

'Do you not think, then, that he might have been trying to straighten it?'

'God bless you! You are doing what you can for him and for me. But it is too heavy a task. What was he doing there at all? If his purpose were innocent, why did he not say so?'

'Precisely. And if it were guilty, why did he not invent a lie? His silence appears to me to cut both ways. There are several singular points about the case. What did the police think of the noise which awoke you from your sleep?'

'They considered that it might be caused by Arthur's closing his bedroom door.'

'A likely story! As if a man bent on felony would slam his door so as to wake a household. What did they say, then, of the disappearance of these gems?'

'They are still sounding the planking and probing the furniture in the hope of finding them.'

'Have they thought of looking outside the house?'

'Yes, they have shown extraordinary energy. The whole garden has already been minutely examined.'

'Now, my dear sir,' said Holmes, 'is it not obvious to you now that this matter really strikes very much deeper than either you or the police were at first inclined to think? It appeared to you to be a simple case; to me it seems exceedingly complex. Consider what is involved by your theory. You suppose that your son came down from his bed, went, at great risk, to your dressing-room, opened your bureau, took out your coronet, broke off by main force a small portion of it, went off to some other place, concealed three gems out of the thirty-nine, with such skill that nobody can find them, and then returned with the other thirty-six into the room in which he exposed himself to the greatest danger of being discovered. I ask you now, is such a theory tenable?'

'But what other is there?' cried the banker, with a gesture of despair. 'If his motives were innocent, why does he not explain them?'

'It is our task to find that out,' replied Holmes; 'so now, if you please, Mr Holder, we will set off for Streatham together, and devote an hour to glancing a little more closely into details.'

My friend insisted upon my accompanying them in their expedition, which I was eager enough to do, for my curiosity and sympathy were deeply stirred by the story to which we had listened. I confess that the guilt of the banker's son appeared to me to be as obvious as it did to his unhappy father, but still I had such faith in Holmes's judgment that I felt that there must be some grounds for hope as long as he was dissatisfied with the accepted explanation. He hardly spoke a word the whole way out to the southern suburb, but sat with his chin upon his breast and his hat drawn over his eyes, sunk in the deepest thought. Our client appeared to have taken fresh heart at the little glimpse of hope which had been presented to him, and he even broke into a desultory chat with me over his business affairs. A short railway journey and a shorter walk brought us to Fairbank, the modest residence of the great financier.

Fairbank was a good-sized square house of white stone, standing back a little from the road. A double carriage sweep, with a snow-clad lawn, stretched down in front to two large iron gates which closed the entrance. On the right side was a small wooden thicket, which led into a narrow path between two neat hedges stretching from the road to the kitchen door, and forming the tradesmen's entrance. On the left ran a lane which led to the stables, and was not itself within the grounds at all, being a public, though little used, thoroughfare. Holmes left us standing at the door, and walked slowly all round the house, across the front, down the tradesmen's path, and so round by the garden behind into the stable lane. So long was he that Mr Holder and I went into the dining room and waited by the fire until he should return. We were sitting there in silence when the door opened and a young lady came in. She was rather above the middle height, slim, with dark hair and eyes, which seemed the darker against the absolute pallor of her skin. I do not think that I have ever seen such deadly paleness in a woman's face. Her lips, too, were bloodless, but her eyes were flushed with crying. As she swept silently into the room she impressed me with a greater sense of grief than the banker had done in the morning, and it was the more striking in her as she was evidently a woman of strong character, with immense capacity for self-restraint.

Disregarding my presence, she went straight to her uncle, and passed her hand over his head with a sweet womanly caress.

'You have given orders that Arthur should be liberated, have you not, dad?' she asked.

'No, no, my girl, the matter must be probed to the bottom.'

'But I am so sure that he is innocent. You know what women's instincts are. I know that he has done no harm and that you will be sorry for having acted so harshly.'

'Why is he silent, then, if he is innocent?'

'Who knows? Perhaps because he was so angry that you should suspect him.'

'How could I help suspecting him, when I actually saw him with the coronet in his hand?'

'Oh, but he had only picked it up to look at it. Oh do, do take my word for it that he is innocent. Let the matter drop and say no more. It is so dreadful to think of our dear Arthur in prison!'

'I shall never let it drop until the gems are found – never, Mary! Your affection for Arthur blinds you as to the awful consequences to me. Far from hushing the thing up, I have brought a gentleman down from London to inquire more deeply into it.'

'This gentleman?' she asked, facing round to me.

'No, his friend. He wished us to leave him alone. He is round in the stable lane now.'

'The stable lane?' She raised her dark eyebrows. 'What can he hope to find there? Ah! this, I suppose, is he. I trust, sir, that you will succeed in proving, what I feel sure is the truth, that my cousin Arthur is innocent of this crime.'

'I fully share your opinion, and I trust, with you, that we may prove it,' returned Holmes, going back to the mat to knock the snow from his shoes. 'I believe I have the honour of addressing Miss Mary Holder. Might I ask you a question or two?'

'Pray do, sir, if it may help to clear this horrible affair up.'

'You heard nothing yourself last night?'

'Nothing, until my uncle here began to speak loudly. I heard that, and I came down.'

'You shut up the windows and doors the night before. Did you fasten all the windows?'

'Yes.'

'Were they all fastened this morning?'

'Yes.'

'You have a maid who has a sweetheart? I think that you remarked to your uncle last night that she had been out to see him?'

'Yes, and she was the girl who waited in the drawing room, and who may have heard uncle's remarks about the coronet.'

'I see. You infer that she may have gone out to tell her sweetheart, and that the two may have planned the robbery.'

'But what is the good of all these vague theories,' cried the banker, impatiently, 'when I have told you that I saw Arthur with the coronet in his hands?'

'Wait a little, Mr Holder. We must come back to that. About this girl, Miss Holder. You saw her return by the kitchen door, I presume?'

'Yes; when I went to see if the door was fastened for the night I met her slipping in. I saw the man, too, in the gloom.'

'Do you know him?'

'Oh yes; he is the greengrocer who brings our vegetables round. His name is Francis Prosper.'

'He stood,' said Holmes, 'to the left of the door – that is to say, farther up the path than is necessary to reach the door?'

'Yes, he did.'

'And he is a man with a wooden leg?'

Something like fear sprang up in the young lady's expressive black eyes. 'Why, you are like a magician,' said she. 'How do you know that?' She smiled, but there was no answering smile in Holmes's thin, eager face.

'I should be very glad now to go upstairs,' said he. 'I shall probably wish to go over the outside of the house again. Perhaps I had better take a look at the lower windows before I go up.'

He walked swiftly round from one to the other, pausing only at the large one which looked from the hall onto the stable lane. This he opened, and made a very careful examination of the sill with his powerful magnifying lens. 'Now we shall go upstairs,' said he, at last.

The banker's dressing-room was a plainly furnished little chamber, with a grey carpet, a large bureau, and a long mirror. Holmes went to the bureau first and looked hard at the lock.

'Which key was used to open it?' he asked.

'That which my son himself indicated – that of the cupboard of the lumber room.'

'Have you it here?'

'That is it on the dressing-table.'

Sherlock Holmes took it up and opened the bureau.

'It is a noiseless lock,' said he. 'It is no wonder that it did not wake you. This case, I presume, contains the coronet. We must have a look at it.' He opened the case, and, taking out the diadem, he laid it upon the table. It was a magnificent specimen of the jeweller's art, and the thirty-six stones were the finest that I have ever seen. At one side of the coronet was a cracked edge, where a corner holding three gems had been torn away.

'Now, Mr Holder,' said Holmes, 'here is the corner which corresponds to that which has been so unfortunately lost. Might I beg that you will break it off.'

The banker recoiled in horror. 'I should not dream of trying,' said he.

'Then I will.' Holmes suddenly bent his strength upon it, but without result. 'I feel it give a little,' said he; 'but, though I am exceptionally strong in the fingers, it would take me all my time to break it. An ordinary man could not do it. Now, what do you think would happen if I did break it, Mr Holder? There would be a noise like a pistol shot. Do you tell me that all this happened within a few yards of your bed, and that you heard nothing of it?'

'I do not know what to think. It is all dark to me.'

'But perhaps it may grow lighter as we go. What do you think, Miss Holder?'

'I confess that I still share my uncle's perplexity.'

'Your son had no shoes or slippers on when you saw him?'

'He had nothing on save only his trousers and shirt.'

'Thank you. We have certainly been favoured with extraordinary luck during this inquiry, and it will be entirely our own fault if we do not succeed in clearing the matter up.

With your permission, Mr Holder, I shall now continue my investigations outside.'

He went alone, at his own request, for he explained that any unnecessary footmarks might make his task more difficult. For an hour or more he was at work, returning at last with his feet heavy with snow and his features as inscrutable as ever.

'I think that I have seen now all that there is to see, Mr Holder,' said he; 'I can serve you best by returning to my rooms.'

'But the gems, Mr Holmes. Where are they?'

'I cannot tell.'

The banker wrung his hands. 'I shall never see them again!' he cried. 'And my son? You give me hopes?'

'My opinion is in no way altered.'

'Then, for God's sake, what was this dark business which was acted in my house last night?'

'If you can call upon me at my Baker Street rooms tomorrow morning between nine and ten I shall be happy to do what I can to make it clearer. I understand that you give me *carte blanche* to act for you, provided only that I get back the gems, and that you place no limit on the sum I may draw.'

'I would give my fortune to have them back.'

'Very good. I shall look into the matter between this and then. Good-bye; it is just possible that I may have to come over here again before evening.'

It was obvious to me that my companion's mind was now made up about the case, although what his conclusions were was more than I could even dimly imagine. Several times during our homeward journey I endeavoured to sound him upon the point, but he always glided away to some other topic, until at last I gave it over in despair. It was not yet three when we found ourselves in our room once more. He hurried to his chamber, and was down again in a few minutes dressed as a common loafer. With his collar turned up, his shiny seedy coat, his red cravat, and his worn boots, he was a perfect sample of the class.

'I think that this should do,' said he, glancing into the glass above the fireplace. 'I only wish that you could come with me, Watson, but I fear that it won't do. I may be on the trail in this matter, or I may be following a will-o'-the-wisp, but I shall soon know which it is. I hope that I may be back in a few hours.' He cut a slice of beef from the joint upon the sideboard, sandwiched it between two rounds of bread, and, thrusting this rude meal into his pocket, he started off upon his expedition.

I had just finished my tea when he returned, evidently in excellent spirits, swinging an old elastic-sided boot in his hand. He chucked it down into a corner and helped himself to a cup of tea.

'I only looked in as I passed,' said he. 'I am going right on.'

'Where to?'

'Oh, to the other side of the West End. It may be some time before I get back. Don't wait up for me in case I should be late.'

'How are you getting on?'

'Oh, so so. Nothing to complain of. I have been out to Streatham since I saw you last, but I did not call at the house. It is a very sweet little problem, and I would not have missed it for a good deal. However, I must not sit gossiping here, but must get these disreputable clothes off and return to my highly respectable self.'

I could see by his manner that he had stronger reasons for satisfaction than his words alone would imply. His eyes twinkled, and there was even a touch of colour upon his sallow cheeks. He hastened upstairs, and a few minutes later I heard the slam of the hall door, which told me that he was off once more upon his congenial hunt.

I waited until midnight, but there was no sign of his return, so I retired to my room. It was no uncommon thing for him to be away for days and nights on end when he was hot upon a scent, so that his lateness caused me no surprise. I do not know at what hour he came in, but when I came down to breakfast in the morning, there he was with a cup of coffee in one hand and the paper in the other, as fresh and trim as possible.

'You will excuse my beginning without you, Watson,' said he; 'but you remember that our client has rather an early appointment this morning.'

'Why, it is after nine now,' I answered. 'I should not be surprised if that were he. I thought I heard a ring.'

It was, indeed, our friend the financier. I was shocked by the change which had come over him, for his face, which was naturally of a broad and massive mould, was now pinched and fallen in, while his hair seemed to me at least a shade whiter. He entered with a weariness and lethargy which was even more painful than his violence of the morning before, and he dropped heavily into the armchair which I pushed forward for him.

'I do not know what I have done to be so severely tried,'

said he. 'Only two days ago I was a happy and prosperous man, without a care in the world. Now I am left to a lonely and dishonoured age. One sorrow comes close upon the heels of another. My niece, Mary, has deserted me.'

'Deserted you?'

'Yes. Her bed this morning had not been slept in, her room was empty, and a note for me lay upon the hall table. I had said to her last night, in sorrow and not in anger, that if she had married my boy all might have been well with him. Perhaps it was thoughtless of me to say so. It is to that remark that she refers in this note: "My Dearest Uncle, I feel that I have brought trouble upon you, and that if I had acted differently this terrible misfortune might never have occurred. I cannot, with this thought in my mind, ever again be happy under your roof, and I feel that I must leave you for ever. Do not worry about my future, for that is provided for; and, above all, do not search for me, for it will be fruitless labour and an ill-service to me. In life or in death, I am ever your loving, Mary." What could she mean by that note, Mr Holmes? Do you think it points to suicide?'

'No, no, nothing of the kind. It is perhaps the best possible solution. I trust, Mr Holder, that you are nearing the end of your troubles.'

'Ha! You say so! You have heard something, Mr Holmes; you have learned something! Where are the gems?'

'You would not think a thousand pounds apiece an excessive sum for them?'

'I would pay ten.'

'That would be unnecessary. Three thousand will cover the matter. And there is a little reward, I fancy. Have you your chequebook? Here is a pen. Better make it out for four thousand pounds.'

With a dazed face the banker made out the required cheque. Holmes walked over to his desk, took out a little triangular piece of gold with three gems in it, and threw it down upon the table.

With a shriek of joy our client clutched it up.

'You have it!' he gasped. 'I am saved! I am saved!'

The reaction of joy was as passionate as his grief had been, and he hugged his recovered gems to his bosom.

'There is one other thing you owe, Mr Holder,' said Sherlock Holmes, rather sternly.

'Owe!' He caught up a pen. 'Name the sum, and I will pay it.'

'No, the debt is not to me. You owe a very humble apology to that noble lad, your son, who has carried himself in this matter as I should be proud to see my own son do, should I ever chance to have one.'

'Then it was not Arthur who took them?'

'I told you yesterday, and I repeat today, that it was not.'

'You are sure of it! Then let us hurry to him at once, to let him know that the truth is known.'

'He knows it already. When I had cleared it all up I had an interview with him, and, finding that he would not tell me the story, I told it to him, on which he had to confess that I was right, and to add the very few details which were not yet quite clear to me. Your news of this morning, however, may open his lips.'

'For Heaven's sake, tell me, then, what is this extraordinary mystery!'

'I will do so, and I will show you the steps by which I reached it. And let me say to you, first, that which it is hardest for me to say and for you to hear: there has been an understanding between Sir George Burnwell and your niece Mary. They have now fled together.'

'My Mary? Impossible!'

'It is, unfortunately, more than possible; it is certain. Neither you nor your son knew the true character of this man when you admitted him into your family circle. He is one of the most dangerous men in England – a ruined gambler, an absolutely desperate villain, a man without heart or conscience. Your niece knew nothing of such men. When he breathed his vows to her, as he had done to a hundred before her, she flattered herself that she alone had touched his heart. The devil knows best what he said, but at least she became his tool, and was in the habit of seeing him nearly every evening.'

'I cannot, and I will not, believe it!' cried the banker, with an ashen face.

'I will tell you, then, what occurred in your house last night. Your niece, when you had, as she thought, gone to your room, slipped down and talked to her lover through the window which leads into the stable lane. His footmarks had pressed right through the snow, so long had he stood there. She told him of the coronet. His wicked lust for gold kindled at the news, and he bent her to his will. I have no doubt that she loved you, but there are women in whom the love of a lover extinguishes all other loves, and I think that she must have been one. She had hardly listened to his instructions when she saw you coming downstairs, on which she closed the window rapidly, and told you about one of the servants' escapade with her wooden-legged lover, which was all perfectly true.

'Your boy, Arthur, went to bed after his interview with you, but he slept badly on account of his uneasiness about his club debts. In the middle of the night he heard a soft tread pass his door, so he rose, and looking out, was surprised to see his cousin walking very stealthily along the passage, until she disappeared into your dressing-room. Petrified with astonishment, the lad slipped on some clothes, and waited there in the dark to see what would come of this strange affair. Presently she emerged from the room again, and in the light of the passage-lamp your son saw that she carried the precious coronet in her hands. She passed down the stairs, and he, thrilling with horror, ran along and slipped behind the curtain near your door, whence he could see what passed in the hall beneath. He saw her stealthily open the window, hand out the coronet to some one in the gloom, and then closing it once more hurry back to her room, passing quite close to where he stood hid behind the curtain.

'As long as she was on the scene he could not take any action without a horrible exposure of the woman whom he loved. But the instant that she was gone he realised how crushing a misfortune this would be for you, and how all-important it was to set it right. He rushed down, just as he was, in his bare feet, opened the window, sprang out into the snow, and ran down the lane, where he could see a dark figure in the moonlight. Sir George Burnwell tried to get away, but Arthur caught him, and there was a struggle between them, your lad tugging at one side of the coronet, and his opponent at the other. In the scuffle, your son struck Sir George, and cut him over the eye. Then something suddenly snapped, and your son, finding that he had the coronet in his hands, rushed back, closed the window, ascended to your room, and had just observed that the coronet had been twisted in the struggle, and was endeavouring to straighten it when you appeared upon the scene.'

'Is it possible?' gasped the banker.

'You then roused his anger by calling him names at a moment when he felt that he had deserved your warmest thanks. He could not explain the true state of affairs without betraying one who certainly deserved little enough consideration at his hands. He took the more chivalrous view, however, and preserved her secret.'

'And that was why she shrieked and fainted when she saw the coronet,' cried Mr Holder. 'Oh, my God! what a blind fool I have been! And his asking to be allowed to go out for five minutes! The dear fellow wanted to see if the missing piece were at the scene of the struggle. How cruelly I have misjudged him!'

'When I arrived at the house,' continued Holmes, 'I at once went very carefully round it to observe if there were any traces in the snow which might help me. I knew that none had fallen since the evening before, and also that there had been a strong frost to preserve impressions. I passed along the tradesmen's path, but found it all trampled down and indistinguishable. Just beyond it, however, at the far side of the kitchen door, a woman had stood and talked with a man, whose round impressions on one side showed that he had a wooden leg. I could even tell that they had been disturbed, for the woman had run back swiftly to the door, as was shown by the deep toe and light heel marks, while Wooden-leg had waited a little, and then had gone away. I thought at the time that this might be the maid and her sweetheart, of whom you had already spoken to me, and inquiry showed it was so. I passed round the garden without seeing anything more than random tracks, which I took to be the police; but when I got into the stable lane a very long and complex story was written in the snow in front of me.

'There was a double line of tracks of a booted man, and a second double line which I saw with delight belonged to a man with naked feet. I was at once convinced from what you had told me that the latter was your son. The first had walked both ways, but the other had run swiftly, and, as his tread was marked in places over the depression of the boot, it was obvious that he had passed after the other. I followed them up, and found that they led to the hall window, where Boots had worn all the snow away while waiting. Then I walked to the other end, which was a hundred yards or more down the lane. I saw where Boots had faced round, where the snow was cut up as though there had been a struggle, and, finally, where a few drops of blood had fallen, to show me that I was not mistaken. Boots had then run down the lane, and another little smudge of blood showed that it was he who had been hurt. When he came to the high road at the other end, I found that the pavement had been cleared, so there was an end to that clue.

'On entering the house, however, I examined, as you remember, the sill and framework of the hall window with my lens, and I could at once see that someone had passed out.

I could distinguish the outline of an instep where the wet foot had been placed in coming in. I was then beginning to be able to form an opinion as to what had occurred. A man had waited outside the window, someone had brought the gems; the deed had been overseen by your son, he had pursued the thief, had struggled with him, they had each tugged at the coronet, their united strength causing injuries which neither alone could have effected. He had returned with the prize, but had left a fragment in the grasp of his opponent. So far I was clear. The question now was, who was the man, and who was it that brought him the coronet?

'It is an old maxim of mine that when you have excluded the impossible, whatever remains, however improbable, must be the truth. Now, I knew that it was not you who had brought it down, so there only remained your niece and the maids. But if it were the maids, why should your son allow himself to be accused in their place? There could be no possible reason. As he loved his cousin, however, there was an excellent explanation why he should retain her secret – the more so as the secret was a disgraceful one. When I remembered that you had seen her at that window, and how she had fainted on seeing the coronet again, my conjecture became a certainty.

'And who could it be who was her confederate? A lover evidently, for who else could outweigh the love and gratitude which she must feel to you? I knew that you went out little, and that your circle of friends was a very limited one. But among them was Sir George Burnwell. I had heard of him before as being a man of evil reputation among women. It must have been he who wore those boots and retained the missing gems. Even though he knew that Arthur had discovered him, he might still flatter himself that he was safe, for the lad could not say a word without compromising his own family.

'Well, your own good sense will suggest what measures I took next. I went in the shape of a loafer to Sir George's house, managed to pick up an acquaintance with his valet, learned that his master had cut his head the night before, and, finally, at the expense of six shillings, made all sure by buying a pair of his cast-off shoes. With these I journeyed down to Streatham, and saw that they exactly fitted the tracks.'

'I saw an ill-dressed vagabond in the lane yesterday evening,' said Mr Holder.

'Precisely. It was I. I found that I had my man, so I came home and changed my clothes. It was a delicate part which I had to play then, for I saw that a prosecution must be avoided to avert scandal, and I knew that so astute a villain would see that our hands were tied in the matter. I went and saw him. At first, of course, he denied everything. But when I gave him every particular that had occurred, he tried to bluster, and took down a life-preserver from the wall. I knew my man, however, and I clapped a pistol to his head before he could strike. Then he became a little more reasonable. I told him that we would give him a price for the stones he held – a thousand pounds apiece. That brought out the first signs of grief that he had shown. "Why, dash it all!" said he, "I've let them go at six hundred for the three!" I soon managed to get the address of the receiver who had them, on promising him that there would be no prosecution. Off I set to him, and after much chaffering I got our stones at a thousand apiece. Then I looked in upon your son, told him that all was right, and eventually got to my bed about two o'clock, after what I may call a really hard day's work.'

'A day which has saved England from a great public scandal,' said the banker, rising. 'Sir, I cannot find words to thank you, but you shall not find me ungrateful for what you have done. Your skill has indeed exceeded all that I have heard of it. And now I must fly to my dear boy to apologise to him for the wrong which I have done him. As to what you tell me of poor Mary, it goes to my very heart. Not even your skill can inform me where she is now.'

'I think that we may safely say,' returned Holmes, 'that she is wherever Sir George Burnwell is. It is equally certain, too, that whatever her sins are, they will soon receive a more than sufficient punishment.'

The Man from Nowhere

Edward D. Hoch

The interested reader may find the tale of Kaspar Hauser's strange life and stranger death related at some length in volume eleven of the *Encyclopedia Britannica*. And perhaps the story of Douglas Zadig's life and death will be there some day, too.

For Douglas Zadig was also a man from nowhere, a man who came out of the mists and died in the snow – just as Kaspar Hauser had over one hundred years ago.

This is the story of Douglas Zadig's last day on earth, and of the people who were with him when he died ...

It was a cold, bleak Friday afternoon in early November when Simon Ark called me at my office. I was in the midst of checking some final galley proofs for our January books, but I tossed them aside when I recognised his voice on the line. 'Simon! How've you been?'

'Busy,' he replied. 'How would you like to go up to Maine for the weekend?'

'Maine? In November? Nobody goes up there except hunters this time of year.'

'Hunters and publishers,' Simon Ark corrected; 'I want to see a man, and since he's a writer of sorts, I thought it might be good to take you along. That is, if you're free …'

I'd learned long ago that an invitation from Simon Ark was never as casual as it sounded. If he was going up to Maine for the weekend, there was a reason for it, and I wanted to be with him. 'I'm free,' I said. 'When should I meet you?'

'Can you be at Grand Central at six? We'll take the New Haven part of the way.'

'I'll be there. At the information booth …'

I called my wife after that, explaining the reason for my sudden trip. She knew Simon Ark almost as well as I did, and she was one of the few people in this world who understood. She said goodbye to me with that little catch in her breath that told me she'd be waiting for whatever adventures I had to relate upon my return.

And then I was off, on a weekend I was never to forget …

I'd first met Simon Ark years before, when I was still a newspaper reporter; and though I'd lost track of him for several years, he'd turned up again recently to renew our friendship. He was an odd man by any standards, a tall, heavy-set figure with an expression that was saintly.

My experiences with him in the past, together with the tales he'd related to me over a beer or a glass of wine, told me that he was someone not really of our world at all. He belonged to the world of the past – to the world of the supernatural, perhaps, but certainly not to the world of twentieth-century America.

He was a man who was searching, searching for what he called the Ultimate Evil, the devil himself. I'd laughed at first, or thought possibly that he was a little crazy; but I didn't laugh anymore, and I knew that if anything he was the sanest man in the world. He found evil everywhere, because there was evil everywhere, and I knew that someday he would have his wish; someday he would confront Satan himself.

That was why I always went with him when he asked. He'd been searching for a long time, and the meeting might never take place in my lifetime; but if it did I wanted to be there, too.

So that was why I was with him as the train rumbled north toward New England that night. 'What's it all about this time, Simon?' I asked finally, when no information was forthcoming.

He gazed out the train window, almost as if he could see something in the darkness besides the irregular patterns of light from buildings and roads.

Presently he asked, 'Did you ever hear of a man called Douglas Zadig?'

The name seemed somehow familiar, but I had to shake my head. 'Who is he?'

'He is a man from nowhere, a man without family or country, a man without a past. You may have read about him some ten years ago, when he walked out of an English mist one night to become an overnight sensation.'

'I remember now,' I said. 'He was a youth of about twenty at the time, and he claimed to have no memory of his past life. He spoke English very poorly, and his clothes were almost rags. The only thing he remembered was that his first name was Douglas. When they found him, he was carrying a worn French copy of Voltaire's novel, *Zadig*, so the newspapers named him Douglas Zadig.'

'You have a good memory for details,' Simon Ark said. 'As you probably remember, this Douglas Zadig has remained a complete mystery. His fingerprints were not on file anywhere in the world; his picture has never been identified by anyone. He is simply a man without a past.'

'I lost track of him a few years back, though,' I told Simon. 'What's he been doing recently?'

'I ran into him a few years ago in London,' Simon Ark continued. 'I was in England to investigate an odd happening in Devonshire, and I happened to hear him speaking at a sort of rally. He's become quite a writer and speaker in some circles – a sort of prophet, I suppose you'd call him.'

'Is this the man we're going up to Maine to see?'

'Quite correct. He came to this country with an American doctor two years ago. The doctor – a man named Adam Hager – has actually adopted him as a son, and the two of them are living in Maine.'

'Odd, but hardly in your field of investigation, is it, Simon?'

The train rumbled on through the small New England towns, along the dark waiting waters of Long Island Sound. Around us, people were drifting into sleep, and the seat lights were being dimmed.

Simon Ark took a slim volume from his pocket and held it out for my examination. I glanced at the cover and saw that the unlikely title was *On the Eternal War Between the Forces of Good and the Forces of Evil*. The author was Douglas Zadig.

Simon Ark returned the book to his pocket. 'The odd thing about this book – as with all of Douglas Zadig's writings and speeches – is that his apparently new philosophy is actually lifted almost word for word from the teachings of a religious leader named Zoroaster, who lived seven centuries before Christ ...'

It took us until Saturday noon to reach our destination, a small town called Katahdin in the northern part of the state. It was cold up here, and a fresh layer of snow already covered the ground. All around us were mountains and lakes and forests, and it seemed impossible that such a place could be only a single night's journey from New York.

There was a small hotel of sorts, where we left what few belongings we'd brought along. It was all but empty now, but in another week I imagined it would be full of sportsmen from Bangor and Boston.

'You fellows hunters?' the room clerk asked us. 'Little early in the season for good hunting.'

'We're hunters of a very special type of game,' Simon Ark replied. 'Can you direct us to the house of Doctor Hager?'

'Sure; it's right at the edge of town, where the road turns. Big white place. You can't miss it.'

'Thank you.'

The house of Doctor Hager was indeed easy to find; and from the look of the barren white fields that surrounded it, I guessed that someone had once tried farming the land.

Doctor Hager himself was average in almost every

respect. He might have been a typical country doctor, but he might just as well have been a big-city businessman. There was a look of shrewdness about his eyes that contrasted with the weak smile that seemed always on his lips.

Simon Ark explained that we were from a New York publishing company, and had come up to speak with Douglas Zadig about the possibility of doing one of his books.

'Come in, by all means,' Doctor Hager urged us. 'I'm sure Douglas will be happy to speak with you. There are so many people interested in his work …'

The house was even larger than it had seemed from outside, and we saw at once that we were not the only visitors. A handsome young woman of perhaps thirty, and an older man with thin, drawn features were sitting in the living room.

Doctor Hager took charge of the introductions, and I learned that the woman was a Mrs Eve Brent, from Chicago. The older man was Charles Kingsley, and I recognised him as a retired manufacturer, whose name was prominent in financial circles.

'These are some New York publishers,' Doctor Hager announced proudly, 'who have come all the way up here to talk with Douglas.' Then, turning to us, he explained, 'Our house here is always open to visitors. Mrs Brent and Mr Kingsley are staying with us for a few weeks to try and find themselves spiritually.'

I had taken the chair next to Mrs Brent, and I asked her where Douglas Zadig was, just to get the conversation started.

'He's upstairs in his room; I think he'll be down shortly.'

'You're a long way from Chicago, aren't you?' I asked.

'My ... my husband died a few years back. Since then, I've just been at loose ends, traveling to Europe and South America; it wasn't until I read one of Douglas Zadig's books that I found myself again.'

I saw that Simon was busy talking with Hager and Mr Kingsley. But all conversation stopped with the sudden entrance of a thin young man whom I knew to be Douglas Zadig.

He was taller than I'd supposed, with gaunt, pointed features of the type that stayed in your memory. There was a slight limp to his walk, and I remembered reading now that he'd had the limp when he first appeared, more than ten years ago in England.

'I'm sorry to be late,' he apologised, in a rich full voice, with barely a trace of English accent. 'But it happened again.'

Whatever it was that had 'happened' was enough to bring gasps from the Doctor and the two guests. Hager rushed to Douglas Zadig's side and quickly examined his head.

'The same side as before, Adam,' the young man said. 'I was shaving, when suddenly I felt this blow on the temple; there's not much blood this time, though.'

'The skin is broken, though,' Doctor Hager said. 'Just like the other time.'

Simon Ark arose from his chair and went forward to examine the young man. 'Just what is the trouble here?' he asked, addressing the question to the four of them.

It was Mrs Brent at my side who answered. 'Douglas has been the victim of two mysterious attacks, both while he was alone in the room. We ... we think it might be the ... devil ...'

I saw Simon Ark's quiet eyes come alive at the word, and I knew that in some mysterious way he'd come into conflict again with the Evil he eternally sought. From outside, a slight wind stirred the barren trees; and through the window I could see a brief gust of snow eddy up into the air.

Charles Kingsley snorted and took out a cigar. 'This whole business is nonsense. We're not living in the Middle Ages anymore; the devil doesn't come around attacking people.'

'I fear you're quite wrong.' Simon Ark spoke quietly. 'Satan is just as real today as he was a thousand years ago; and there's no reason to suppose that his tactics have changed any in that time. If I were more certain he was among us, in fact, I'd suggest a rite of exorcism.'

'We'd need a priest for that,' Mrs Brent said; 'there isn't one within miles of here.'

Simon Ark shook his head. 'In the early days of Christianity, it was quite common for lay persons to exorcise the devil. But I would not want to attempt it under the present circumstances.'

Douglas Zadig spoke from the doorway, where he'd remained during Simon Ark's brief examination. 'Just what do you mean by that, sir? You talk oddly for a book publisher.'

'I have other professions. I refer to the peculiar doctrine you preach as to the eternal war between the two great forces of good and evil. It reminds one somewhat of the teachings of Zoroaster.'

The young man seemed to pale slightly at the name. 'I ... I have read about his doctrines, of course. But if you'd completed your study of my teachings and published works, I think you'd find that my theory of evil holds that, as a force, it is part of God, and is willed by Him – not that it is a separate and distinct power.'

'Oh, come now, Mr Zadig,' Simon Ark said with almost a chuckle, 'Thomas Aquinas disproved that idea seven hundred years ago. In case you're not familiar with it, I refer you to chapters thirty-nine and ninety-five in Book One of his *Summa Contra Gentiles*. For a preacher of a new religion, you seem to be quite confused as to your own doctrine.'

Douglas Zadig turned on him with blazing eyes. 'I need not listen to these insults in my own house,' he said, and turned from the room. Doctor Hager ran after him and followed him onto the front porch.

Kingsley and Mrs Brent seemed shocked at Simon Ark's tactics; I walked over close enough to speak to him without their hearing us. 'Perhaps you were a little hard on the fellow, Simon; I'm sure he means no harm.'

'Whether he *means* harm or not, the fact remains that false teachings like that can always cause harm.'

Doctor Hager returned to us then, and through the window we could see Douglas Zadig walking off across a snow-covered field, his open jacket flapping in the breeze. 'He's gone for a walk,' the doctor informed us; 'he wants to be alone with his thoughts.'

Simon Ark walked to the window and watched him until he was out of sight over a hill of snow.

'Really,' Mrs Brent said, 'I think you owe him an apology when he returns. In his own way, he's a great man.'

Simon Ark turned from the window and faced the four of

us. 'Have any of you ever heard the story of Kaspar Hauser?' he asked quietly. And when he saw our blank expressions, he went on, 'Kaspar Hauser was a German youth of about sixteen, who appeared suddenly in Nuremberg in May of 1828. He was dressed as a peasant, and seemed to remember nothing of his past life. In his possession were found two letters, supposedly written by the boy's mother and his guardian. A professor in Nuremberg undertook his education, and he remained there and in Ansbach until his death in 1833. Twice before his death, while he was living with the professor, he suffered mysterious wounds; and his death from a stab wound while he was walking in a park during the winter has never been explained.'

Doctor Hager spoke from between tightened lips. 'Just what are you driving at?'

'I am suggesting that Douglas Zadig's life, his appearance out of nowhere in England ten years ago, his friendship with you, Doctor, and even the two odd wounds he has recently suffered, follow very closely the life of Kaspar Hauser.'

Mrs Brent was still beside me, and her fingers dug unconsciously into my arm. 'Perhaps you're right. What does that prove?'

'Don't any of you see it?' Simon Ark asked. 'This man we all know as Douglas Zadig has no life of his own. Everything he has done and said has been done and said before in this world. He bears the name of a fictional character from French literature; he teaches a doctrine of a man dead nearly three thousand years, and he lives the life of a man from the nineteenth century. I don't propose to explain it – I am only stating the facts ...'

There was silence when he finished speaking, and the four of us who were with him in the room looked at each other with questioning glances. There was something here which was beyond our understanding. Something ...

Doctor Hager broke the silence. 'How ... how did this man ... this Kaspar Hauser die?'

'He was stabbed to death while walking alone in a park. There were no other footprints in the snow, and yet the wound could not have been self-inflicted. The mystery has never been solved.'

As if with one body our eyes went toward the window where last we'd seen Douglas Zadig walking. And I knew there was but a single thought in our minds.

Doctor Hager pulled a coat from the closet and threw it over his shoulders. 'No, not that way,' he said, giving voice to the fear that was in all our minds. 'He'll come back the other way, at the rear of the house.'

We ran out, Hager and Simon Ark in the lead, closely followed by Kingsley, Mrs Brent and myself. We gave only a passing glance to the single set of footprints leading off over the hill, and then we ran around the back of the big white house.

It was cold, but somehow we didn't notice the cold. We saw only the snow – clear and white and unmarked ahead of us – and far away in the distance across the field, the lone figure of Douglas Zadig walking back toward us.

He walked quickly, with the steady gait of a young, vigorous man. The thin layer of snow did not impede his feet, and his short jacket flapped in the breeze as if it were a summer's day. When he saw us he waved a greeting, and seemed to walk a little faster toward us.

He was perhaps a hundred yards away when it happened. He stopped short as if struck by a blow, and his hands flew to his left side. And even at that distance, we could see the look of shock and surprise on his face.

He staggered, almost fell, and then continued staggering toward us, his hands clutching at his side. 'I've been stabbed,' he shouted, 'I've been stabbed.' And already we could see the bloody trail he was leaving in the snow …

Doctor Hager was the first to break the spell, and he dashed forward to meet the wounded man, with the rest of us in close pursuit. When Hager was still some twenty yards from him, Douglas Zadig fell to his knees in the snow; and now the blood was reddening his shirt and gushing out between his fingers. He looked at us once more with that surprised expression, and then he toppled over in the snow.

Hager was the first to reach him, and he bent over quickly and turned the body back to examine the wound. The he let it fall again and looked up at us.

'He's dead …' he said simply.

We knew it was impossible, and we looked down at the impossible and perhaps we prayed.

'He must have been shot,' Eve Brent said, but then Doctor Hager showed us the wound and it was clearly that of a knife.

'He stabbed himself,' Charles Kingsley said, but I knew that Kingsley didn't even believe it himself. There was no knife in the wound, no knife back there in the snow; and Hager settled it by pointing out that such a wound would be difficult to self-inflict, and impossible while the five of us watched him.

We went back to where the bloodstains started, and searched in the snow for something, anything – even the footprints of an invisible man. But there was nothing. The snow was unmarked, except for the bloodstains and the single line of footprints.

And then we stood there and looked at the body and looked at each other and waited for somebody else to say something.

'I suggest we call the local police, or the state troopers,' Simon Ark said finally.

And so we left the body of Douglas Zadig where it lay in the snow and went back into the house. And waited for the police.

And when they came – a bent old man, who was the local barber and also at times the constable, and a wiser one, who was the town doctor and also its coroner, we knew no more.

Could the wound have been inflicted by someone on the other side of the hill, before he came into view? That was my question, but the half-formed theory in my mind died even before it was born. The blood had only started at the point where we'd seen him grip his side; and besides that both doctors agreed that such a wound would cause almost instantaneous death. It was a wonder he'd even managed to walk as far he did.

And presently the barber, who was the constable, and the doctor who was the coroner, left, taking the body of Douglas Zadig with them.

Simon Ark continued to gaze out the window at the occasional snowflakes that were drifting down from above. Mrs Brent and I managed to make coffee for the others, but for a long time no one spoke.

Presently I heard Simon Ark mumble, 'The man from nowhere ... Nowhere ...' And seeing me watching him, he continued, 'Dear, beauteous death, the jewel of the just! Shining nowhere but in the dark; what mysteries do lie beyond thy dust, could man outlook that mark!'

When he saw my puzzled expression, he explained, 'The lines are not original with me. They were written back in the seventeenth century by Henry Vaughan.'

'Does that tell you what killed Douglas Zadig out there in the snow?'

He smiled at me, something he rarely did. 'The answer to our mystery might better be found in Shakespeare than in Vaughan.'

'Then you do know!'

'Perhaps ...'

'I read a story once, about a fellow who was murdered with a dagger made of ice.'

'That melted and left no trace? Well, you'd hardly expect a dagger of ice to melt when the outside temperature is below freezing, would you?'

'I guess not,' I admitted. 'But if it wasn't done in any of the ways we've mentioned, then it must have been supernatural. Do you really mean that Douglas Zadig was possessed of the devil?'

But Simon Ark only repeated his favourite word. 'Perhaps ...'

'I don't care,' Charles Kingsley was saying, in the loud voice I'd come to expect from him. 'I'm not a suspect, and I don't intend to stay here any longer. I came because I believed in the teachings and writings of Douglas Zadig; now that he's dead there's no reason for me to remain any longer.'

Doctor Hager shrugged and gave up the argument. 'You're certainly free to leave any time you want to, Mr Kingsley. Believe me, this awful tragedy strikes me a much greater blow than anyone else.'

Mrs Brent had taken out a chequebook and her pen. 'Well, I'll still give you the money as I promised, Doctor Hager. If nothing else perhaps you can erect a memorial of some sort.'

I could see that she was serious. I had known Douglas Zadig for only a short time on the final day of his life, but I could see that he'd had a profound effect on the lives of these people and others like them. To me he had been only a name half-remembered from the news stories of ten years ago, but to some he had become apparently the preacher of a new belief.

And then Simon Ark spoke again. 'I would like you people to remain for another hour if you would. I think I will be able to show you the manner in which Douglas Zadig died.'

'If you can do that,' Kingsley said, 'it's worth waiting for. But if there really is some sort of devil around here, I sure don't want to stay.'

'I promise you that I'll protect you all from the force that struck down Douglas Zadig,' Simon Ark said. 'I have one question, though: Doctor Hager, do you keep any chickens here?'

'Chickens?' Hager repeated with a puzzled frown. 'Why, no; there's a place down the road that raises them, though. Why?'

'I wondered,' he replied, and then he would say no more. After that, he disappeared into a remote section of the house and the four of us were left alone. We knew that the state police would be arriving before long, to continue the investigation; and I could understand why Kingsley and Mrs Brent were anxious to get away.

They were beginning to grow restless again when Simon Ark reappeared, this time holding in his hands the small ansated cross he always carried. 'If you people will accompany me outside, I believe I will be able to show you how Douglas Zadig met his death.'

'You mean you know who killed him.'

'In a way I suppose I was responsible for his death,' Simon Ark answered. 'The least I can do is to avenge it.'

We followed him outside, to the snow-covered field very near the spot where Douglas Zadig had died just an hour earlier. The four of us paused at the edge of the snow, but Simon Ark walked on, until he was some fifty feet away from us.

Then he stood there, looking up at the bleak November sky and at the distant trees and mountains. And he seemed to be very much alone …

He held the strange ansated cross above his head, and chanted a few words in the Coptic language I had come to know so well.

From somewhere a large bird swooped in a gigantic circle overhead. It might have been an eagle, or a vulture, lured north into the cold weather by some unknown quirk of nature. We watched it until it disappeared into a low brooding cloud bank, and then our eyes returned to Simon Ark.

He stood there, chanting in the strange tongue, as if calling for some demons from the dark past. He stood there for what seemed like an eternity, and what must have been the longest five minutes of my life.

And then it happened.

Again.

He dropped his hands suddenly to his side, and when they came away we could see the blood. He took a single step forward and then collapsed on his face in the snow, one outstretched hand still clutching the ansated cross.

We rushed forward behind Adam Hager, and I could feel my knees growing weak at the sight before us. Simon Ark, whom I had come to think of as almost an invincible man, had been struck down by the same force that had killed Douglas Zadig …

Doctor Hager reached him first, and felt for his heart. And then …

… In a moment I'll never forget, Simon Ark suddenly came alive, and rolled over in the snow, pinning Hager beneath him.

And we all saw, in Hager's outstretched helpless hand, the gleaming blade of a thin steel dagger …

'They were just a couple of small-time swindlers who came close to hitting the big money.' Simon Ark said later, when the state police had taken away the cursing, struggling figure of Doctor Hager.

We were back inside – Kingsley, Mrs Brent, several police officers, and myself – and listening to Simon Ark's explanation. Somehow the tension of the past few hours was gone, and we were a friendly group of people who might have been discussing the results of the day's football games.

'It's always difficult to imagine yourself as the victim of a swindler,' he was saying, 'but I saw at once that Zadig and Hager had invited you two here for the purpose of getting money from you. We might never know how many dozens were here before you, people who'd read Zadig's book and written to him. If you'll check further, I think you'll find that the book's publication was paid for by Zadig and Hager, and that most of his speaking engagements were phony, too – like his occasional limping.'

'He did ask us for money to carry out various projects,' Kingsley admitted.

'As I've already told you,' Simon Ark continued, 'the very fact that his name, his life, and his so-called doctrine were copied from the past made me suspect a swindle of some sort. There was just nothing original about the man; his was a life copied out of an encyclopedia. I suppose after he met Hager in London, the two of them thought up the scheme. I imagine you'll find that Hager has tried this sort of thing before under various names.'

'But what about the murder?' Mrs Brent wanted to know. 'Why should Hager kill his partner in crime?'

'I fear it was because of my arrival. My detailed questions about Zadig's teachings caught them both off guard; and Hager, especially, knew that I might uncover their whole phony plot. When I mentioned the parallels between the attacks on Zadig and Kaspar, as well as those between the doctrines of Zadig and Zoroaster, Hager knew I was getting too close. When he and Zadig went out on the porch together before, I imagine they set up the final act of the Hauser drama, in which Zadig was to be wounded by a devil that had taken possesion of him. I suppose this was the final try for the money, and perhaps they'd done the whole performance before.'

'Only this time it was real,' I said; 'this time Hager really killed him …'

'Correct. You'll remember it was Hager who asked how Hauser had been killed – and Hager who got us out of the house, so we could have front row seats for the final act. The actual mechanics of the murder are simple, once you know they were both swindlers. There's an old trick among confidence men – I believe it's called a "cackle-bladder" – a small membranous bag filled with chicken blood or the like, which the swindler crushes to his body in order to appear wounded, after his confederate has fired a blank pistol at him. Douglas Zadig, walking toward us across the field, simply burst the bladder on his side and did a good job of acting. Hager, who naturally was expecting it all, easily managed to move fastest and reach the "body" first. At this point, to make it look as realistic as possible, Hager was to wound Zadig slightly with a spring-knife hidden up his sleeve …'

He paused, and we remembered the scene in the snow; and the horror of what was coming dawned on us all.

'And then, while Douglas Zadig braced himself so as to remain motionless when the knife cut into him, his partner released the spring-knife up his sleeve, and sent the steel blade deep into Zadig's side, straight for the heart ...'

Charles Kingsley stirred slightly, and Mrs Brent was beginning to look sick. But there wasn't much more, and Simon Ark continued. 'Both doctors told us such a wound would have caused almost instantaneous death, and that made me wonder about the wounded man walking as far as he did. Anything's possible, of course, but it seemed far more likely that Hager had killed him as he bent over the body.'

'But,' I objected, 'why did he have the nerve to try to kill you in the same way? When you pulled the trick with the chicken blood he must have realised you knew.'

'It wasn't chicken blood,' Simon Ark corrected with a slight smile. 'I was forced to use ordinary ketchup, but I knew Hager would try to kill me, even though he realised I was only waiting to grab the knife from his sleeve. He had no choice, really. Once I was on to his trick, I had only to explain it; and an analysis of the various bloodstains on Zadig's shirt would have proved me correct. His only chance was to be faster with his spring-knife than I was with my hands. Luckily, he wasn't, or you might have had a second impossible death on your hands.'

He said it as if he meant it; but somehow I had the feeling that his life had never really been in danger. I had the feeling that it would be awfully difficult to kill Simon Ark.

And so we departed from the little town in Maine, and journeyed back toward the slightly warmer wilds of Manhattan. A search of the house had turned up nearly a hundred thousand dollars in contributions from Zadig's swindled followers, and we began to think that Hager had possibly been thinking of that, too, when he plunged the knife into his partner's side.

'One thing, though, Simon,' I said as the train thundered through the New England night. 'Just where did Douglas Zadig ever come from? What happened in that London mist ten years ago?'

'There are things that are never explained,' he answered simply. 'But several explanations present themselves. The copy of the novel in French suggests – now that we know the man's true character – that even at this early age he was trying to fool the public into thinking him French instead of English. I don't know the real answer, and probably never will; but if a young man had avoided military service during England's darkest hours, he might well have had to think up a scheme to protect himself in a post-war world full of returning veterans.'

'Of course!' I agreed. 'He was a draft-dodger; that would explain why his fingerprints weren't on file with the army, or elsewhere!'

But Simon Ark was gazing out the window, into the night, and he replied in a quiet voice. 'There are other possible explanations, of course, but I prefer not to dwell on them. Douglas Zadig is dead, like Kasper Hauser before him, and there are some things better left unexplained, at least in this world.'

And after that he said no more about it ...

The Avenging Chance

Anthony Berkeley

When he was able to review it in perspective Roger Sheringham was inclined to think that the Poisoned Chocolate Case, as the papers called it, was perhaps the most perfectly planned murder he had ever encountered. Certainly he plumed himself more on its solution than on that of any other. The motive was so obvious, when you knew where to look for it – but you didn't know; the method was so significant, when you had grasped its real essentials – but you didn't grasp them; the traces were so thinly covered, when you had realised what was covering them – but you didn't realise. But for the merest piece of bad luck, which the murderer could not possibly have foreseen, the crime must have been added to the classical list of great mysteries.

This was the story of the case, as Chief Inspector Moresby told it one evening to Roger in the latter's rooms in the Albany a week or so later. Or rather, this is the raw material of Moresby's story as it passed through the crucible of Roger's vivid imagination:

On Friday morning, the fifteenth of November, at half past ten in the morning, Graham Beresford walked into his club in Piccadilly, the very exclusive Rainbow Club, and asked for his letters. The porter handed him one and a couple of circulars. Beresford walked over to the fireplace in the big lounge to open them.

While he was doing so, a few minutes later, another member entered the club, a Sir William Anstruther, who lived in rooms just round the corner in Berkeley Street and spent most of his time at the Rainbow. The porter glanced at the clock, as he always did when Sir William entered, and, as always, it was exactly half past ten to the minute. The time was thus definitely fixed by the porter beyond all doubt. There were three letters for Sir William and a small parcel, and he also strolled over to the fireplace, nodding to Beresford but not speaking to him. The two men only knew each other very slightly, and had probably never exchanged more than a dozen words in all.

Having glanced through his letters Sir William opened the parcel and, after a moment, snorted with disgust. Beresford looked at him, and Sir William thrust out a letter which had been enclosed in the parcel, with an uncomplimentary remark upon modern trade methods. Concealing a smile (Sir William's ways were a matter of some amusement to his fellow members), Beresford read the letter. It was from a big firm of chocolate manufacturers, Mason & Sons, and set forth that they were putting on the market a new brand of liqueur chocolates designed especially to appeal to men; would Sir William do them the honour of accepting the enclosed two-pound box and letting the firm have his candid opinion on them?

'Do they think I'm a blank chorus-girl?' fumed Sir William. 'Write 'em testimonials about their blank chocolates, indeed! Blank 'em! I'll complain to the blank committee. That sort of blank thing can't blank well be allowed here.' Sir William, it will be gathered, was a choleric man.

'Well, it's an ill wind so far as I'm concerned,' Beresford soothed him. 'It's reminded me of something. My wife and I had a box at the Imperial last night and I bet her a box of chocolates to a hundred cigarettes that she wouldn't spot the villain by the end of the second act. She won. I must remember to get them this morning. Have you seen it, by the way – *The Creaking Skull*? Not a bad show.'

'Not blank likely,' growled Sir William, unsoothed. 'I've got something better to do than sit and watch a lot of blank fools with phosphorescent paint on their faces popping off silly pop-guns at each other. Got to get a box of chocolates, did you say? Well, take this blank one. I don't want it.'

For a moment Beresford demurred politely and then, most unfortunately for himself, accepted. The money so saved meant nothing to him, for he was a wealthy man; but trouble was always worth saving.

By an extraordinarily lucky chance neither the outer wrapper of the box nor its covering letter were thrown into the fire, and this was the more fortunate in that both men had tossed the envelopes of their letters into the flames. Sir William did, indeed, make a bundle of wrapper, letter and string, but he handed it over to Beresford with the box, and the latter simply dropped it inside the fender. This bundle the porter subsequently extracted and, being a man of orderly habits, put it tidily away in the waste-paper basket, whence it was retrieved later by the police. The bundle, it may be said at once, comprised two out of the only three material clues to the murder, the third of course being the chocolates themselves.

Of the three unconscious protagonists in the impending tragedy, Sir William was without doubt the most remarkable. Still a year or two under fifty he looked, with his flaming red face and thick-set figure, a typical country squire of the old school, and both his manners and his language were in accordance with tradition. There were other resemblances too, but always with a difference. The voices of the country squires of the old school were often slightly husky towards late middle-age; but it was not with whiskey. They hunted, and so did Sir William. But the squires only hunted foxes; Sir William was more catholic. Sir William, in short, was no doubt a thoroughly bad baronet. But there was nothing mean about him. His vices, like such virtues as he had, were all on the large scale. And the result, as usual, was that most other men, good or bad, liked him well enough (except a husband here and there, or a father or two) and women openly hung on his husky words.

On comparison with him Beresford was rather an ordinary man, a tall, dark, not unhandsome fellow of two-and-thirty, quiet and reserved; popular in a way but neither inviting nor apparently reciprocating anything beyond a rather grave friendliness. His father had left him a rich man, but idleness did not appeal to him. He had inherited enough of the parental energy and drive not to allow his money to lie softly in gilt-edged securities and had a finger in a good many business pies, out of sheer love of the game.

Money attracts money. Graham Beresford had inherited it, he made it, and, inevitably, he had married it too. The daughter of a late ship-owner in Liverpool, with not far off half a million in her own right. That half-million might have made some poor man incredibly happy for life, but she had chosen to bring it to Beresford, who needed it not at all. But the money was incidental, for he needed her and would have married her just as inevitably (said his friends) if she had not a farthing.

She was so exactly his type. A tall, rather serious-minded, highly cultured girl, not so young that her character had not had time to form (she was twenty-five when Beresford married her, three years ago), she was the ideal wife for him. A bit of a Puritan, perhaps, in some ways, but Beresford, whose wild oats, though duly sown, had been a sparse crop, was ready enough to be a Puritan himself by that time, if she was.

To make no bones about it, the Beresfords succeeded in achieving that eighth wonder of the modern world, a happy marriage.

And into the middle of it there dropped, with irretrievable tragedy, the box of chocolates. Beresford gave her the chocolates after the meal as they were sitting over their coffee in the drawing room, explaining how they had come into his possession. His wife made some laughing comment on his meanness in not having bought a special box to pay his debt, but approved the brand and was interested to try the new variety. Joan Beresford was not so serious-minded as not to have a healthy feminine interest in good chocolates.

She delved with her fingers among the silver-wrapped sweets, each bearing the name of its filling in neat blue lettering, and remarked that the new variety appeared to consist of nothing but Kirsch and Maraschino taken from the firm's ordinary brand of liqueur chocolates. She offered him one, but Beresford, who had no interest in chocolates and did not believe in spoiling good coffee, refused. His wife unwrapped one and put it in her mouth, uttering the next moment a slight exclamation.

'Oh! I was wrong. They are different. They're twenty times as strong. Really, it almost burns. You must try one, Graham. Catch!' She threw one across to him and Beresford, to humour her, consumed it. A burning taste, not intolerable but far too strong to be pleasant, followed the release of the liquid filling.

'By Jove,' he exclaimed, 'I should think they are strong. They must be filled with neat alcohol.'

'Oh, they wouldn't do that, surely,' said his wife, unwrapping another. 'It must be the mixture. I rather like them. But that Kirsch one tasted far too strongly of almonds; this may be better. You try a Maraschino too.' She threw another over to him.

He ate it and disliked it still more. 'Funny,' he remarked, feeling the roof of his mouth with the tip of his tongue. 'My tongue feels quite numb.'

'So did mine at first,' she agreed. 'Now it's tingling rather nicely. But there doesn't seem to be any difference between the Kirsch and the Maraschino. And they do burn! The almond flavouring's much too strong too. I can't make up my mind whether I like them or not.'

'I don't,' Beresford said with decision. 'I shouldn't eat any more of them if I were you. I think there's something wrong with them.'

'Well, they're only an experiment, I suppose,' said his wife.

A few minutes later Beresford went out, to keep a business appointment in the City. He left her still trying to make up her mind whether she liked the new variety or not. Beresford remembered that conversation afterwards very clearly, because it was the last time he saw his wife alive.

That was roughly half past two. At a quarter to four Beresford arrived at his club from the City in a taxi, in a state of collapse. He was helped into the building by the driver and the porter, and both described him subsequently as pale to the point of ghastliness, with staring eyes and livid lips, and his skin damp and clammy. His mind seemed unaffected, however, and when they had got him up the steps he was able to walk, with the porter's help, into the lounge.

The porter, thoroughly alarmed, wanted to send for a doctor at once, but Beresford, who was the last man in the world to make a fuss, refused to let him, saying that it must be indigestion and he would be all right in a few minutes. To Sir William Anstruther, however, who was in the lounge at the time, he added after the porter had gone: 'Yes, and I believe it was those infernal chocolates you gave me, now I come to think of it. I thought there was something funny about them at the time. I'd better go and find out if my wife's all right.'

Sir William, a kind-hearted man, was much perturbed at the notion that he might be responsible for Beresford's condition and offered to ring up Mrs Beresford himself, as the other was plainly in no fit state to move. Beresford was about to reply when a strange change came over him. His body, which had been leaning back limply in his chair, suddenly heaved rigidly upright; his jaws locked together, the livid lips drawn back in a horrible grin, and his hands clenched on the arms of his chair. At the same time Sir William became aware of an unmistakable smell of bitter almonds.

Believing that the man was dying under his eyes, Sir William raised an alarmed shout for the porter and a doctor. The other occupants of the lounge hurried up, and between them they got the convulsed body of the unconscious man into a more comfortable position. They had no doubt that Beresford had taken poison, and the porter was sent off post-haste to find a doctor. Before the latter could arrive a telephone message was received at the club from an agitated butler asking if Mr Beresford was there, and if so would he come home at once as Mrs Beresford had been taken seriously ill. As a matter of fact she was already dead.

Beresford did not die. He had taken less of the poison than his wife, who after his departure must have eaten at least three more of the chocolates, so that its action in his case was less rapid and the doctor had time to save him. Not that the latter knew then what the poison was. He treated him chiefly for prussic acid poison, on the strength of the smell of bitter almonds, but he wasn't sure and threw in one or two others things as well. Anyhow it turned out in the end that he could not have had a fatal dose, and by about eight o'clock that

night he was conscious; the next day he was practically con-
valescent. As for the unfortunate Mrs Beresford, the doctor
arrived too late to save her and she passed away very rapidly
in a deep coma.

At first it was thought that the poisoning was due to a terrible accident on the part of the firm of Mason & Sons. The
police had taken the matter in hand as soon as Mrs Beresford's
death was reported to them and the fact of poison established, and it was only a very short time before things had
become narrowed down to the chocolates as the active agent.
Sir William was interrogated, the letter and wrapper were
recovered from the waste-paper basket, and, even before the
sick man was out of danger, a detective inspector was asking
for an interview just before closing time with the managing
director of Mason & Sons. Scotland Yard moves quickly.

It was the police theory at this stage, based on what Sir
William and two doctors had been able to tell them, that by
an act of criminal carelessness on the part of one of Mason's
employees, an excessive amount of oil of bitter almonds had
been included in the filling mixture of the chocolates, for
that was what the doctors had decided must be the poisoning
ingredient. Oil of bitter almonds is used a good deal, in the
cheaper kinds of confectionery, as a flavouring. However,
the managing director quashed this idea at once. Oil of
bitter almonds, he asserted, was never used by Mason's.
The inspector then produced the covering letter and asked
if he could have an interview with the person or persons
who had filled the sample chocolates, and with any others
through whose hands the box might have passed before it
was dispatched.

That brought matters to a head. The managing director read the letter with undisguised astonishment and at once declared that it was a forgery. No such letter, no such samples had been sent out by the firm at all; a new variety of liqueur chocolates had never even been mooted. Shown the fatal chocolates, he identified them without hesitation as their ordinary brand. Unwrapping and examining one more closely, he called the inspector's attention to a mark on the underside, which he suggested was the remains of a small hole drilled in the case through which the liquid could have been extracted and the fatal filling inserted, the hole afterwards being stopped up with softened chocolate, a perfectly simple operation.

The inspector agreed. It was now clear to him that somebody had been trying deliberately to murder Sir William Anstruther.

Scotland Yard doubled its activities. The chocolates were sent for analysis, Sir William was interviewed again, and so was the now conscious Beresford. From the latter the doctor insisted that the news of his wife's death must be kept till the next day, as in his weakened condition the shock might be fatal, so that nothing very helpful was obtained from him. Nor could Sir William, now thoroughly alarmed, throw any light on the mystery or produce a single person who might have any grounds for trying to kill him. The police were at a dead end.

Oil of bitter almonds had not been a bad guess at the noxious agent in the chocolates. The analysis showed that this was actually nitrobenzene, a kindred substance. Each chocolate in the upper layer contained exactly six minims, the remaining space inside the case being filled with a mixture of Kirsch and Maraschino. The chocolates in the lower layers, containing the other liqueurs to be found in one of Mason's two-pound boxes, were harmless.

'And now you know as much as we do, Mr Sheringham,' concluded Chief Inspector Moresby; 'and if you can say who sent those chocolates to Sir William, you'll know a good deal more.'

Roger nodded thoughtfully. 'It's a brute of a case. The field of possible suspects is so wide. It might have been anyone in the whole world. I suppose you've looked into all the people who have an interest in Sir William's death?'

'Well, naturally,' said Moresby. 'There aren't many. He and his wife are on notoriously bad terms and have been living apart for the last two years, but she gets a good fat legacy in his will and she's the residuary legatee as well (they've got no children). But her alibi can't be got round. She was at her villa in the South of France when it happened. I've checked that, from the French police.'

'Not another Marie Lafarge case, then,' Roger murmured. 'Though of course there never was any doubt as to Marie Lafarge really being innocent, in any intelligent mind. Well, who else?'

'His estate in Worcestershire's entailed and goes to a nephew. But there's no possible motive there. Sir William hasn't been near the place for twenty years, and the nephew lives there, with his wife and family, on a long lease at a nominal rent, so long as he looks after the place properly. Sir William couldn't turn him out if he wanted to.'

'Not a male edition of the Mary Ansell case, then,' Roger commented. 'Well, two other possible parallels occur to me. Don't they to you?'

'Well, sir,' Moresby scratched his head. 'There's the Molineux case, of course, in New York, where a poisoned phial of bromo-seltzer was sent to a Mr Cornish at the Knickerbocker Club, with the result that a lady to whom he gave some at his boarding house for a headache died and Cornish himself, who only sipped it because she complained of it being bitter, was violently ill. That's as close a parallel as I can call to mind.'

'By Jove, yes.' Roger was impressed. 'And it had never occurred to me at all. It's a very close parallel indeed. Have you acted on it at all? Molineux, the man who was put on trial, was a fellow member of the same club, if I remember, and it was said to be a case of jealousy. Have you made enquiries about any possibilities like that among Sir William's fellow members at the Rainbow?'

'I have, sir, you may be sure; but there's nothing in it along those lines. Not a thing,' said Moresby with conviction. 'What were the other two possible parallels you had in mind?'

'Why, the Christina Edmunds case, for one. Feminine jealousy. Sir William's private life doesn't seem to be immaculate. I daresay there's a good deal of off with the old light-o'-love and on with the new. What about investigations round that idea?'

'Why, that's just what I have been doing, Mr Sheringham, sir,' retorted Chief Inspector Moresby reproachfully. 'That was the first thing that came to me. Because if anything does stand out about this business it is that it's a woman's crime. Nobody but a woman would send poisoned chocolates to a man. Another man would never think of it. He'd send a poisoned sample of whiskey, or something like that.'

'That's a very sound point, Moresby,' Roger meditated. 'Very sound indeed. And Sir William couldn't help you?'

'Couldn't,' said Moresby, not without a trace of resentment, 'or wouldn't. I was inclined to believe at first that he might have his suspicions and was shielding some woman. But I don't know. There may be nothing in it.'

'On the other hand, there may be quite a lot. As I feel the case at present, that's where the truth lies.'

Moresby looked as if a little solid evidence would be more to his liking than any amount of feelings about the case. 'And your other parallel, Mr Sheringham?' he asked, rather dispiritedly.

'Why, Sir William Horwood. You remember that some lunatic sent poisoned chocolates not so long ago to the Commissioner of Police himself. A good crime always gets imitated. One could bear in mind the possibility that this is a copy of the Horwood case.'

Moresby brightened. 'It's funny you should say that, Mr Sheringham, sir, because that's about the conclusion I'm being forced to myself. In fact I've pretty well made up my mind. I've tested every other theory there is, you see. There's not a solitary person with an interest in Sir William's death, so far as I can see, whether it's from motives of gain, revenge, hatred, jealousy or anything else, whom I haven't had to rule out of the question. They've all either got complete alibis or I've satisfied myself in some other way that they're not to blame. If Sir William isn't shielding someone (and I'm pretty sure now that he isn't) there's nothing else for it but some irresponsible lunatic of a woman who's come to the conclusion that this world would be a better place without Sir William Anstruther in it – some social or religious fanatic, who's probably never even seen Sir William personally. And if that's the case,' sighed Moresby, 'a fat lot of chance we have of laying hands on her.'

Roger reflected for a moment. 'You may be right, Moresby. In fact I shouldn't be at all surprised if you were. But if I were superstitious, which I'm not, do you know what I should believe? That the murderer's aim misfired and Sir William escaped death for an express purpose of Providence: so that he, the destined victim, should be the ironical instrument of bringing his own intended murderer to justice.'

'Well, Mr Sheringham, would you really?' said the sarcastic chief inspector, who was not superstitious either.

Roger seemed rather taken with the idea. '*Chance, the Avenger.* Make a good film title, wouldn't it? But there's a terrible lot of truth in it. How often don't you people at the Yard stumble on some vital piece of evidence out of pure chance? How often isn't it that you are led to the right solution by what seems a series of sheer coincidences? I'm not belittling your detective work; but just think how often a piece of brilliant detective work which has led you most of the way but not the last vital few inches, meets with some remarkable stroke of sheer luck (thoroughly well-deserved luck, no doubt, but *luck*), which just makes the case complete for you. I can think of scores of instances. The Milsom and Fowler murder, for example. Don't you see what I mean? Is it chance every time, or is it Providence avenging the victim?'

'Well, Mr Sheringham,' said Chief Inspector Moresby, 'to tell you the truth, I don't mind what it is, so long as it lets me put my hands on the right man.'

'Moresby,' laughed Roger, 'you're hopeless, I thought I was raising such a fruitful topic. Very well, we'll change the subject. Tell me why in the name of goodness the murderess (assuming that you're right every time) used nitrobenzene, of all surprising things?'

'There, Mr Sheringham,' Moresby admitted, 'you've got me. I never even knew it was so poisonous. It's used a good deal in various manufactures, I'm told, confectionery for instance, and as a solvent; and its chief use is in making aniline dyes. But it's never reckoned among the ordinary poisons. I suppose she used it because it's so easy to get hold of.'

'Isn't there a line of attack there?' Roger suggested. 'The inference is that the criminal is a woman who is employed in some factory or business, the odds favouring an aniline dye establishment, and who knew of the poisonous properties of nitrobenzene because the employees have been warned about it. Couldn't you use that as a point of departure?'

'To interrogate every employee of every establishment in this country that uses nitrobenzene in any of its processes, Mr Sheringham? Come, sir. Even if you're right the chances are we should all be dead before we reached the guilty person.'

'I suppose we should,' regretted Roger, who had thought he was being rather clever.

They discussed the case for some time longer, but nothing further of importance emerged. Naturally it had not been possible to trace the machine on which the forged letter had been typed, nor to ascertain how the piece of Mason's notepaper had come into the criminal's possession. With regard to this last point, Roger suggested, as an outside possibility, that it might not have been Mason's notepaper at all but a piece with a heading especially printed for the occasion, which might give a pointer towards a printer as being concerned in the crime. He was chagrined to learn that this brilliant idea had occurred to Moresby as a mere matter of routine, and the notepaper had been definitely identified by Merton's, the printers concerned, as their own work. He produced the piece of paper for Roger's inspection, and the latter commented on the fact that the edges were distinctly yellowed, which seemed to suggest that the sheet was an old one.

Another idea occurred to Roger. 'I shouldn't be surprised, Moresby,' he said, with a certain impressiveness, 'if the murderer never *tried* to get hold of this sheet at all. In other words, it was the chance possession of it which suggested the whole method of the crime.'

It appeared that this notion had also occurred to Moresby. If it were true, it only helped to make the crime more insoluble than before. From the wrapper, a piece of ordinary brown paper with Sir William's name and address handprinted on it in large capitals, there was nothing at all to be learnt beyond the fact that the parcel had been posted at the office in Southampton Street, Strand, between the hours of eight thirty and nine thirty p.m. Except for the chocolates themselves, which seemed to offer no further help, there was nothing else whatsoever in the way of material clues.

Whoever coveted Sir William's life had certainly no intention of purchasing it with his or her own.

If Moresby had paid his visit to Roger Sheringham with any hope of tapping that gentleman's brains, he went away disappointed. Rack them as he might, Roger had been unable to throw any effective light on the affair.

To tell the truth Roger was inclined to agree with the chief inspector's conclusion, that the attempted murder of Sir William Anstruther and the actual death of the unfortunate Mrs Beresford must be laid to the account of some irresponsible criminal lunatic, actuated by a religious or social fanaticism. For this reason, although he thought about it a good deal during the next few days, he made no attempt to take the case in hand. It was the sort of affair, necessitating endless enquiries, that a private person would have neither the time nor the authority to carry out, which can only be handled by the official police. Roger's interest in it was purely academic.

It was hazard, two chance encounters, which translated this interest from the academic to the personal.

The first was at the Rainbow Club itself. Roger was lunching there with a member, and inevitably the conversation turned on the recent tragedy. Roger's host was inclined to plume himself on the fact that he had been at school with Beresford and so had a more intimate connection with the affair than his fellow members. One gathered, indeed, that the connection was a trifle closer even than Sir William's. Roger's host was that kind of man.

'And just as it happened I saw the Beresfords in their box at the Imperial that night. Noticed them before the curtain went up for the first act. I had a stall. I may even have seen them making that fatal bet.' Roger's host took on an even more portentous aspect. One gathered that it was by no means improbably due to his presence in the stalls that the disastrous bet was made at all.

As they were talking a man entered the dining room and walked past their table. Roger's host became abruptly silent. The newcomer threw him a slight nod and passed on. The other leant forward across the table.

'Talk of the devil! That was Beresford himself. First time I've seen him in here since it happened. Poor devil! It knocked him all to pieces, you know. I've never seen a man so devoted to his wife. Did you notice how ghastly he looked?' All this in a hushed, tactful whisper, that would have been far more obvious to the subject of it, had he happened to have been looking their way, than the loudest shouts.

Roger nodded shortly. He had caught a glimpse of Beresford's face and been shocked by it even before he learned his identity. It was haggard and pale and seamed with lines of bitterness, prematurely old. 'Hang it all,' he now thought, much moved, 'Moresby really must make an effort. If the murderer isn't found soon it'll kill that chap too.'

He said aloud, somewhat at random and certainly without tact: 'He didn't exactly fall on your neck. I thought you two were such bosom friends?'

His host looked uncomfortable. 'Oh, well, you must make allowances, just at present,' he hedged. 'Besides, we weren't *bosom* friends exactly. As a matter of fact he was a year or two senior to me. Or it might have been three. We were in different houses, too. And he was on the modern side of course, while I was a classical bird.'

'I see,' said Roger, quite gravely, realising that his host's actual contact with Beresford at school had been limited, at the very most, to that of the latter's toe with the former's hinder parts.

He left it at that.

The next encounter took place the following morning. Roger was in Bond Street, about to go through the distressing ordeal of buying a new hat. Along the pavement he suddenly saw bearing down on him Mrs Verreker-le-Flemming. Mrs Verreker-le-Flemming was small, exquisite, rich and a widow, and she sat at Roger's feet whenever he gave her the opportunity. But she talked. She talked, in fact, and talked, and talked. And Roger, who rather liked talking himself, could not bear it. He tried to dart across the road, but there was no opening stream. He was cornered.

Mrs Verreker-le-Flemming fastened on him gladly. 'Oh, Mr Sheringham! *Just* the person I wanted to see. Mr Sheringham, *do* tell me. In confidence. *Are* you taking up this dreadful business of *poor* Joan Beresford's death? Oh, don't – *don't* tell me you're not!' Roger was trying to do so, but she gave him no chance. 'It's too dreadful. You must – you simply *must* find out who sent those chocolates to that dreadful Sir William Anstruther. You *are* going to, aren't you?'

Roger, the frozen and imbecile grin of civilised intercourse on his face, again tried to get a word in; without result.

'I was horrified when I heard of it – simply horrified. You see, Joan and I were such very close friends. Quite intimate. We were at school together – Did you say anything, Mr Sheringham?'

Roger, who had allowed a faint groan to escape him, hastily shook his head.

'And the awful thing, the truly *terrible* thing is that Joan brought the whole business on herself. Isn't that *appalling*?'

Roger no longer wanted to escape. 'What did you say?' he managed to insert, incredulously.

'I suppose it's what they call tragic irony. Certainly it was tragic enough, and I've never heard anything so terribly ironical. You know about that bet she made with her husband of course, so that he had to get her a box of chocolates, and if he hadn't Sir William would never have given him the poisoned ones and he'd have eaten them and died himself and good riddance? Well, Mr Sheringham –' Mrs Verreker-le-Flemming lowered her voice to a conspirator's whisper and glanced about her in the approved manner. 'I've never told anybody else this, but I'm telling you because I know you'll appreciate it. You're interested in irony, aren't you?'

'I adore it,' Roger said mechanically. 'Yes?'

'Well – *Joan wasn't playing fair.*'

'How do you mean?' Roger asked, bewildered.

Mrs Verreker-le-Flemming was artlessly pleased with her sensation. 'Why, she ought not to have made that bet at all. It was a judgment on her. A terrible judgment, of course, but the appalling thing is that she did bring it on herself, in a way. She'd seen the play before. We went together, the very first week it was on. She *knew* who the villain was all the time.'

'By Jove!' Roger was as impressed as Mrs Verreker-le-Flemming could have wished. 'Chance the Avenger, with a vengeance. We're none of us immune from it.'

'Poetic justice, you mean?' twittered Mrs Verreker-le-Flemming, to whom these remarks had been somewhat obscure. 'Yes, it was, wasn't it? Though really, the punishment was out of all proportion to the crime. Good gracious, if every woman who cheats over a bet is to be killed for it, where would any of us be?' demanded Mrs Verreker-le-Flemming with unconscious frankness.

'Umph!' said Roger, tactfully.

'But Joan Beresford! That's the extraordinary thing. I should never have thought Joan *would* do a thing like that. She was such a *nice* girl. A little close with money, of course, considering how well off they were, but that isn't anything. Of course it was only fun, and pulling her husband's leg, but I always used to think Joan was such a *serious* girl, Mr Sheringham. I mean, ordinary people don't talk about honour, and truth, and playing the game. Well, she paid herself for not playing the game, poor girl, didn't she? Still, it all goes to show the truth of the old saying, doesn't it?'

'What old saying?' said Roger, hypnotised by this flow.

'Why, that still waters run deep. Joan must have been deep, I'm afraid.' Mrs Verreker-le-Flemming sighed. It was evidently a social error to be deep. 'I mean, she certainly took me in. She can't have been quite so honourable and truthful as she was always pretending, can she? And I can't help wondering whether a girl who'd deceive her husband in a little thing like that might not – oh, well, I don't want to say anything against poor Joan now she's dead, poor darling, but she can't have been quite such a plaster saint after all, can she? I mean,' said Mrs Verreker-le-Flemming, in hasty extenuation of these suggestions, 'I do think psychology is so very interesting, don't you, Mr Sheringham?'

'Sometimes, very,' Roger agreed gravely. 'But you mentioned Sir William Anstruther just now. Do you know him, too?'

'I used to,' Mrs Verreker-le-Flemming replied, with an expression of positive vindictiveness. 'Horrible man! Always running after some woman or other. And when he's tired of her, just drops her – biff! – like that. At least,' added Mrs Verreker-le-Flemming hastily, 'so I've heard.'

'And what happens if she refuses to be dropped?'

'Oh, dear, I'm sure I don't know. I suppose you've heard the latest?' Mrs Verreker-le-Flemming hurried on, perhaps a trifle more pink than the delicate aids to nature on her cheeks would have warranted. 'He's taken up with that Bryce woman now. You know, the wife of the oil man, or petrol, or whatever he made his money in. It began about three weeks ago. You'd have thought that dreadful business of being responsible, in a way, for poor Joan Beresford's death would have sobered him up a little, wouldn't you? But not a bit of it; he …'

'I suppose Sir William knew Mrs Beresford pretty well?' Roger remarked casually.

Mrs Verreker-le-Flemming stared at him. 'Sir William? No, he didn't know Joan at all. I'm sure he didn't. I've never heard her mention him.'

Roger shot off on another tack. 'What a pity you weren't at the Imperial with the Beresfords that evening. She'd never have made that bet if you had been.' Roger looked extremely innocent. 'You weren't, I suppose?'

'I?' queried Mrs Verreker-le-Flemming in surprise. 'Good gracious, no. I was at the new revue at the Pavilion. Lady Gavelstoke had a box and asked me to join her party.'

'Oh, yes. Good show, isn't it? I thought that sketch *The Sempiternal Triangle* very clever. Didn't you?'

'*The Sempiternal Triangle?*' wavered Mrs Verreker-le-Flemming.

'Yes, in the first half.'

'Oh! Then I didn't see it. I got there disgracefully late, I'm afraid. But then,' said Mrs Verreker-le-Flemming with pathos, 'I always do seem to be late for simply everything.'

Once more Roger changed the subject. 'By the way, I wonder if you've got a photograph of Mrs Beresford?' he asked carelessly.

'Of Joan? Yes, I have. Why, Mr Sheringham?'

'You haven't got one of Sir William too, by any chance?' asked Roger, still more carelessly.

The pink on Mrs Verreker-le-Flemming's cheeks deepened half a shade. 'I – I think I have. Yes, I'm almost sure I have. But ...'

'Would you lend them to me some time?' Roger asked, with a mysterious air, and looked around him with a frown in the approved manner.

'Oh, Mr Sheringham! Yes, of course I will. You mean – you mean you *are* going to find out who sent those chocolates to Sir William?'

Roger nodded, and put his finger to his lips. 'Yes. You've guessed it. But not a word, Mrs Verreker-le-Flemming. Oh, excuse me, there's a man on that bus who wants to speak to me. *Scotland Yard,*' he hissed in an impressive whisper.

'Goodbye.' He dived for a passing bus and clung on with difficulty. With awful stealth he climbed up the steps and took his seat, after an exaggerated scrutiny of the other passengers, beside a perfectly inoffensive man in a bowler hat. The man in the bowler hat, who happened to be a clerk in the employment of a builder's merchant, looked at him resentfully: there were plenty of quite empty seats all round them.

Roger bought no new hat that morning.

For probably the first time in her life Mrs Verreker-le-Flemming had given somebody a constructive idea.

Roger made good his opportunity. Getting off the bus at the corner of Bond Street and Oxford Street, he hailed a taxi, and gave Mrs Verreker-le-Flemming's address. He thought it better to take advantage of her permission at a time when he would not have to pay for it a second time over.

The parlour-maid seemed to think there was nothing odd in his mission, and took him up to the drawing room at once. A corner of the room was devoted to the silver-framed photographs of Mrs Verreker-le-Flemming's friends, and there were many of them. Roger, who had never seen Sir William in the flesh, had to seek the parlour-maid's help. The girl, like her mistress, was inclined to be loquacious, and to prevent either of them getting ideas into their heads which might be better not there, he removed from their frames not one photograph but five, those of Sir William, Mrs Beresford, Beresford himself, and two strange males who appeared to belong to the Sir William period of Mrs Verreker-le-Flemming's collection. Finally he obtained, by means of a small bribe, a likeness of Mrs Verreker-le-Flemming herself and added that to his collection.

For the rest of the day he was very busy.

His activities would have seemed, no doubt, to Mrs Verreker-le-Flemming not merely baffling but pointless. He paid a visit to a public library, for instance, and consulted a work of reference, after which he took a taxi and drove to the offices of the Anglo-Eastern Perfumery Company, where he enquired for a certain Mr Joseph Lea Hardwick and seemed much put out on hearing that no such gentleman was known to the firm and was certainly not employed in any of their numerous branches. Many questions had to be put about the firm and its branches before he consented to abandon the quest. After that he drove to Messrs. Weall and Wilson, the well-known institution which protects the trade interests of individuals and advises its subscribers regarding investments. Here he entered his name as a subscriber, and explaining that he had a large sum of money to invest, filled in one of the special enquiry forms which are headed Strictly Confidential.

Then he went to the Rainbow Club, in Piccadilly.

Introducing himself to the porter without a blush as connected with Scotland Yard, he asked the man a number of questions, more or less trivial, concerning the tragedy. 'Sir William, I understand,' he said finally, as if by the way, 'did not dine here the evening before?'

There it appeared that Roger was wrong. Sir William had dined in the club, as he did about three times a week.

'But I quite understood he wasn't here that evening?' Roger said plaintively.

The porter was emphatic. He remembered quite well. So did a waiter, whom the porter summoned to corroborate him.

Sir William had dined rather late, and had not left the dining room till about nine o'clock. He spent the evening there too, the waiter knew, or at least some of it, for he himself had taken him a whiskey-and-soda in the lounge not less than half an hour later.

Roger retired.

He retired to Merton's, in a taxi.

It seemed that he wanted some new notepaper printed, of a very special kind, and to the young woman behind the counter he specified at great length and in wearisome detail exactly what he did want. The young woman handed him the book of specimen pieces and asked him to see if there was any style there which would suit him. Roger glanced through it, remarking garrulously to the young woman that he had been recommended to Merton's by a very dear friend, whose photograph he happened to have on him at that moment. Wasn't that a curious coincidence? The young woman agreed that it was.

'About a fortnight ago, I think my friend was in here last,' said Roger, producing the photograph. 'Recognise this?'

The young woman took the photograph, without apparent interest. 'Oh, yes. I remember. About some notepaper too, wasn't it? So that's your friend. Well, it's a small world. Now this is a line we're selling a good deal of just now.'

Roger went back to his rooms to dine. Afterwards, feeling restless, he wandered out of the Albany and turned down Piccadilly. He wandered round the Circus, thinking hard, and paused for a moment out of habit to inspect the photographs of the new revue hung outside the Pavilion. The next thing he realised was that he had got as far as Jermyn Street and was standing outside the Imperial Theatre. The advertisements of *The Creaking Skull* informed him that it began at half past eight. Glancing at his watch he saw that the time was twenty-nine minutes past that hour. He had an evening to get through somehow. He went inside.

The next morning, very early for Roger, he called Moresby at Scotland Yard.

'Moresby,' he said without preamble, 'I want you to do something for me. Can you find me a taximan who took a fare from Piccadilly Circus or its neighbourhood at about ten past nine on the evening before the Beresford crime, to the Strand somewhere near the bottom of Southampton Street, and another who took a fare back between those points. I'm not sure about the first. Or one taxi might have been used for the double journey, but I doubt that. Anyhow, try to find out for me, will you?'

'What are you up to now, Mr Sheringham?' Moresby asked suspiciously.

'Breaking down an interesting alibi,' replied Roger serenely. 'By the way, I know who sent those chocolates to Sir William. I'm just building up a nice structure of evidence for you. Ring up my rooms when you've got those taximen.'

He strolled out, leaving Moresby positively gaping after him. Roger had his annoying moments.

The rest of the day he spent apparently trying to buy a second-hand typewriter. He was very particular that it should be a Hamilton No. 4. When the shop people tried to induce him to consider other makes he refused to look at them, saying that he had had the Hamilton No. 4 so strongly recommended to him by a friend, who had bought one about three weeks ago. Perhaps it was at this very shop? No? They hadn't sold a Hamilton No. 4 for the last three months? How odd.

But at one shop they had sold a Hamilton No. 4 within the last month, and that was odder still.

At half past four Roger got back to his rooms to await the telephone message from Moresby. At half past five it came.

'There are fourteen taxi drivers here, littering up my office,' said Moresby offensively. 'They all took fares from the Strand to Piccadilly Circus at your time. What do you want me to do with 'em, Mr Sheringham?'

'Keep them till I come, Chief Inspector,' returned Roger with dignity. He had not expected more than three at the most, but he was not going to let Moresby know that. He grabbed his hat.

The interview with the fourteen was brief enough, however. To each grinning man (Roger deduced a little heavy humour on the part of Moresby before his arrival) he showed in turn a photograph, holding it so that Moresby could not see it, and asked if he could recognise his fare. The ninth man did so, without hesitation. At a nod from Roger, Moresby dismissed the others.

'How dressed?' Roger asked the man laconically, tucking the photograph away in his pocket.

'Evening togs,' replied the other, equally laconic.

Roger took a note of his name and address and sent him away with a ten-shilling tip. 'The case,' he said to Moresby, 'is at an end.'

Moresby sat at his table and tried to look official. 'And now, Mr Sheringham, sir, perhaps you'll tell me what you've been doing.'

'Certainly,' Roger said blandly, seating himself on the table and swinging his legs. As he did so, a photograph fell unnoticed out of his pocket and fluttered, face downwards, under the table. Moresby eyed it but did not pick it up. 'Certainly, Moresby,' said Roger. 'Your work for you. It was a simple case,' he added languidly, 'once one had grasped the essential factor. Once, that is to say, one had cleared one's eyes of the soap that the murderer had stuffed into them.'

'Is that so, Mr Sheringham?' said Moresby politely. And yawned.

Roger laughed. 'All right, Moresby. We'll get down to it. I really have solved the thing, you know. Here's the evidence for you.' He took from his note-case an old letter and handed it to the chief inspector. 'Look at the slightly crooked s's and the chipped capital H. Was that typed on the same machine as the forged letter from Mason's, or was it not?'

Moresby studied it for a moment, then drew the forged letter from a drawer of his table and compared the two minutely. When he looked up there was no lurking amusement in his eyes. 'You've got it in one, Mr Sheringham,' he said soberly. 'Where did you get hold of this?'

'In a second-hand typewriter shop in St Martin's Lane. The machine was sold to an unknown customer about a month ago. They identified the customer from that photograph. By a lucky chance this machine had been used in the office after it had been repaired, to see that it was OK, and I easily got hold of that specimen of its work. I'd deduced, of course, from the precautions taken all through this crime, that the typewriter would be bought for that one special purpose and then destroyed, and so far as the murderer could see there was no need to waste valuable money on a new one.'

'And where is the machine now?'

'Oh, at the bottom of the Thames, I expect,' Roger smiled. 'I tell you, this criminal takes no unnecessary chances. But that doesn't matter. There's your evidence.'

'Humph! It's all right so far as it goes,' conceded Moresby. 'But what about Mason's paper?'

'That,' said Roger calmly, 'was extracted from Merton's book of sample notepapers, as I'd guessed from the very yellowed edges might be the case. I can prove contact of the criminal with the book, and there is a gap which will certainly turn out to have been filled by the piece of paper.'

'That's fine,' Moresby said more heartily.

'As for that taximan, the criminal had an alibi. You've heard it broken down. Between ten past nine and twenty-five past, in fact during the time when the parcel must have been posted, the murderer took a hurried journey to that neighbourhood, going probably by bus or underground, but returning, as I expected, by taxi, because time would be getting short.'

'And the murderer, Mr Sheringham?'

'The person whose photograph is in my pocket,' Roger said unkindly. 'By the way, do you remember what I was saying the other day about Chance the Avenger, my excellent film title? Well, it's worked again. By a chance meeting in Bond Street with a silly woman I was put, by the merest accident, in possession of a piece of information which showed me then and there who had sent those chocolates addressed to Sir William. There were other possibilities of course, and

I tested them, but then and there on the pavement I saw the whole thing, from first to last. It was the merest accident that this woman should have been a friend of mine, of course, and I don't want to blow my own trumpet,' said Roger modestly, 'but I do think I deserve a little credit for realising the significance of what she told me and recognising the hand of Providence at work.'

'Who was the murderer, then, Mr Sheringham?' repeated Moresby, disregarding for the moment this bashful claim.

'It was so beautifully planned,' Roger went on dreamily. 'We were taken in completely. We never grasped for one moment that we were making the fundamental mistake that the murderer all along intended us to make.'

He paused, and in spite of his impatience Moresby obliged. 'And what was that?'

'Why, that the plan had miscarried. That the wrong person had been killed. That was just the beauty of it. The plan had *not* miscarried. It had been brilliantly successful. The wrong person was not killed. Very much the right person was.'

Moresby gaped. 'Why, how on earth do you make that out, sir?'

'Mrs Beresford was the objective all the time. That's why the plot was so ingenious. Everything was anticipated. It was perfectly natural that Sir William would hand the chocolates over to Beresford. It was foreseen that we should look for the criminal among Sir William's associates and not the dead woman's. It was probably even foreseen that the crime would be considered the work of a woman; whereas really, of course, chocolates were employed because it was a woman who was the objective. Brilliant!'

Moresby, unable to wait any longer, snatched up the photograph and gazed at it incredulously. He whistled. 'Good heavens! But Mr Sheringham, you don't mean to tell me that – Sir William himself!'

'He wanted to get rid of Mrs Beresford,' Roger continued, gazing dreamily at his swinging feet. 'He had liked her well enough at the beginning, no doubt, though it was her money he was after all the time. But she must have bored him dreadfully very soon. And I really do think there is some excuse for him there. Any woman, however charming otherwise, would bore a normal man if she does nothing but prate about honour and playing the game. She'd never have overlooked the slightest peccadillo. Every tiny lapse would be thrown up at him for years.

'But the real trouble was that she was too close with her money. She sentenced herself to death there. He wanted it, or some of it, pretty badly; and she wouldn't part. There's no doubt about the motive. I made a list of the firms he's interested in and got a report on them. They're all rocky, every one of them. They all need money to save them. He'd got through all he had of his own, and he had to get more. Nobody seems to have gathered it, but he's a rotten businessman. And half a million – Well!

'As for the nitrobenzene, that was simple enough. I looked it up and found that beside the uses you told me, it's used largely in perfumery. And he's got a perfumery business. The Anglo-Eastern Perfumery Company. That's how he'd know about it being poisonous of course. But I shouldn't think he got his supply from there. He'd be cleverer than that. He probably made the stuff himself. I discovered, quite by chance, that he has at any rate an elementary knowledge of chemistry (at least, he was on the modern side at Selchester) and it's the simplest operation. Any schoolboy knows how to treat benzol with nitric acid to get nitrobenzene.'

'But,' stammered Moresby, 'but Sir William – he was at Eton.'

'Sir William?' said Roger sharply. 'Who's talking about Sir William? I told you the photograph of the murderer was in my pocket.' He whipped out the photograph in question and confronted the astounded chief inspector with it. 'Beresford, man! Beresford's the murderer, of his own wife.' Roger studied the other's dumbfounded face and smiled secretly. He felt avenged now for the humour that had been taking place with the taximen.

'Beresford, who still had hankerings after a gay life,' he went on more mildly, 'didn't want his wife but did want her money. He contrived this plot, providing, as he thought, against every contingency that could possibly arise. He established a mild alibi, if suspicion ever should arise, by taking his wife to the Imperial, and slipped out of the theatre at the first interval (I sat through the first act of the dreadful thing myself last night to see when the interval came). Then he hurried down to the Strand, posted his parcel, and took a taxi back. He had ten minutes, but nobody was going to remark if he got back to the box a minute or two late; you may be able to find that he did.

'And the rest simply followed. He knew Sir William came to the club every morning at ten thirty, as regularly as clockwork; he knew that for a psychological certainty he could get the chocolates handed over to him if he hinted for them; he knew that the police would go chasing after all sorts of false trails starting from Sir William. That's one reason why he chose him. He could have shadowed anyone else to the club if necessary. And as for the wrapper and the forged letter, he carefully didn't destroy them because they were calculated not only to divert suspicion but actually to point away from him to some anonymous lunatic. Which is exacttly what they did.'

'Well, it's very smart of you, Mr Sheringham,' Moresby said, with a little sigh but quite ungrudgingly. 'Very smart indeed. By the way, what was it the lady told you that showed you the whole thing in a flash?'

'Why, it wasn't so much what she actually told me as what I heard between her words, so to speak. What she told me was that Mrs Beresford knew the answer to that bet; what I deduced was that, being the sort of person she sounded to be, it was almost incredible that Mrs Beresford should have made a bet to which she knew the answer. Unless she had been the most dreadful little hypocrite (which I did not for a moment believe), it would have been a psychological impossibility for her. *Ergo*, she didn't. *Ergo*, there never was such a bet. *Ergo*, Beresford was lying. *Ergo*, Beresford wanted to get hold of those chocolates for some reason other than he stated. And, as events turned out, there was only one other reason. That was all.

'After all, we only had Beresford's word for the bet, didn't we? And only his word for the conversation in the drawing room – though most of that undoubtedly happened. Beresford must be far too good a liar not to make all possible use of the truth. But of course he wouldn't have left her till he'd seen her take, or somehow made her take, at least six of the chocolates, more than a lethal dose. That's why the stuff was in those meticulous six-minim doses. And so that he could take a couple himself, of course. A clever stroke, that. Took us all in again. Though of course he exaggerated his symptoms considerably.'

Moresby rose to his feet. 'Well, Mr Sheringham, I'm much obliged to you, sir. I shall make a report of course to the assistant commissioner of what you've done, and he'll thank you officially on behalf of the department. And now I shall have to get busy, because naturally I shall have to check your evidence myself, if only as a matter of form, before I apply for a warrant against Beresford.' He scratched his head. 'Chance, the Avenger, eh? Yes, it's an interesting notion. But I can tell you one pretty big thing Beresford left to Chance, the Avenger, Mr Sheringham. Suppose Sir William hadn't handed over the chocolates after all? Supposing he'd kept them, to give to one of his own ladies? That was a nasty risk to take.'

Roger positively snorted. He felt a personal pride in Beresford by this time, and it distressed him to hear a great man so maligned.

'Really, Moresby! It wouldn't have had any serious results if Sir William had. Do give my man credit for being what he is. You don't imagine he sent the poisoned ones to Sir William, do you? Of course not! He'd send harmless ones, and exchange them for the others on his way home. Dash it all, he wouldn't go right out of his way to present opportunities to Chance.

'If,' added Roger, 'Chance really is the right word.'

A Present for Ivo

Ellis Peters

If Sara Boyne had not taken her duties as the secretary of the Shelvedon Teachers' Christmas Committee so seriously, the curious affair at Shelvedon would probably have remained a mystery, a rankling reproach to the local police, to this day. But Sara, in addition to being very young and earnestly pretty, was conscientious, and new to the responsibilities of office.

The committee was collectively responsible for the organisation of the great Shelvedon Christmas party, held annually in the castle on Christmas Eve for all the school children of the little borough; but in practice the onus fell fairly and squarely upon the secretary. And if Sara took on a job, she did it thoroughly.

The night before the party she lay awake half the night, checking over everything in her mind. Was there a present for each child, duly selected and wrapped by his or her class teacher? Did the tree look pretty enough?

In some towns it would have been unthinkable to hang all the parcels on the tree overnight, and stand the tree in the open courtyard of the castle, which was also the town hall and civic offices, at the mercy of any passer-by, and protected only by the occasional perambulations of a constable on his beat. But in Shelvedon it was part of a proud tradition, and nothing had ever been stolen, and no one entertained any fears that anything ever would be.

And the food for the party tea – was there really enough of it? Were Tom Fielding's decorations too adult to please? Roger Brecon had been sweet about the fairy lights, too – fancy a solicitor being so knowledgeable about electricity! Sara, who wasn't vain but knew that she was attractive, could not help wondering whether Roger's interest in the party was on her account.

She awoke with the first hint of dawn to the conviction that the carol sheets had been forgotten. Shelvedon parents, coming at half past six to fetch their children home, liked to stay for a final half-hour of carol singing. She must go along very early to the castle and bring down the leaflets from the cupboard upstairs, in case they should be overlooked later.

That was how she came to leave home immediately after lunch, though the party was not due to start until half past three.

On her way to the castle she bought an evening paper – the first edition was on the streets at noon – to see what it had to say about the junior school nativity play, in which some of her own hopeful pupils had starred. Not until she had sunned herself in the praise of her charges did she suddenly register the shock of the staring headlines which had the place of honour on the front page.

SHELVEDON CHRONICLE STOLEN
Daring midnight raid on town museum

During the night the town museum, housed in one ward of the castle, has been broken into by means of the removal of a pane of glass from which the burglar alarm could be reached and switched off. An expert job, arguing a preliminary reconnaissance, and considerable experience of all kinds of safety devices. By chance the constable on his beat made a round of the buildings, found the window unfastened, and observed the vacant pane, whereupon he immediately gave the alarm, and kept close watch on the building until the arrival of reinforcements who could cover all exits from the castle.

The report went on to say that the museum had then been searched, but the thief must already have vacated this wing, and the search had to be extended to all the civic offices and the arcades of the castle, before a man was run to earth in the open undercroft of the rear gatehouse.

He was sitting on one of the benches, apparently asleep, and claimed that he had no recollection of how he had got there, though he admitted earlier he had been drinking in the Black Bull. The man had been detained and it was understood that he was well known to the police. However, nothing incriminating was found on him.

Examination of the museum premises had revealed that only one item was missing: the world-famous *Shelvedon Chronicle*, the most perfect fourteenth-century manuscript of its kind in existence, a local history written by the monk Anselmus of Shelvedon Priory, and particularly renowned for its beautiful illuminations.

The manuscript of the *Chronicle* had not been recovered. Enquiries were being pursued both in Shelvedon and elsewhere, as this was the latest of many such thefts of extremely valuable antiques and works of art during the last six months, and the police suspected what must be an organisation of a national scale for their acquisition and consequent disposition.

Sara stood gaping at the improbable paragraphs with all the consternation and disbelief of a Londoner reading of the theft of the Crown Jewels. The *Shelvedon Chronicle* lay alone in a black velvet-lined case in the museum, with a small strip-light shining upon its exquisite, jewel-like initial letters and minute pictures.

A steel frame closed down over the glass case at night. How could it be stolen? Only an expert could have done it. A national scale? International, more likely, thought Sara, impervious for the moment to the frosty sharpness of the air and to a rapid ring of footsteps crossing the glazed cobbles.

A tall young man in a duffle coat was reaching up into the branches of the tree, setting the chains of lights tinkling.

'Hallo!' said Sara, embarrassed and delighted to recognise her helpful amateur electrician. 'Have you got this affair on your mind as badly as that, too?'

Roger Brecon swung round, the needles showering down over him as he turned his head. 'Oh, hallo, Sara! My goodness, you startled me!' But his surprise struck her as slightly overdone. 'Where did you spring from?'

'I didn't spring. I was here. I was reading the paper.'

'Whatever brings you here so early, anyhow?'

'I just couldn't rest. I wanted to make sure everything was all right. I forgot to bring down the carol sheets yesterday. Anyhow, what about you? It isn't even your headache, really.'

He laughed, twitching a bright red parcel into a better position, and stepped back to observe the general effect. 'I just wanted to make sure they really light up. After all, I was the one who fixed them up. I'd look a fine fool if they didn't work.'

But they did work; the whole tree leaped into brilliance and colour at a flick of his finger. He stared up at it delightedly, and then bestowed upon Sara the most radiant and intimate of smiles.

They were silent, looking at each other with slightly flushed faces and slightly dazzled eyes, when Tom Fielding came slithering across the cobbles with casual skating strides of his long legs, a newspaper crumpled up under his arm. His black forelock bobbed over the broad brown forehead, and his lean cheeks were red from scurrying through the frost after Sara.

'Hi!' said Tom, pulling up in a long glissade, Roger still hidden from him by the tree. 'Your sense of duty will be the death of you. Did you remember to eat any lunch, or were you too worried about the ice-cream for the kids? Seen the news? Crime marches on!'

'I was just reading it. Isn't it terrible? Somehow you never expect that sort of thing to happen in your own town.'

She was annoyed with herself for sounding embarrassed, and her rising colour caused Tom to scowl suddenly in suspicion. He took a couple of steps to the right, and his line of vision embraced Roger Brecon.

'Oh, it's you!' Tom remarked, with no enthusiasm at all. His lowering brows added: It would be!

'Hallo, Fielding,' said Roger, with more civility but no more warmth. 'A bad business, this museum affair!'

'Oh, I don't know, might be quite good business for you. I heard you'd just stalked out of the police station – don't tell me you're turning the client down? Think of the capital there must be behind an organisation big enough to market stuff like the *Shelvedon Chronicle*!'

'Did this man you're talking about really want you to be his solicitor?' asked Sara, fascinated.

'They charged him, and he asked for a solicitor.' It was clear from his flush of annoyance that Roger had no wish to talk about it. 'He didn't seem to care who it was – said a local man would do, and picked me out at random. I didn't know anything about the case until they notified me he was asking me to act for him.'

'And are you going to?' Sara couldn't help asking.

'No, of course not, how can I? You'd have thought the police would have seen that for themselves. I'm a councillor, and the *Chronicle* is municipal property. I'm even on the museum sub-committee. It wouldn't be proper for me to involve myself in the case legally.' He was red with irritation now. 'Hadn't we better get those carol sheets down, Sara?'

'Didn't you take a good look at him?' asked Tom, happily pursuing what he saw to be an unwelcome subject. 'Surely you wanted at least to *see* the one that got away?'

'I didn't even know what it was all about until I was there. It was only decent to see him, and explain why I couldn't act for him. Sara, I'm just going to straighten that one chain – you go ahead, I'll follow you in a moment.'

'I'll hold the steps for you,' volunteered Tom, maliciously obliging. Even willing to let me out of his sight, thought Sara, as she scurried indoors and through the entrance hall, rather than stop baiting Roger. Well, let him get on with it. Roger could hold his own.

The decorations leaped into beauty as she switched on the lights, and the laden tables shone with jellies and trifles and cakes. She ran up to the small committee room in the gate tower, unlocked the cupboard, and brought down her carol leaflets. There was really nothing else to be done.

Surprised that the two young men had not yet followed her indoors, she took an apple from the bowl of fruit on the nearest table, and went out, peacefully munching it, to see what they were up to.

'Well, well!' said Tom, observing the apple. 'Eve in person! Now which of us two, Brecon, old boy, would you say was cast for the serpent?'

'Which of us,' snapped Roger bitterly, 'looks more like a snake in the grass?' And he strode away from the tree and took Sara by the arm, turning her back towards the hall. 'Come on, Sara, let's get inside. Here come the others.'

Paul Hartland and two of his juniors from the Modern School were just unloading a car on the pavement outside the gatehouse, and little Miss Price from the infants department was trotting across the courtyard with her arms full of sheet music.

Then, quite suddenly, came the first of the children, with dazzled eyes fixed on the tree. And the tenth great Annual

Joint Christmas Party for the schoolchildren of Shelvedon began.

Everybody agreed the party was the most complete success so far, and the best organised. They played games first – active games and quiet games alternately – then they ate an enormous tea, and after it came the puppet show, the conjurer, and the ventriloquist, to keep the guests reasonably still and engrossed while the tea settled; while the helpers snatched a brief rest, too, and Tom Fielding sneaked away and clambered into his beard and his scarlet gown, ready for the climax.

Then out they all trooped, already warmly packed into their outdoor clothes, to cluster round the lighted tree. Tom's assistants climbed about the tree handing down parcels, while he called up eager owners to receive them. He was a voluble and effective Father Christmas. The one real con-solation, he claimed, was that inside all that red flannel he didn't feel the cold.

Then the parents came, and the town band, and the time-honoured half-hour of carol singing began, under the coloured lights and the floating balloons; and before anyone was really ready for it – which was the right time for it to happen – the party was over. With a noise like the descent of the evening starlings upon Trafalgar Square the children of Shelvedon were on their way home.

Sara stood under the ravaged tree, speeding the departing guests as they withdrew.

'Good night, Jimmy! Happy Christmas! Good night, Alison! Good night, Pat! Did you have a good time? A happy Christmas …'

'You seem to know every kid in Shelvedon personally,' said Roger, grinning from behind her shoulder.

An under-sized boy in a navy flannel duffle beamed up at her demurely over his large, flat parcel and gave the string an extra twist round his wrist. 'Miss Boyne, I got a book!'

'You haven't opened it yet,' she said, smiling. 'How do you know it's a book?'

'Oh, yes, Miss Boyne, I have. I did it up again carefully, so it won't get wet even if it snows. The man on the wireless said it would snow.'

Plainly he hoped for the prophecy to be fulfilled. 'And do you like your present, Ivo?'

Large eyes, black-fringed, shone in the shadow of his hood. 'Miss Boyne, it's *beautiful*! It's a *beautiful* book!'

'Funny little thing,' said Roger as the small figure trotted away over the scintillating cobbles. 'Who is he?'

'He's an orphan, in the county's care – name's Ivo Jenkins. He's boarded out with old Mrs Freeman – you know, at Cross Farm Cottage. She's very good to him, but she's rather old. I wish he had more young, stimulating company, he's such a reserved, serious child.'

'One of yours, I see,' said Roger, gently laughing at her. He stretched and sighed, looking after the last stragglers as they withdrew under a barrage of dancing balloons, leaving the courtyard suddenly quiet and desolate. 'I should have liked to stay and help you tidy up, Sara, but I've got to go to a dinner tonight, and I promised I'd go home first.'

'You've done enough,' said Sara. 'You've been most helpful. Thanks for everything!'

She had almost hoped that he would make some tentative

reference to the New Year's Eve dance, but he didn't. He simply smiled, wished her a happy Christmas, and fled.

She turned away with a sigh, and went to join her weary fellow-workers who were clearing up the debris. Just then Tom emerged, scarlet and perspiring, from his beard. He stripped off his robes, and began to gather up the coloured heaps of tinsel and wrappings under the tree. 'Hallo, what's this? There's something buried in the soil here!'

Sara went to his side. The earth in the tub had certainly been disturbed, and Tom's vigorous gesture had swept aside the fallen needles and exposed a corner of brown paper.

'It's a box – no, a book!' He tugged it clear and brushed away the needles that clung to it. An oblong package wrapped loosely in a single fold of stiff paper, which fell away as he turned it in his hands, revealed the vividly coloured dust-jacket of a book. '*Boys Gigantic Adventure Annual*! Oh, lord!' said Tom blankly. 'Has somebody been forgotten? One of the absentees?'

'No, I'm positive! Besides, this was for one of my boys. I remember it perfectly. But how on earth did it get there do you suppose?'

'Sara!' Tom stared at her reproachfully. '*You* didn't choose this for some poor kid, did you?' Just because he taught art at the Secondary Modern and the Technical College, she thought indignantly, he didn't have to be so damned superior about other people's taste.

'Yes, I did! What's the matter with it? But ...' She gaped helplessly towards the gateway, through which young Ivo Jenkins had vanished some ten minutes ago. 'But he *had* his book! He just told me he'd looked at it, and it was beautiful.'

'Couldn't have meant this,' said Tom, averting his eyes from it. 'Anyhow, he buried it decently. Probably disapproved of the art work – and who could blame him? Obviously he was just being nice to you – thought you didn't know any better.'

Sara experienced an urge, by no means new to her where Tom Fielding was concerned, to box his ears. 'I tell you he *liked* it! A beautiful book, he said!' She heard him saying it again, and knew that he had meant it; and quite suddenly the confusion in her mind was all blown away by a staggering thought.

This annual was undoubtedly the book she'd chosen for him; what, then, had he been clutching so tightly under his arm as he took leave of her? What was the beautiful book that had caused his serious eyes to shine so brilliantly in the shadow of his hood?

She clutched at Tom's arm, forgetting all her irritation with him. 'Tom! – *how big* is the *Shelvedon Chronicle*!'

Tom turned a face stricken into ludicrous consternation, and stared at her wildly, making the same mental leap she had just made. *'Just about as big as this thing*!' They stood gaping at each other, trying to grasp the monstrous implications. 'It couldn't be! Things like that don't happen!'

'But they have happened! It disappeared from the museum, didn't it? And the police closed all the ways out of the castle, and then made a thorough search for the thief, didn't they? And found a man with a criminal record in just that line …'

'Right here inside the courtyard!'

'But without the *Chronicle*,' said Tom. 'You realise what that means? They had him penned inside here, unable to get clean away with the goods, but with a few minutes' respite while they combed out the museum buildings.

'Long enough for him to swop his loot for a similar-sized parcel on the Christmas tree, wrap it and leave it to be collected later – by himself or someone else. Without it, he stood a chance of getting off. He'd only to hang the *Chronicle* on the tree, and hide it, and let himself be picked up. What else could he do?'

'But how could he get a message through to anyone else?' protested Sara breathlessly, swept away by this reconstruction.

'I don't know. There are ways; maybe he had a confederate outside the enclave, maybe he managed to get some sort of signal through.'

'Then one thing's certain,' said Sara. 'He'd let them know the name on the parcel, otherwise they could hunt all day. And if he did manage to get word through, why haven't they collected it?'

'Maybe they have. Maybe that's some fresh substitute young Ivo's carrying home now. Or perhaps they simply didn't get here in time. The precincts would be rather popular this morning, while the offices were open. And this afternoon conscience brought us along so early ...'

'Then they'll be looking for Ivo now,' said Sara with fierce finality, and grew pale at what she herself had said. It wasn't the *Shelvedon Chronicle* she was thinking of, it was that funny, old-fashioned little boy with the quiet manners and the impenetrable reserve, trotting home through the frosty evening with thousands of pounds' worth of skill and beauty and devotion under his arm.

'A beautiful book!' said Tom with awe. 'My God, he was right!'

They exchanged one bemused, incredulous glance.

'Come on!' said Tom, seizing her by the arm. 'At least, we've got to make sure. See him safely home, and beg a look at his book, just in case.'

'And take him this!' Sara grabbed up the *Boys Gigantic Adventure Annual* as she was towed away at the end of Tom's long arm.

'*That*!' Tom snorted as he slid into the car and reached for the starter. 'A boy who falls for the *Chronicle* won't think the *Gigantic Adventure Annual* a fair exchange.'

'This is entirely appropriate for his age group,' said Sara indignantly, slamming the door on her side as the engine obediently hiccupped into life.

'Only unfortunately he doesn't seem to be entirely appropriate to it himself.'

'You don't know him! I do! I chose it specially for him, because he's far too prim and quiet. I want to encourage him to think adventurously,' she said, all the more aggressively because Tom always made her feel self-conscious about her beliefs.

Tom swung the car out through the gateway. They threaded their way rapidly through the late Christmas shoppers and the lighted windows fell behind them. Through the archway in the town wall the black sky lowered at them, heavy with cloud. The first desultory flakes of the promised snow were already falling.

'Perhaps there's no one to collect,' said Sara. 'Perhaps

there wasn't any message. Maybe he's just been hoping they couldn't hold him, so that he could pick it up himself. It may be just a one-man job, after all.'

'Not a chance! He can't be any more than a very small cog in a very large system of wheels. What would an ordinary thug want with a thing like the *Chronicle*! No, this is no one-man job. It ties in with all those other thefts of works of art, just as the newspaper said.'

'Isn't it queer,' she said, 'to think there are people willing to spend a fortune on a thing they'll never be able to show off to anyone? What do they get out of gloating over them in secret?'

'If I had the chance to gloat over the *Chronicle* in secret, and feel I owned it, I might be able to tell you. They exist, all right. Plenty of them, if you know where to look.'

He put his foot down hard as soon as they were well out of the shopping streets and through the gate. The high, windy road, fringed with semi-detached houses at first, soon fell into darkness between the occasional older cottages. Not three miles away to the right, keen in the strong salt scent of the wind, was the sea.

'Wouldn't Ivo be with some of the other children? The little Grettons have to come out this way, nearly as far as Cross Farm.'

'They left well ahead of him. No, I'm afraid he'll be alone.' He was so often alone, partly from habit, partly from choice.

She wished he lived with some large, cheerful family in the town, where he'd be jockeyed into mixing with other children whether he liked it or not. But foster-homes are where you can find them. And the old lady was very good to him. Sara found herself thinking of Ivo with an indignant, anxious affection, as though she had only become aware of his deprivations when danger was added to them.

The road ran between hedges and fields now, and the street lighting was all left behind, but it was only a quarter of a mile to Cross Farm. And suddenly Sara gave a breathless laugh of sheer relief, and pointed ahead. 'There he is! He's all right!'

The small figure, bent purposefully forward in an old man's trotting walk, scurried along the footpath with his parcel tucked under his arm.

Tom heaved an audible sigh, and relaxed the pressure of his foot on the accelerator. The next moment he had to jam it hard upon the brake, for out of a side road on the right a large, old, dark-bodied car drove suddenly across his path, and turned into the road ahead of him, cutting off his view of the child trotting briskly into the distance.

It all happened in an instant. The big car drew alongside the hurrying child, and slowed there smoothly, and an arm and shoulder, no more than a vague black movement in the murky dusk, leaned out and plucked the parcel from under his arm.

Ivo's scared squeal sounded thinly through the moan of the snow-laden wind, and sharpened into a yell of pain as the strong cord dragged sharply at his wrist. Sara, remembering how tightly he had wound the string round to anchor his treasure, gasped in sympathy. It must have been the sound of Tom accelerating furiously that decided what happened next. If only the string had broken Ivo would have been safe, but the string did not break, and delay was impossible.

The man in the passenger seat transferred his grip suddenly from the book to the boy's arm, and hoisted him bodily into the car, which shot away into the night with a roar of a powerful engine, Tom's old Morris throbbing on its tail.

Sara heard herself repeating the car number breathlessly, memorising it because she had no opportunity of writing it down.

Tom said nothing at all. His jaw was set, and his foot had the accelerator pedal flattened to the floor of the car, and every ounce of energy he possessed was devoted to hurling them along after the kidnappers. Sara hooked an arm over the back of the seat to steady herself as they rocked round the corner into the Westensea road, and met the squalls of thin, sharp snow head-on.

The rear light ahead winked at them through the murk, and seemed if anything a shade nearer. The speedometer needle was wobbling furiously around sixty-five; it crept up towards seventy, in a flash of desperation lunged above seventy, and lurched back shuddering at its own temerity.

Past the Mitre Inn now, and round the long curve, turning with the curve of the coastline. Two miles or so more, and they'd be entering the suburbs of Westensea, and the big fellow would be forced to slow down. They'd get him there, if they had to ram him to do it. If he kept up this speed the police would join in the chase, and he wouldn't risk that, with what he had on board.

'He's stopping!' panted Sara. The big car seemed to have drawn into the hedge and slowed considerably, if not stopped. The driver opened his door, and seemed to be getting out, though he clung close to the body of the car.

Tom didn't lift his foot until the first tiny flash against the blackness of the night and the deeper blackness of the car warned him. The report was lost in the protests of his own sorely tried motor, but he recognised the signs, and slowed for an instant, then, realising that if he stopped he would merely present a sitting target, he gritted his teeth, trod hard down again, and wrenched the wheel round to drive full at the enemy. Head-on he'd have a better chance of upsetting the marksman's aim.

The second shot, by luck or skill, got their right front tyre, and brought them round with a horrible, lurching plunge towards the ditch.

Tom, wrestling frantically with the wheel, wrenched the Morris back onto the road, and somehow managed to pull it up without disaster on a front tyre slashed to ribbons; but by the time they had tumbled, panting and trembling, out into the snow the big car was pulling away at speed, and before they had breath enough to speak it had vanished completely in the direction of Westensea.

Tom caught Sara by the shoulders, and held her for a moment against his heart. 'Sara, you're all right? You're not hurt?' The alarm and ardour in his voice hardly registered until later, she was so intent upon the chase.

'I'm all right! A bit shaken, that's all. Now what do we do? We *can't* let them get away!'

'We're not going to. I've got to change this wheel. Thank God the spare's all right! I can manage alone – only a twenty-minute job! Sara, darling, could you run on alone? You're not afraid? We can't be far out of the town, there must be a call-box soon, or a house with a phone.

'Call the police, tell them the car number, and where it's headed. As soon as I've changed the wheel I'll come on after you and pick you up, and we'll go on together and report, see if we can help at all. After you've called them, walk back towards me. Or if the snow gets bad stay in shelter somewhere by the side of the road and watch out for me. Can you do that?'

'Yes, of course!' She was glad to have something active to do, glad to be still in the hunt. She set off at a rapid run, head-down into the snow. Not until she had left Tom and the Morris well behind did she realise that she was still clutching the *Gigantic Adventure Annual* under her arm. She tucked it inside her coat to keep it dry, and ran on.

The first larger house, after several isolated cottages, lay back from the road behind a screen of trees and shrubberies. There was a wide carriage-gate, and a small wicket beside it, and the overhead wires, thrumming angrily in the wind, turned inward with the drive towards the house.

As she pushed open the wicket gate she thought it might be wise to leave Tom an indication of where she had halted, in case he came along before she was back on the road. No use leaving boy scout's signs in this obliterating blizzard. She detached the gaudy cover of the *Gigantic Adventure Annual* and impaled it firmly on one of the top spikes of the iron gate, so that it stood up and faced the road like a professional sign.

Then she ran up the drive, and rang the bell at the front door of a large, complacent Victorian house in two-coloured brick.

There was what seemed a long interval before a light came on inside the porch, and high heels tapped up to the door.

The woman who opened it was dressed in a smart black suit, and had the cool, noncommittal manner of a housekeeper or a secretary.

At Sara's request to use the telephone she raised her eyebrows very slightly, but waved the intruder civilly into the porch out of the snow.

'It's urgent,' Sara found herself saying, 'or I wouldn't trouble you.' Possibly the eyebrows had intimidated her a little. 'I want to call the police,' she added breathlessly.

'Not an accident?' the woman in black asked, with quick sympathy.

'Well, no, but ...'

'I'm sorry, of course you mustn't lose any time. One moment, I'll tell Professor Brayburn.' And she left Sara standing in the hall, and vanished through one of a bewildering array of doors.

After a few minutes the same door opened once again, and out bustled a small, benevolent, grey-haired man, peering kindly at Sara over the rims of bifocals.

His face was rosy and elderly, and instantly familiar, though it took her a moment or two to relate both face and name to her memories of three or four summers ago, when she had last seen him.

It had been at a rally of adult educationalists, at the University of Westchester, and the Professor of English Literature had moved benignly among guests at tea. She felt herself suddenly back among known, safe, comforting things; the lurking car and the gunman on the lonely road seemed as remote as the moon.

'My dear young lady, of course, of course, come into my

study, you'll be more comfortable at the extension in there. Such a night! Terrible!' He waved her before him into a brown, book-lined room full of deep leather chairs, and indicated the telephone.

Sara lifted the receiver. The line was quite dead. She tried dialling the operator, joggled the rest, waited, tried again. But nothing happened. The heavy, dead silence closed on her hearing like a vice.

Professor Brayburn, surprised by the delay, looked in from the next room. 'Dear, dear, is there some trouble on the line? It was all right an hour or so ago.'

'It seems to be dead. No response at all.'

He bustled across with a concerned face to try it for himself, and had to admit defeat. 'That's extraordinary – surely there's not been enough snow to bring down wires? My dear child, I'm so sorry! Can I ...'

'Oh, I can't put you out any more. You've been most kind. My friend will soon be along to pick me up, and we can go on into the town.'

'But my dear, you can't possibly go out again in this, it's still snowing heavily. Won't you at least let me give you a warm drink, and wait a little, and see if it stops?'

'It's most kind of you, but I can't. My friend might miss me if I don't go to the road. He won't know where I am, you see ...'

She was moving steadily towards the door as she spoke, preparing to bow herself out as gracefully as she could, when she stepped upon something that felt sharp and hard in the pile of the Persian carpet, something that stabbed through the sole of her shoe. She withdrew her foot and looked down, quite involuntarily, to see what she had trodden on. A button. A wooden toggle button from a duffle coat, with a girdle of red string still circling its middle.

The thick, strong cord by which it had been attached to the coat had torn loose, bringing with it a few threads of dark blue flannel; and the button was not big enough to have come from a man's coat. A child's, then; a navy blue one – *Ivo's*!

She tore her eyes from it instantly, but she was too late. Across three yards of charged air they encountered Professor Brayburn's old, faded, benevolent blue eyes, and she knew that he had followed her glance, and understood all its implications.

She made a gallant attempt. She took another tentative step towards the door, and said, 'Good night, and thank you very much. I'm sorry I've troubled you for nothing.'

But with that the door opened, and the black-clad secretary slid through it, and after her, circling gently, one to the left and the other to the right, like dancers, two large and silent men in dark overcoats.

They drew into a tight semicircle between Sara and the door.

'What a pity!' said the Professor sadly. 'Such a nice young lady, too! But we can hardly let you go running off into the night now, knowing what you know – can we?'

The door closed behind her, and she heard the key turn in the lock. The soft footsteps of the man with the gun receded down the staircase.

The room, heavily furnished but with that impersonal look of a bedroom which is seldom slept in, was dimly lit by one inadequate electric bulb under a fringed shade. On the big bed, draped with a dark tapestry cover, Ivo sat staring at her in astonishment and uncertainty through the tears he had just hurriedly scrubbed away.

'Miss Boyne, you mustn't be scared. I'll look after you! Was it you, Miss Boyne, in the car with Mr Fielding, following them? They haven't got him, too, have they?' He slid off the tall bed and stood in front of her, quivering gently like a terrier on a scent. 'Was he hurt when they fired the gun? What happened?'

She told him. Putting the whole crazy sequence into words somehow clarified it for her, too, and she found in it more to reassure her than she had expected. 'So you see, he's sure to come, as soon as he's changed the wheel. Even if he misses seeing my sign as he comes by, he'll go straight to the police when he doesn't find me. And once they start looking for us properly, they're sure to start from where the car was halted, so they'll soon be here. They can't miss us, really Ivo.'

'But suppose Mr Fielding sees it the first time, and comes here by himself?' asked the all-too-knowing child, staring at her with those unblinking eyes of his. 'There's at least *four* of them. I think there may be more.'

'Mr Fielding will almost certainly call the police first,' said Sara, all the more firmly because of the sinking feeling he'd given her. 'Why, *all* your buttons are gone!' she said, surveying the duffle coat that hung open over Ivo's Sunday suit.

'I pulled them off. I left one in the car, in case we ever have to identify it,' he explained simply, 'because there might be a lot of big black cars like it, and they could change the number plates, couldn't they? And one in the garden here.'

Somewhat staggered, Sara sat down on the bed, and drew him down beside her. 'Ivo, I want to ask you about the book you had from the Christmas tree.'

His face burned up into indignation. 'They took it away from me! They can't do that, it's stealing. It's my book!'

'Ivo, dear, I'm afraid it may not be. You see, I think it was stolen already, from the town museum, and put in the place of the book that was meant for you. Tell me what it was like.'

He gave her one dismayed glance, and then obeyed, shutting his eyes the better to see it again. 'It was in a folding leather case, without any fastener. Inside it had a beautiful leather cover, and the paper was funny, but nice to feel. I couldn't read the letters, they were funny, too, but they made lovely patterns, and the big ones were done with colours, with birds, and animals, and people. And there were lots of little pictures, with people with queer dresses like in the history books.'

'It is a history book, Ivo, a wonderful one, made hundreds of years ago. Somebody stole it from the museum, and then he wanted to hide it because the police were after him, and he hid it in the parcel meant for you.'

'What will they do with us?' asked Ivo.

That was what Sara was wondering, too. She hoped he had not realised the full implications of their position, but she was afraid he had.

'Oh, take us and leave us somewhere miles from home, while they make their getaway. Or leave us locked up here – that would give them time to vanish, too, before anyone finds us.'

'But if that old man who lives here has got to vanish,' said the disconcerting child after a moment's thought, 'that means he'll lose his house, and his job, and everything. And then he wouldn't be any use to them again, would he? I mean, if the police knew who he is, and are looking for him, and all that? I don't think he'll like that. And the people he's working for – they won't like it, either, will they?'

They would not, and she knew it. There was too much at stake. To leave Ivo and herself to tell what they knew, however much later, meant to sacrifice at least all this local part of a carefully-built organisation. No, the game was far too big. They would be quietly disposed of. Not here, though! This house was too close to the scene of the latest theft.

Furthermore, it would be very much easier and safer to remove them to some more discreet place for disposal alive. They would be taken away from here, she felt sure. In this blizzard? There was too great a chance of a car getting stuck in the drifts. No, nothing would happen until the snow stopped. Tom and the police had a little grace in which to find them, and she and Ivo a short respite in which to help themselves.

She was uncomfortably aware that Ivo was adding up the probabilities no less accurately than she, and it was largely to distract him if she could, and avoid confirming his conclusions at all costs, that she jumped up briskly, and began to look round their prison.

First of all she crossed over to the window, pulled back the thick, dusty curtains, and hoisted the heavy lower sash. Its weight was greater than she had expected, and as soon as she relaxed her upward pressure she saw why, for instantly it surged down again, and she had only just time to catch it before it crashed.

Both sash-cords were broken so she let it slide down the last few inches, quietly, and looked round for something with which to prop it open.

There was an enormous book on the old-fashioned table in the corner, a family Bible. She propped it under one end of the sash, and through the opening the snow blew in thinning eddies.

Sara hoisted the sash of the heavy window cautiously higher, inserting her shoulder under it, and stacking the *Boys Gigantic Adventure Annual* on top of the Bible. When she gently lowered the weight upon this precarious erection it settled and held fast, giving her reasonable room to lean out and inspect their position.

'We're on the garden side,' said Ivo apologetically. 'I looked. We couldn't signal to the road from here.'

Sara looked down upon a depressingly blank wall. 'We're only on the first floor,' she said strenuously.

'The bed isn't made up,' said the practical child, even more sadly. 'No sheets or blankets, only that big cover. And the curtains!'

The curtains were old brocade, far too thick to knot successfully without losing half their length. And even if curtains and bedcover could be joined together, how were they to be anchored? The furniture offered no help, the bed had no posts, only a solid footboard.

Then, looking round with more optimism than she felt, she perceived for the first time in her life the true beauty and utility of Victorian furnishing. Instead of a neat little track and plastic runners, the curtains were slung by metal rings from an enormous mahogany pole, as long as a tilting lance and as thick as her wrist.

This pole, she discovered, was at least three feet longer than the width of the window frame, and the very pins by which the rings were secured to the fabric of the curtains were of solid brass, and thick as skewers.

She began almost to believe in what she was doing. She hoisted a chair across to the window, and piled several volumes of a discarded encyclopaedia on top of the chair, and climbed precariously to the swaying crest. Large curved brackets supported the curtain pole.

She had to exert all her strength, thus straining upward, to lift clear one end, and then the sudden shifting of weight sent all the rings rattling and chiming down the pole in a fine shower of dust and almost toppled her from her perch. Ivo flew to prop her up, and stretched up his puny arms to nurse the weight while she climbed down and moved her ladder to the other end. There was no need to explain anything to him, he was already ahead of her in spirit, his eyes glittering with excitement.

The pole, braced across the open window to take the weight upon those huge, solid rings, was the safest anchorage they could have found anywhere. Sara stripped off one of the heavy curtains, rings and all, and with the brass pin attached to the rings secured it firmly to the curtain which still dangled in place. She pulled at the join, first gingerly, then more confidently. A few threads strained warningly, but nothing gave.

Then Ivo dragged the tapestry cover from the bed.

Attaching that was not so easy. There were no more spare pins, and after one attempt she gave up the idea of tying it on. There remained only the two looped curtain cords. She used them to bind the thick fabrics together as tightly as she could, and hoped they wouldn't slip. The thickness of the hems would certainly help to hold them fast.

By that time she really believed in the machinery of escape. She had the awkward bundle coiled in her arms on the snowy window sill when she checked for a moment to say: 'Turn out the light!'

When it was out, the whole face of the house below her lay black and unpeopled. The Professor and his henchmen were all at the front, there was no one to observe the dangling curtains snaking down the wall and past the ground-floor window.

Past it? She was afraid that even when the whole length was paid out the end still swung only just level with the upper panes of the downstairs window. From above it was difficult to tell by how many feet it hung clear of the ground, but she was afraid it must be almost six feet.

'All right, Ivo, put the light on again. It looks a long way to drop. Do you think you can manage? Are you good at climbing?'

The snort he gave was the most contemptuous sound she had ever heard! He leaned out and peered down the wall. 'Do it on my head! Plenty of snow to drop in!' He was already balanced on his stomach with both legs waving out of the window, and both hands locked fast on the pole, when he checked. 'Sorry, Miss Boyne,' he said, abashed. 'Ladies first!'

Sara looked at the distant ground, and the absurd rope, and shut her eyes. 'I'm not sure it will bear me. You go, quickly! When you get down, get into cover at once, and go down the drive to the road. You must go into the town, to the police, and tell them everything, do you understand?'

'But what about you?' His solemn eyes stared anxiously across the window sill.

'Never mind me, I shall be all right until the police come. Go on down, quickly!'

She was so intent on seeing him safely down that she never heard the door of the room open behind her. The first she knew of it was the sudden pull of the ice-cold wind surging more strongly into the room, and a bellow of alarm and indignation that made her leap round wildly to face the doorway. One of the two gunmen, the taller, came plunging across to the window in three great strides. She saw the dark-blue gleam of the revolver barrel in his right hand, and screamed, 'Quickly, Ivo!' Then the man swung his left arm and struck her out of his way, and she was flung against the wall, and slid to her knees, shaken and dazed.

It took her a moment to realise what he meant to do. In her world such things had never happened before. It took time to adjust herself to them. He was leaning well out from the open window, looking down the still jerking rope. He took hold of it for an instant as if he meant to try and haul it up again with its burden, then abandoned the idea, for Ivo was now so near to the end of it that he had only to slither down the last foot or so and let go. Instead, the right hand that held the gun steadied deliberately, pointed the barrel downwards and took aim.

She flung herself forward on her knees, gripped the spine of the *Boys Gigantic Adventure Annual* in both hands, and wrenched it from its place. The family Bible, pulled askew with it, toppled majestically to the floor, just before the falling window could strike it. Instead, it struck the leaning man across the small of the back with a crunch like that of a tree falling, just as he fired. Shot and scream, and the awful, crushed sound of the sash thudding into his ribs, all came together. Where the shot went nobody knew, but the gun flew out of his paralysed hand and dropped into the snow and one muted yell of triumph from the invisible garden eased Sara's heart once for all of any terror that Ivo had been hit.

His movements were so implicit in that joyful shout that she almost saw him drop like a hunting cat upon the fallen gun, and dive with it into the snowy shrubberies, that threshed for one moment after his vanishing, and then were still.

She stood petrified in the middle of the room, clutching the battered annual, and staring at the trapped man in fascinated horror.

He had left the door wide open. Sara turned and darted through it. Instinctively she turned towards the staircase, and scurried down it. At the foot she suffered a moment of terror, because the woman in black was standing by the hall door, peering out into the drive. No quick way out there. She drew back hastily, and backed through the nearest doorway in the shadow of the stairs, into an unlighted room. Somewhere she could hear the humming of a car.

The curtains of the room were not drawn, and her eyes, aided by the reflected glow from the snow outside, gradually grew accustomed to the darkness. The place seemed to be a little rear parlour, looking on to the same silent, bushy garden she had seen from above. She felt her way to the window, and put down the *Boys Gigantic Adventure Annual* while she quietly eased back the catch and freed the lower sash. Before she could raise it there were rapid footsteps at the door, and the rattle of the knob turning.

She had no time to think or plan. She dropped to the carpet and crept under the chenille-covered table, just as the door opened and the light was snapped on.

The neatly-shod elderly feet entering could belong to no one but Professor Brayburn. Sara cowered in her hiding-place, and watched him approach her across the room; and for one awful moment she believed he had seen her, and was coming to coax her out of cover with his gentle, regretful, almost apologetic voice.

But she saw he was only making for the window, just as she had done. When he reached it she was even able to peep from under the chenille folds, and watch him. He had a leather case under his arm, something like a flat briefcase. Her heart gave a lurch as she realised what it must be.

A folding case minus fastener, Ivo had said. Was the Professor just in the act of putting his plunder safely away somewhere in this room? It didn't look like that. He had laid it down on the edge of the table – she heard the tiny, dull sound it made on the chenille pile.

Now he had left the table and gone back to the door for a moment. He opened it a crack, and curious sounds came in. Wasn't that a car again? More a roar than a purr this time, surely, in the drive. It sounded like more than one car. Then suddenly a shot, or at least something that sounded like a shot.

She no longer understood anything that was happening, it was all a terrifying confusion. The Professor was quietly closing and locking the door.

Now he had turned his back on her, and was bending over the drawers of a writing desk across the room. Sara reached up a timid hand, and groped along the edge of the table until she found the leather case. She lifted it gently down, and drew it into the shelter of the tablecloth with her.

The flap opened quietly, the vellum, supple as velvet, slid softly out upon the floor. She slipped the battered annual into the case, and gingerly hoisted it back on to the table. They'd reckoned it a fair exchange once, so why not a second time?

The Professor had not turned. He was busy stuffing his pockets with small, rustling bundles from the drawers of the desk. Sara retired undetected into the darkest corner under the table, hugging the *Shelvedon Chronicle* to her heart. Now it only remained to get safely out of here!

But that, it appeared, was just what the Professor was doing. She ought to have known. Why else should he be wearing a long black overcoat and a scarf? And why else should he be methodically filling his pockets with money, and quietly withdrawing into a locked back room with the *Chronicle*?

The cars, then, and of course the shot – these were wonderfully relevant. They must mean that Tom had got through to the police, that the hunt was up, and this house written off – at least by the Professor.

His underlings, apparently, were expendable. For now

he was hoisting the creaking lower sash of the window, and picking up his precious leather folder, and sliding, with an agility surprising in one of his sober years and appearance, out into the snowy garden.

Sara crept from under the table, and clambered resolutely over the sill in his wake. She waded through the deep snow under the window, and followed his track into the thick darkness of some fir trees.

Behind them, from somewhere on the other side of the house, came a few brief, staccato shouts, a shot, a confusion of sounds.

Then there were other sounds, much nearer, the snapping of a twig, trodden inadvertently under the snow, a soft, slithering fall from other branches, behind her now. She was following the Professor, but someone else was following her.

Frightened of what this might mean, she began to hurry and then, remembering how precious and how dangerous was the thing she carried, she took off the scarf, wrapped it about the unprotected leather cover, and halted for a moment to thrust it into the middle of a big, round holly bush at the side of the path.

She was not ten yards past the holly bush, and hesitating in momentary panic, unsure of her direction, when hands reached out of the obscurity behind and grasped her by the shoulders. She opened her lips to scream and her captor clapped one palm over them and hissed frantically, 'Sara, darling, don't! It's me, Roger! Don't make a noise!' He withdrew his hand and she gasped in a quavering sob of relief, 'Roger, thank goodness! I thought it was *them*!'

Sara clung to him, trembling with reaction, looking up at his strained and anxious face, so close to her own. 'How did you get here? How did you know where we were? Where's Tom?'

'Later!' he whispered back urgently. 'No time now to tell you. Come on, this way, quickly!' And he folded his arm round her, and dragged her on through the bushes, away from the house. She hung back for a moment. 'But the police – I heard cars ...'

'Not police cars! It's more of the gang. They're in trouble, but so are we if we run into them before the police arrive. Come on! Let's get out of here, quick!'

'And Ivo ...' panted Sara, almost swept off her feet by the masterful and most reassuring arm about her waist. 'He got out safely – I told him to get to the road and go on into the town ...'

'I know! We'll take care of Ivo. Let's get you safely out of here first. Come on, run for it! My car's down here.'

She had neither breath nor time to say a word more, or she would probably have told him what she had done with the *Chronicle*.

Round the curve of the path, shrouded in trees, there was a long, low, creosote-brown shed. Open garage doors had scooped new arcs out of the piled snow, and someone was hurriedly shovelling away the remains of the drift which had formed in front of them. With a sudden sickening downward lurch of her heart she recognised Professor Brayburn. The old man had imposed upon Roger!

He possibly thought they were all escaping from the same alien danger, carrying the rescued *Chronicle* with them. She tried to halt, but Roger dragged her onward.

'Roger, stop! The Professor – he was with them – he's in it! Don't let him …'

He must have heard, he must have understood, but he didn't stop. His grip tightened upon her arm, he drew her into the shed, and held her hard against the side of his familiar grey Jaguar. He looked over her shoulder at the Professor with a white, strained grin and said, 'Insurance! The kid's evidence won't be worth much.'

'Admirable!' said Professor Brayburn, giving her a brief glance bereft now of all benignity. 'She'll come in handy if there's any bargaining to be done, too – but I hope it won't come to that.' And he opened the rear door of the car, and slid rapidly into it, fastening a hand on her wrist to draw her after him.

She hung back, trembling, too dazed to understand what was happening.

'Roger, what are you doing? Roger, you can't …'

'Get in!' he said peremptorily, and thrust her bodily into the car. She fell against the Professor, and he took her by the arms and held her fast as she fought to reach the handle of the door. Roger got into the car, and started the engine.

Bitterly through all her rage and hurt she remembered how she had admired and envied the car's rapid getaway and breathless acceleration when he had driven her home from the Hallowe'en dance.

They lunged forward out of the garage, and crunched into the snow, turning away from the house. Down the steps, down the path, shouts echoed distantly, and small black figures came running, too late. The nearest of them, tall, long-legged, running like a hare and shouting like a maniac, was already recognisable. She screamed, 'Tom! Tom!' But he couldn't possibly reach them – she might never see him again.

The car heeled round the curve of the narrow drive, gathering speed. Far behind, another car roared into action. Close at hand, Tom Fielding took a flying leap at the rear door, and was flung off and sent sprawling into the snow by the wing. Nothing could intercept the Jaguar now.

Between the enclosing trees the shot was flung back and forth in a loud, stammering repetition. The car swerved violently to the left, plunging like a wild horse under Roger's startled hands. Sara heard the squeal of the front tyre, the horrid scraping of wings against branches; then with a shattering crash the Jaguar flattened its nose against a tree, and settled sideways into the snow.

By the time Sara had got the door open and tumbled out into Tom's arms the police were all round them, and everything was under control. The Professor emerged unhurt into the welcoming hands of constables. From the driving seat they lifted out Roger Brecon, stunned, shaken and bruised, but without more serious injuries. And then, as though by common consent, everyone looked round for the source of the shot.

Ivo Jenkins came swaggering out of the bushes, glowing with excitement and pride, and brandishing his captured revolver in a manner which caused the policeman to exclaim in horror.

'Give that to me!' Tom said.

Ivo looked mutinous for one moment, but he was resigned to the fact that the scales are loaded against the young.

'Sorry!' said Tom. 'Very hard, I know, but the law's the law.' And discreetly ignoring a muttered comment which had sounded to him like: 'Just like a bloomin' teacher!' he added generously, 'Jolly good shot, all the same, had you been practising Ivo? Congratulations!'

'I *am* a good shot,' said the marksman, expanding into good-humour again. 'Did you find my book? Did they have it in the car with them, Miss Boyne?'

Sara had almost forgotten the *Chronicle*. She smiled for the first time, rather wryly, as she saw the sergeant lift the leather case triumphantly out of the car, and laughed aloud at his dumbfounded face as Tom drew from it the *Boys Gigantic Adventure Annual*.

'It's all right,' she said, suddenly, ceasing to laugh because of the childlike disappointment in Tom's face. 'It's all right, I know where the real *Chronicle* is. I hid it myself.'

Her only regret, and for personal reasons it was admittedly a vindictive one, was that Roger Brecon wasn't present to see her draw the precious bundle from its refuge and put it safely into the hands of the police.

'They wouldn't use Brecon's car or him for the snatch job, naturally,' said the police sergeant as they stood in the main garage a little later. 'It was far too conspicuous, and he was too well known in the district. He had to rush out here and send someone else to get the book back from the kid. An old, unobtrusive job like this of Brayburn's was much more the mark. Once the London registration was whipped off again, a big, dark, elderly car could be any one of hundreds.

'I know one thing, if it hadn't been for Buster here, with his toggle buttons, we couldn't have proved this was the right car without digging up the number plates – unless the other two or the girl choose to talk. I don't imagine they will. Organisations as big as this take care of their pensioners, as a matter of business, and besides, selling them out would be suicide. On the other hand, they're not likely to hold out anything that can shop the Professor for years, once they know he was leaving them to rot. Well, one centre of the organisation's wiped out anyhow, and one of their experts immobilised, and we've got the *Shelvedon Chronicle* back.

'Well, young man, we'd better see about that telephone extension that so conveniently wouldn't work. I bet it will for us. The sooner we get in touch with your folks, and send you safely home, the better.'

'I'm not tired, thank you very much,' said Ivo politely, if not very truthfully. But he climbed contentedly into the back seat of Tom's car when he was told, and curled up in the corner with his marvellous memories.

'I tell you what,' said the sergeant in a low voice, looking warily after him, 'that one may have pulled off all his buttons in a good cause, but take it from me, I never saw a kid who more certainly had his buttons *on*!'

Ivo fell asleep on the drive home, and only opened his eyes again when Tom lifted him gently out of the car and carried him into the cottage, where Mrs Freeman was waiting to fuss over him and put him to bed. 'I shall have something for Christmas instead of the beautiful book, shan't I? Something just as nice? But I wanted that!' And his mouth drooped for a moment.

'You'll have two somethings. And you shall choose any book you like, or anything else within reason.'

'Can I have a gun?' asked Ivo, waking up fully for a moment.

'No, you certainly can't!' said Tom very firmly indeed. 'You've cost me ten years of my life tonight with the one you borrowed. Suppose Miss Boyne had been hurt badly when the car crashed?' But remembering what might well have happened to Sara if the car had not crashed, he was not disposed to dwell upon that.

'All right,' conceded Ivo, recognising one of those blank walls in which the young cannot yet hope to find a convenient door, 'I'll have a book, if I can pick my own.'

They were silent as they drove on towards Sara's home. Too much had happened too suddenly. They sat side by side in the car, and couldn't think of the right things to say.

'*Boys Gigantic Adventure Annual*, indeed!' said Tom abruptly. 'I told you he didn't need any stimulants, he's an adventurer born. Took to it like a duck to water.'

'Yes,' said Sara in a low voice. 'I was wrong about a lot of things, wasn't I?'

'I'm sorry!' Tom said hastily, 'I didn't mean to say *I told you so* – really I didn't.' And he added hesitantly: 'Sara, I *am* sorry! I never thought Roger could be crooked. They think he must have been the one who provided all the necessary information about the burglar alarms, you know – he's on the museum committee. And the burglar got his message out by asking for a local solicitor, and then choosing him, of course. That's why he came rushing to the castle as soon as he got away from the police station. But you were earlier still, and he never had a chance to pick up the loot.'

'You know what I thought, don't you?' said Sara, turning

her brown, honest eyes upon him and blushing to the roots of her hair. 'I thought he'd followed me because he – liked me. I was nearly as wild with you for butting in as he was. And all the time he was only exasperated with both of us for getting in the way.'

'We did it jolly effectively, anyhow,' said Tom, scarlet in his turn. He coasted to a stop outside Sara's front door, and the quiet, snowy darkness of the street folded round their mutual embarrassment. 'Sara,' said Tom huskily, '*He* may not have been following you because he – liked you – but *I* was! I've been doing it for months!'

By that time she was in his arms, without any clear idea of how she had got there, without any clear idea of anything, except that the castle clock had just begun to strike midnight, and all the bells of Shelvedon had burst into a triumphant and entirely appropriate peal of exultation. In the clamour his words were lost. He gave up the attempt to talk, and kissed her instead.

Some time later, between the loud reverberations of the bells, she heard him mumble happily, 'Bless that kid! We'll adopt him for this!' Not that he was expressing a serious intention at that stage, of course. Still, Mrs Freeman was old, and Ivo was very young, and it was at least the germ of an idea. She put it away somewhere at the back of her mind, to be pondered over later.

'Happy Christmas, dear Tom! Happy Christmas!' she murmured, and settled her cheek more comfortably upon his shoulder.

Rumpole and the
Health Farm Murder

John Mortimer

Christmas comes but once a year, and it is usually preceded by Christmas cards kept in the prison officers' cubby holes around the Old Bailey and 'Away In A Manger' bleating through Boots, where I purchase for my wife Hilda (known to me as She Who Must Be Obeyed) her ritual bottle of lavender water, which she puts away for later use, while she gives me another tie which I add to my collection of seldom-worn articles of clothing. After the turkey, plum pudding and a bottle or two of Pommeroy's Château Thames Embankment I struggle to keep my eyes open during the Queen's Speech.

Nothing like this happened over the Christmas I am about to describe.

Hilda broke the news to me halfway through December.

'I have booked us in for four days over Christmas, Rumpole, at Minchingham Hall.'

What, I wondered, was she talking about? Did She Who Must have relatives at this impressive-sounding address?

I said, 'I thought we'd spend this Christmas at home, as usual.'

'Don't be ridiculous, Rumpole. Don't you ever think about your health?'

'Not really. I seem to function quite satisfactorily.'

'You really think so?'

'Certainly. I can get up on my hind legs in court when the occasion demands. I can stand and cross-examine, or make a speech lasting an hour or two. I've never been too ill to do a good murder trial. Of course, I keep myself fortified by a wedge of veal and ham pie and a glass or two of Pommeroy's Very Ordinary during the lunchtime adjournment.'

'Slices of pie and red wine, Rumpole. How do you think that makes you feel?'

'Completely satisfied. Until teatime, of course.'

'Teatime?'

'I might slip into the Tastee-Bite on Fleet Street for a cup of tea and a slice of Dundee cake.'

'All that does is make you fat, Rumpole.'

'You're telling me I'm fat?' The thought hadn't really occurred to me, but on the whole it was a fair enough description.

'You're on the way to becoming obese,' she added.

'Is that a more serious way of saying I'm fat?'

'It's a very serious way of saying it. Why, the buttons fly off your waistcoat like bullets. And I don't believe you could run to catch a bus.'

'Not necessary. I go by Tube to the Temple Station.'

'Let's face it, Rumpole, you're fat and you're going to do something about it. Minchingham Hall is the place for you,' she said, sounding more and more like an advert. 'So restful, you'll leave feeling marvellous. And now that you've finished the long fraud case ...'

'You mean,' I thought I was beginning to see the light, 'this Minchingham place is a hotel?'

'A sort of hotel, yes.'

Again I should have asked for further particulars, but it was time for the news so I merely said, 'Well, I suppose it means you won't have to cook at Christmas.'

'No, I certainly won't have to do that!' Here She Who Must gave a small laugh, that I can only describe as merciless, and added, 'Minchingham Hall is a health farm, Rumpole. They'll make sure there's less of you by the time you leave. I've still got a little of the money Auntie Dot left me in her will and I'm going to give you the best and the healthiest Christmas you've ever had.'

'But I don't need a healthy Christmas. I don't feel ill.'

'It's not only your health, Rumpole. I was reading about it in a magazine at the hairdresser's. Minchingham Hall specialises in spiritual healing. It can put you in touch with yourself.'

'But I've met myself already.'

'Your *true* self, Rumpole. That's who you might find in "the restful tranquillity of Minchingham Hall",' she quoted from the magazine.

I wondered about my true self. Had I ever met him? What would he turn out to be like? An ageing barrister who bored

235

on about his old cases? I hoped not – and if that were all he was, I'd rather not meet him. And as for going to the health farm, 'I'll think it over,' I told Hilda.

'Don't bother yourself, Rumpole,' she said. 'I've already thought.'

'Tell me quite honestly, Mizz Probert,' I said in the corridor in front of Number Six Court at the Old Bailey, 'would you call me fat?'

Mizz Liz, a young barrister and my pupil, was defending Colin Timson who, in a pub fight with a rival gang, the Molloys, was alleged to have broken a bottle and wounded Brian Molloy in the arm.

'No, I wouldn't call you that.'

'Wouldn't you?' I gave her a grateful smile.

'Not to your face, I wouldn't. I wouldn't be so rude,' Mizz Liz Probert replied.

'But behind my back?'

'Oh, I might say it then.'

'That I'm fat?'

'Well, yes.'

'But you've nothing against fat men?'

'Well, nothing much, I suppose. But I wouldn't want a fat boyfriend.'

'You know what Julius Caesar said?'

'I've no idea.'

'Let me have men about me that are fat; / Sleek-headed men and such as sleep o' nights.'

Mizz Probert looked slightly mystified, and as the prosecuting counsel, Soapy Sam Ballard QC, the Head of our

Chambers, approached, I went on paraphrasing Julius Caesar. 'Yond Ballard has a lean and hungry look; / He thinks too much: such men are dangerous.'

As Ballard came up I approached him. 'Look here, Ballard, I've been meaning to talk to you about the Timson case,' I said. 'We all know the bottle broke and Brian Molloy fell on to it by accident. If we plead guilty to affray will you drop the grievous bodily harm?'

'Certainly not.'

'But surely, Ballard, you could be generous. In the spirit of Christmas?'

'The spirit of Christmas has got nothing to do with your client fighting with a broken bottle.'

'Goodwill and mercy to all men except Colin Timson. Is that it?'

'I'm afraid it is.'

'You should go away somewhere to have your spiritual aura cleansed, Ballard. Spend Christmas somewhere like a health farm.'

The result of all this was that the young Timson went to prison and I went to the health farm.

On Christmas Eve we took a train to Norwich and then a taxi across flat and draughty countryside (the wind, I thought, blew directly from the Russian Steppes, unbroken by any intervening mountains).

Minchingham, when we got there, appeared to be a village scattered around a grey-walled building that reminded me, irresistibly, of Reading Gaol. This was Minchingham Hall, the scene of this year's upcoming Christmas jubilations.

The woman at the reception desk was all grey – grey hair, grey face and a grey cardigan pulled down over her knuckles to keep her hands warm,

She told us that Oriana was giving someone a 'treatment' and would be down soon to give us a formal welcome and to hug us.

'Did you say "hug"?' I couldn't believe my ears.

'Certainly, Mr Rumpole. People travel here from all over England to be hugged by Oriana Mandeville. She'll suffuse you with "good energy". It's all part of the healing process. Do take a seat and make yourselves comfortable.'

We made ourselves uncomfortable on a hard bench beside the cavernous fireplace and, in a probably far too loud whisper, I asked Hilda if she knew the time of the next train back to London.

'Please, Rumpole!' she whispered urgently. 'You promised to go through with this. You'll see how much good it's going to do you. I'm sure Oriana will be with us in a minute.'

Oriana was with us in about half an hour. A tall woman with a pale, beautiful face and a mass of curling dark hair, she was dressed in a scarlet shirt and trousers. This gave her a military appearance – like a female member of some revolutionary army. On her way towards us she glanced at our entry in the visitors' book on the desk and then swooped on us with her arms outstretched.

'The dear Rumbelows!' Her voice was high and enthusiastically shrill. 'Helena and Humphrey. Welcome to the companionship of Minchingham Hall! I can sense that you're both going to respond well to the treatments we have on offer. Let me hug you both. You first, Helena.'

'Actually, it's Hilda.' Her face was now forcibly buried in the scarlet shirt of the taller Oriana. Having released my wife her gaze now focused on me.

'And now you, Humphrey.'

'My first name's Horace,' I corrected her. 'You can call me Rumpole.'

'I'm sorry. We're so busy here that we sometimes miss the details. Why are you so stiff and tense, Horace?' Oriana threw her arms around me in a grip which caused me to stiffen in something like panic. For a moment my nose seemed to be in her hair, but then she threw back her head, looked me straight in the eye and said, 'Now we've got you here we're really going to teach you to relax, Horace.'

We unpacked in a bedroom suite as luxurious as that in any other country hotel. In due course, Oriana rang us to invite us on a tour of the other, less comfortable attractions of Minchingham Hall.

There were a number of changing rooms where the visitors, or patients, stripped down to their underpants or knickers and, equipped with regulation dressing gowns and slippers, set out for their massages or other treatments. Each of these rooms, so Oriana told us, was inhabited by a 'trained and experienced therapist' who did the pummelling.

The old building was centred around the Great Hall where, below the soaring arches, there was no sign of medieval revelry. There was a 'spa bath' – a sort of interior whirlpool – and many mechanical exercise machines. Soft music played perpetually and the lights changed from cold blue to warm purple. A helpful blonde girl in white trousers and a string of beads came up to us.

'This is Shelagh,' Oriana told us. 'She was a conventional nurse before she came over to us and she'll be giving you most of your treatments. Look after Mr and Mrs Rumbelow, Shelagh. Show them our steam room. I've got to greet some new arrivals.'

So Oriana went off, presumably to hug other customers, and Shelagh introduced us to a contraption that looked like a small moving walkway which you could stride down but which travelled in the opposite direction, and a bicycle that you could exhaust yourself on without getting anywhere.

These delights, Hilda told me, would while away the rest of my afternoon while she was going to opt for the relaxing massage and sunray therapy. I began to wonder, without much hope, if there were anywhere in Minchingham Hall where I could find something that would be thoroughly bad for me.

The steam room turned out to be a building – almost a small house – constructed in a corner of the Great Hall. Beside the door were various dials and switches which, Shelagh told us, regulated the steam inside the room.

'I'll give you a glimpse inside,' Shelagh said, and she swung the door open. We were immediately enveloped in a surge of heat which might have sprung from an equatorial jungle. Through the cloud we could see the back of a tall, perspiring man wearing nothing but a towel around his waist.

'Mr Airlie!' Shelagh called into the jungle. 'This is Mr and Mrs Rumpole. They'll be beginning their treatments tomorrow.'

'Mr Rumpole. Hi!' The man turned and lifted a hand.

'Join me in here tomorrow. You'll find it's heaven. Absolute heaven! Shut the door, Shelagh, it's getting draughty.'

Shelagh shut the door on the equatorial rainforest and returned us to a grey Norfolk afternoon. I went back to my room and read Wordsworth before dinner. There may have been a lot wrong with the English countryside he loved so much – there was no wireless, no telephone, no central heating and no reliable bus service. But at least at that time they had managed to live without health farms.

Before dinner all the guests were asked to assemble in the Great Hall for Oriana to give us a greeting. If I had met myself at Minchingham Hall I also met the other visitors. The majority of them were middle-aged and spreading, as middle-aged people do, but there were also some younger, more beautiful women – who seemed particularly excited by the strange environment – and a few younger men.

Oriana stood, looking, I thought, even more beautiful than ever as she addressed us. 'Welcome to you all on this Eve of Christmas and welcome especially to our new friends. When you leave you are going, I hope, to be more healthy than when you arrived. But there is something even more important than physical health. There is the purification of our selves so that we can look inward and find peace and tranquillity. Here at Minchingham we call that "bliss". Let us now enjoy a short period of meditation and then hug our neighbours.'

I meditated for what seemed an eternity on the strange surroundings, the state of my bank balance and whether there was a chance of a decent criminal defence brief in the New Year. My reverie was broken by Oriana's command to hug. The middle-aged, fairly thin, balding man next to me took me in his arms.

'Welcome to Minchingham, Rumpole. Graham Banks. You may remember I instructed you long ago in a dangerous-driving case.'

It was the first time in my life that I'd been hugged by a solicitor. As it was happening, Oriana started to hum and the whole company joined in, making a noise like a swarm of bees. There may have been some sort of signal, but I didn't see it, and we processed as one in what I hoped was the direction of the dining room. I was relieved to find that I was right. Perhaps things were looking up.

The dining room at Minchingham Hall was nowhere near the size of the Great Hall but it was still imposing. There was a minstrels' gallery where portraits hung of male and female members of the Minchingham family – who had inhabited the hall, it seemed, for generations before the place had been given over to the treatment industry.

Before the meal I was introduced to the present Lord Minchingham, a tall, softly spoken man in a tweed suit who might have been in his late fifties. His long nose, heavy eyelids and cynical expression were echoed in the portraits on the walk.

'All my ancestors – the past inhabitants of Minchingham Hall,' he explained and seemed to be dismissing them with a wave of his hand. Then he pointed to a bronze angel with its wings spread over a map of the world as it was known in the seventeenth century. 'This is a small item that might amuse you, Mr Rumpole. You see, my ancestors were great travellers and they used this to plan in which direction they would take their next journey,' and he showed me how the angel could be swivelled round over the map. 'At the moment I've got her pointing upwards as they may well be in heaven. At least, some of them.'

When we sat down to dinner Hilda and I found ourselves at a table with Graham Banks (the solicitor who had taken me in his arms earlier) and his wife. Banks told us that he was Oriana's solicitor and he was at pains to let me know that he now had little to do with the criminal law.

'Don't you find it very sordid, Rumpole?' he asked me.

'As sordid and sometimes as surprising as life itself,' I told him, but he didn't seem impressed.

Lord Minchingham also came to sit at our table, together with the corpulent man I had last seen sweating in the steam room, who gave us his name as Fred Airlie.

Dinner was hardly a gastronomic treat. The aperitif consisted of a strange, pale yellowish drink, known as 'yak's milk'. We were told it is very popular with the mountain tribes of Tibet. It may have tasted fine there, but it didn't, as they say of some of the finest wines, travel well. In fact it tasted so horrible that as I drank it I closed my eyes and dreamed of Pommeroy's Very Ordinary.

The main course, indeed the only course, was a small portion of steamed spinach and a little diced carrot, enough, perhaps, to satisfy a small rodent but quite inadequate for a human.

It was while I was trying to turn this dish, in my imagination, into a decent helping of steak and kidney pie with all the trimmings that I was hailed by a hearty voice from across the table.

'How are you getting on, Rumpole? Your first time here, I take it?' Fred Airlie asked me.

I wanted to say, 'The first and, I hope, the last,' but I restrained myself. 'I'm not quite sure I need treatments,' was what I said.

'The treatments are what we all come here for,' Airlie boomed at me. 'As I always say to Oriana, your treatments are our treats!'

'But fortunately I'm not ill.'

'What's that got to do with it?'

'Well, I mean, it's bad enough being treated when you're ill. But to be treated when you're not ill ...'

'It's fun, Rumpole. This place'll give you the greatest time in the world. Anyway, you look as though you could lose half a stone. I've lost almost that much.'

'Ah! Is that so?' I tried to feign interest.

'You've come at a fortuitous moment,' Airlie said. 'Oriana is going to give us a special Christmas dinner.'

'You mean turkey?'

'Turkey meat is quite low in calories,' Airlie assured me.

'And bread sauce? Sprouts? Roast potatoes?'

'I think she'd allow a sprout. So cheer up, Rumpole.'

'And Christmas pud?'

'She's found a special low-calorie one. She's very pleased about that.'

'Wine?' I sipped my glass of water hopefully.

'Of course not. You can't get low-calorie wine.'

'So the traditional Christmas cheer is, "Bah, humbug".'

'Excuse me?' Airlie looked puzzled.

'A touch of the Scrooge about the health farm manageress,

is there?' It was no doubt rude of me to say it, and I wouldn't, probably, have uttered such a sacrilegious thought in those sanctified precincts if Oriana had been near.

For a moment or two Airlie sat back in his chair, regarding me with something like horror, but another voice came to my support.

'Looking around at my ancestors on these walls,' Lord Minchingham murmured, as though he was talking to himself, 'it occurs to me that they won several wars, indulged in complicated love affairs and ruled distant territories without ever counting the calories they consumed.'

'But that was long ago,' Airlie protested.

'It was indeed. Very, very long ago.'

'You can't say Oriana lacks the Christmas spirit. She's decorated the dining room.'

There were indeed, both in the dining room and the Great Hall, odd streamers placed here and there and some sprigs of holly under some of the pictures. These signs had given me some hopes for a Christmas dinner, hopes that had been somewhat dashed by my talk with Airlie.

'In my great-grandfather's day,' Minchingham's voice was quiet but persistent, 'a whole ox was roasted on a spit in the Great Hall. The whole village was invited.'

'I think we've rather grown out of the spit-roasting period, haven't we?' Airlie was smiling tolerantly. 'And we take a more enlightened view of what we put in our mouths. Whatever you say about it, I think Oriana's done a wonderful job here. Quite honestly, I look on this place as my home. I haven't had much of a family life, not since I parted company with the third Mrs Airlie. This has become my home and Oriana and all her helpers are my family. So, Mr Rumpole, you're welcome to join us.' Airlie raised his glass and took a swig of yak's milk, which seemed to give him the same good cheer and feeling of being at one with world as I got from a bottle of Château Thames Embankment.

'And let me tell you this.' He leaned forward and lowered his voice to a conspiratorial whisper. 'When I go, all I've got will go to Oriana, so she can build the remedial wing she's so keen on. I've told her that.'

'That's very good of you.' Minchingham seemed genuinely impressed. 'My old father was very impressed with Oriana when he did the deal with her. But he wasn't as generous as you.'

'I'm not generous at all. It's just a fair reward for all the good this place has done me.' He sat back with an extremely satisfied smile.

I've always found people who talk about their wills in public deeply embarrassing, as though they were admitting to inappropriate love affairs or strange sexual behaviour. And then I thought of his lost half stone and decided it must have had enormous value to bring such a rich reward to the health farm.

Thomas Minchingham left us early. When he had gone, Airlie told us, 'Tom Minchingham rates Oriana as highly as we all do. And, as he told us, his father did before him.'

Whether it was hunger or being in a strange and, to me, curiously alien environment, I felt tired and went to bed early. Hilda opted for a discussion in the Great Hall on the 'art of repose', led by two young men who had become Buddhist monks. I had fallen asleep some hours before she got back and, as a consequence, I woke up early.

I lay awake for a while as a dim morning light seeped through the curtains. My need for food became imperative and I thought I might venture downstairs to see if breakfast was still a custom at Minchingham Hall.

When I turned on the lights the dining room had been cleared and was empty. I thought I could hear sounds from the kitchen but I was stopped by a single cry, a cry of panic or a call for help. I couldn't tell which. I only knew that it was coming from the Great Hall.

When I got there, I saw the nurse Shelagh, already dressed, standing by the door to the steam room. The door was open and hot steam was billowing around. Looking into the room I saw Fred Airlie lying face down; a pool of blood had formed under his forehead.

Shelagh came towards me out of the mist.

'Is he hurt badly?' I asked her.

'Is he hurt?' she repeated. 'I'm afraid he's dead. He couldn't get out, you see.'

'Why couldn't he? The door opens.'

Shelagh bent down and picked up a piece of wood, about a foot long; it could have been part of a sawn-off chair leg. As she held it out to me she said, 'Someone jammed the door handle with this on the outside. That's how I found it when I came down.'

She showed me how the wood had been jammed into the oval circle of the door handle. Fred Airlie had been effectively locked into a steam-filled tomb and left there to die.

'I think you'd better call someone, don't you?' I said to Shelagh. She agreed and went at once to the small closet that held the telephone. I waited for her to come back and, once she arrived, told her that I was going to my room and would make myself available if needed.

It was Christmas morning. The bells of the village church rang out the usual peals of celebration. The sun rose cheerfully, flecking the empty branches of the trees with an unusually golden light. In our bedroom Hilda and I exchanged presents. I received my tie and socks with appropriate gasps of surprise and delight and she greeted her lavender water in the same way. It was difficult to remember that, in the apparently peaceful health farm, a man had been done horribly to death while we were asleep.

'I don't know what it is about you, Rumpole,' She Who Must Be Obeyed told me, 'but you do seem to attract crime wherever you go. You often say you're waiting for some good murder case to come along.'

'Do I say that?' I felt ashamed.

'Very often.'

'I suppose that's different,' I tried to excuse myself. 'I get my work long after the event. Served up cold in a brief. There are names, photographs of people you've never met. It's all laid out for a legal argument. But we had dinner with Fred Airlie. He seemed so happy,' I remembered.

'Full of himself.' He had clearly failed to charm She Who Must Be Obeyed. 'When you go downstairs, Rumpole, just you try to keep out of it. We're on holiday, remember, and it's got absolutely nothing to do with you.'

When I got downstairs again there was a strange and unusual quietness about the Great Hall and the dining room. The steam-room door was closed and there was a note pinned to it that said it was out of order. A doctor had been sent for and had gone away after pronouncing Airlie dead. An ambulance had called and removed the body.

Oriana was going around her patients and visitors, doing her best to spread calm. As I sat down to breakfast (fruit, which I ate, and special low-calorie muesli, which I avoided) Graham Banks, the solicitor, came and sat down beside me. He seemed, I thought, curiously enlivened by the night's events. However, he began by accusing me of a personal interest.

'I suppose this is just up your street, isn't it, Rumpole?'

'Not really. I wouldn't want that to happen to anyone,' I told him.

Banks thought this over and poured himself a cup of herbal tea (the only beverage on offer). 'You know that they're saying someone jammed the door so Airlie couldn't escape?'

'Shelagh told me that.'

'They must have done it after midnight when everyone else was asleep.'

'I imagine so.'

'Airlie often couldn't sleep so he took a late-night steam bath. He told me that, so he must have told someone else. Who, I wonder?'

'Yes. I wonder too.'

'So someone must have been about, very early in the morning.'

'That would seem to follow.'

There was a pause then, while Banks seemed to think all this over. Then he said, 'Rumpole, if they find anyone they think is to blame for this ...'

'By "they" you mean the police?'

'They'll have to be informed, won't they?' Banks seemed to be filled with gloom at the prospect.

'Certainly they will. And as the company's solicitor, I think you're the man to do it,' I told him.

'If they suspect someone, will you defend them, whoever it is?'

'If I'm asked to, yes.'

'Even if they're guilty?'

'They won't be guilty until twelve honest citizens come back from the jury room and pronounce them so. In this country we're still hanging on to the presumption of innocence, if only by the skin of our teeth.'

There was a silence for a while as Banks got on with his breakfast. Then he asked me, 'Will I have to tell them what Airlie said about leaving his money to Oriana?'

'If you think it might be relevant.'

The solicitor thought this over quietly while he chewed his spoonful of low-calorie cereal. Then he said, 'The truth of the matter is that Minchingham Hall's been going through a bit of a bad patch. We've spent out on a lot of new equipment and the amount of business has been, well, all I can say is, disappointing. We're not really full up this Christmas. Of course, Oriana's a wonderful leader, but not enough people seem to really care about their health.'

'You mean they cling to their old habits, like indulging in turkey with bread sauce and a few glasses of wine?' I couldn't resist the jab.

He ignored me. 'The fact is, this organisation is in desperate need of money.'

I let this information hang in the air and we sat in silence for a minute or two, until Graham Banks said, 'I was hungry during the night.'

'I know exactly what you mean.' I began to feel a certain sympathy for the solicitor.

'My wife was fast asleep so I thought I'd go down to the kitchen and see if they'd left anything out. A slice of cheese or something. What are you smiling at?'

'Nothing much. It's just so strange that well-off citizens like you will pay good money to be reduced to the hardships of the poor.'

'I don't know about that. I only know I fancied a decent slice of cheese. I found some in the kitchen, and a bit of cake.'

'Did you really? Does that mean that the kitchen staff are allowed to become obese?'

'I only know that when I started back up the stairs I met Oriana coming down.' He was silent then, as if he was already afraid that he'd said too much.

'What sort of time was that?' I asked him.

'I suppose it was around one in the morning.'

'Had she been to bed?'

'I think so. She was in a dressing gown.'

'Did she say anything?'

'She said she'd heard some sort of a noise and was going down to see if everything was all right.'

'Did you help her look?'

'I'm afraid not. I went straight on up to bed. I suddenly felt tired.'

'It must have been the unexpected calories.'

'I suppose so.'

Banks fell silent again. I waited to see if there was going to be more. 'Is that it?' I asked.

'What?'

'Is that all you want to tell me?'

'Isn't it enough?' He looked up at me, I thought pleadingly. 'I need your advice, Rumpole. Should I tell the police all that? After all, I'm a friend of Oriana. I've known her and been her friend for years. I suppose I'll have to tell them?'

I thought that with friends like that Oriana hardly needed enemies. I knew that the solicitor wouldn't be able to keep his story to himself. So I told him to tell the police what he thought was relevant and see what they would make of it. I was afraid I knew what their answer would be.

Someone, I wasn't sure who at the time, had been in touch with the police and two officers were to come at two thirty to interview all the guests. Meanwhile two constables were sent to guard us. Hilda and I wanted to get out of what had now become a Hall of Doom and I asked for, and got, permission to walk down to the village. The young officer in charge seemed to be under the mistaken impression that barristers don't commit murder.

Minchingham village was only half a mile away but it seemed light years from the starvation, the mechanical exercises and the sudden deathtrap at the Hall. The windows of the cottages were filled with Christmas decorations and children were running out of doors to display their presents. We went into the Lamb and Flag and made our way past a Christmas tree, into the bar. There was something here that had been totally absent at Minchingham Hall – the smell of cooking.

Hilda seemed pleased to be bought a large gin and tonic. Knowing that the wine on offer might be even worse than Pommeroy's, I treated myself to a pint of stout.

'We don't have to be back there till two thirty,' I told her.

'I wish we never had to be back.'

I felt for She Who Must in her disappointment. The visit to Minchingham Hall, designed to produce a new slim and slender Rumpole, had ended in disaster. I saw one positive advantage to the situation.

'While we're here anyway,' I said, 'we might as well have lunch.'

'All right,' Hilda sighed in a resigned sort of way. 'If you don't *mind* being fat, Rumpole.'

'I suppose I could put up with it,' I hoped she realised I was facing the prospect heroically, 'for another few years. Now, looking at what's chalked up on the blackboard, I see that they're offering steak pie, but you might go for the pizza.'

It was while we were finishing our lunch that Thomas Minchingham came into the pub. He had some business with the landlord and then he came over to our table, clearly shaken by the turn of events.

'Terrible business,' he said. 'It seems that the police are going to take statements from us.'

'Quite right,' I told him. 'We're on our way back now.'

'You know, I never really took to Airlie, but poor fellow, what a ghastly way to die. Shelagh rang and told me the door was jammed from the outside.'

'That's right. Somebody did it.'

'I suppose it might be done quite easily. There's all that wood lying around in the workshop. Anyone could find a bit of old chair leg ... I say, would you mind if I joined you? It's all come as the most appalling shock.'

'Of course not.'

So His Lordship sat and consumed the large brandy he'd ordered. Then he asked, 'Have they any idea who did it?'

'Not yet. They haven't started to take statements. But when they find out who benefits from Airlie's will, they might have their suspicions.'

'You don't mean Oriana?' he asked.

'They may think that.'

'But Oriana? No! That's impossible.'

'Nothing's impossible,' I said. 'It seems she was up in the night. About the time Airlie took his late-night steaming. Her solicitor, Graham Banks, was very keen to point out all the evidence against her.'

Minchingham looked shocked, thought it over and said, 'But *you* don't believe it, do you, Mr Rumpole?'

'I don't really believe anything until twelve honest citizens come back from the jury room and tell me that it's true.' I gave him my usual answer.

The Metropolitan Police call their country comrades 'turnips', on the assumption that they are not very bright and so incapable of the occasional acts of corruption that are said to demonstrate the superior ingenuity of the 'townees'.

I suppose they might have called Detective Inspector Britwell a turnip. He was large and stolid with a trace of that country accent that had almost disappeared in the area around Minchingham. He took down statements slowly and methodically, licking his thumb as he turned the pages in his notebook. I imagined he came from a long line of Britwells who were more used to the plough and the axe than the notebook and pencil. His sidekick, Detective Sergeant Watkins, was altogether more lively, the product, I imagined, of a local sixth form college and perhaps a university. He would comment on his superior's interviews with small sighs and tolerant smiles and he occasionally contributed useful questions.

They set up their headquarters in the dining hall, far from the treatment area, and we waited outside for our turns.

Graham Banks was called first and I wondered if he would volunteer to be the principal accuser. When he came out he avoided Oriana, who was waiting with the rest of us, and went upstairs to join his wife.

Thomas Minchingham was called in briefly and I imagined that he was treated with considerable respect by the turnips. Then Shelagh went in to give the full account of her discovery of Airlie and the steam-room door.

While we were waiting Oriana came up to me. She seemed, in the circumstances, almost unnaturally calm, as though Airlie's murder was nothing but a minor hitch in the smooth running of Minchingham Hall. 'Mr Rumpole,' she began, 'I'm sorry I got your name wrong. Graham has told me you are a famous barrister. He says you are something of a legend around the courts of justice.'

'I'm glad to say that I have acquired that distinction,' I told her modestly, 'since the day, many years ago, when I won the Penge Bungalow murder case alone and without a leader.'

There was a moment's pause as she thought it over. I

looked at her, a tall, rather beautiful woman, dedicated to the healing life, who was, perhaps, a murderess.

'I'm entitled to have a lawyer present, when I'm answering their questions?'

'Certainly.'

'Can I ask you to be my lawyer, Mr Rumpole?'

'I would have to be instructed by a solicitor.'

'I've already spoken to Graham. He has no objections.'

'Very well, then. You're sure you don't want Graham to be present as well?'

'Would you, Mr Rumpole,' she gave a small, I thought rather bitter, smile, 'in all the circumstances?'

'Very well,' I agreed. 'But in any trial I might be a possible witness. After all, I did hear what Airlie said. I might have to ask the judge's permission.'

'Don't let's talk about any trial yet.' She put a slim hand on mine and her smile became sweeter. 'I would like to think you were on my side.'

I was called next into the dining room and the turnip in charge looked hard at me and said, without a smile, 'I suppose you'll be ready to defend whoever did this horrible crime, Mr Rumpole.'

'In any trial,' I told him, 'I try to see that justice is done.' I'm afraid I sounded rather pompous and my remark didn't go down too well with the Detective Inspector.

'You barristers are there to get a lot of murderers off. That's been our experience down here in what you'd call "the sticks".'

'We are there to make an adversarial system work,' I told him, 'and as for Minchingham, I certainly wouldn't call it "the sticks". A most delightful village, with a decent pub to its credit.'

When I had gone through what I remembered of the dinner-time conversation, the DI said they would see Oriana next.

'She has asked me to stay here with her,' I told the DI, 'as her legal representative.'

There was a silence as he looked at me, and he finally said, 'We thought as much.'

Oriana gave her statement clearly and well. The trouble was that it did little to diminish or contradict the evidence against her. Yes, the Minchingham Hall health farm was in financial difficulties. Yes, Airlie had told her he was leaving her all his money, and she didn't improve matters by adding that he had told her that his estate, after many years as a successful stockbroker, amounted to a considerable fortune. Yes, she got up at about one in the morning because she thought she heard a noise downstairs, but, no, she didn't find anything wrong or see anybody. She passed the steam room and didn't think it odd that it was in use as Airlie would often go into it when he couldn't sleep at night. No, she saw nothing jamming the door and she herself did nothing to prevent the door being opened from the inside.

At this point the Detective Sergeant produced the chair leg, which was now carefully wrapped in cellophane to preserve it as the prosecution's Exhibit A. The DI asked the question.

'This was found stuck through the handle of the door to the steam room. As you know, the door opens inwards so this chair leg would have jammed the door and Mr Airlie could not have got out. And the steam dial was pushed up as high as it would go. Did you do that?'

Oriana's answer was a simple, 'No.'

'Do you have any idea who did?'

'No idea at all.'

It was at this point that she was asked if she would agree to have her fingerprints taken. I was prepared to make an objection, but Oriana insisted that she was quite happy to do so. The deed was done. I told the officers that I had seen the chair leg for a moment when the nurse showed it to me, but I hadn't held it in my hand, so as not to leave my own prints on it.

At this DI Britwell made what I suppose he thought was a joke. 'That shows what a cunning criminal you'd make, Mr Rumpole,' he said, 'if you ever decided to go on to the wrong side of the law.'

The DI and the DS laughed at this and once more Oriana gave a faintly amused smile. The turnips told us that they planned to be back again at six p.m. and that until then the witnesses would be carefully guarded and would not be allowed to leave the Hall.

'And that includes you this time, Mr Rumpole,' Detective Inspector Britwell was pleased to tell me.

Oriana made a request. A school choir with their music master were coming to sing carols at four o'clock. Would they be allowed in? Rather to my surprise DI Britwell agreed, no doubt infected by the spirit of Christmas.

As I left the dining room I noticed that the little baroque angel had been swivelled round. She was no longer pointing vaguely upward, and her direction now was England, perhaps somewhere in the area of Minchingham Hall.

The spirit of Christmas seemed to descend on Minchingham more clearly during that afternoon than at any other time during our visit. The Great Hall was softly lit, the Christmas decorations appeared brighter, the objects of exercise were pushed into the shadows, the choir had filed in and the children's voices rose appealingly.

'Silent night,' they sang, 'holy night, / All is calm, all is bright, / Round yon Virgin Mother and Child / Holy Infant so tender and mild / Sleep in heavenly peace ...'

I sat next to Shelagh the nurse, who was recording the children's voices on a small machine. 'Just for the record,' she said. 'I like to keep a record of all that goes on in the hall.'

A wonderful improvement, I thought, on her last recorded event. And then, because the children were there, we were served Christmas tea, and a cake and sandwiches were produced. It was a golden moment when Minchingham Hall forgot the calories!

When it was nearly six o'clock Detective Inspector Britwell arrived. He asked me to bring Oriana into the dining hall and I went with her to hear the result of any further action he might have taken. It came, shortly and quickly.

'Oriana Mandeville,' he said. 'I am arresting you for the wilful murder of Frederick Alexander Airlie. Anything you say may be taken down and used in evidence at your trial.'

I awoke very early on Boxing Day, when only the palest light was seeping through a gap in the curtains. The silent night and holy night was over. It was time for people all over the country to clear up the wrapping paper, put away the presents, finish up the cold turkey and put out tips for the postman. Boxing Day is a time to face up to our responsibilities. My wife, in the other twin bed, lay sleeping peacefully.

Hilda's responsibilities didn't include the impossible defence of a client charged with murder when all the relevant evidence seemed to be dead against her.

I remembered Oriana's despairing, appealing look as Detective Inspector Britwell made her public arrest. 'You'll get me out of this, won't you?' was what the look was saying, and at that moment I felt I couldn't make any promises.

I bathed, shaved and dressed quietly. By the time I went downstairs it had become a subdued, dank morning, with black, leafless trees standing against a grey and unsympathetic sky.

There seemed to be no one about. It was as if all the guests, overawed by the tragedy that had taken place, were keeping to their rooms in order to avoid anything else that might occur.

I went into the echoing Great Hall, mounted a stationary bike and started pedalling on my journey to nowhere at all. I was trying to think of any possible way of helping Oriana at her trial. Would I have to listen to the prosecution witnesses and then plead guilty in the faint hope of getting the judge to give my client the least possible number of years before she might be a candidate for parole? Was that all either she or I could look forward to?

I had just decided that it was when I heard again, in that empty hall, the sound of the children's voices singing 'Once In Royal David's City'. I got off the bike and went to one of the treatment rooms. Nurse Shelagh was alone there, sitting on a bed and listening to her small tape recorder.

When she saw me she looked up and wiped the tears from her eyes with the knuckles of her hands. She said, 'Forgive me, Mr Rumpole. I'm being silly.' And she switched off the music.

'Not at all,' I told her. 'You've got plenty to cry about.'

'She told me you're a famous defender. You'll do all you can for her, won't you, Mr Rumpole?'

'All I can. But it might not be very much.'

'Oriana wouldn't hurt anyone. I'm sure of that.'

'She's a powerful woman. People like her are continually surprising.'

'But you will do your best, won't you?'

I looked at Shelagh, sadly unable to say much to cheer her up. 'Could you turn me into a slim, slender barrister in a couple of days?' I asked her.

'Probably not.'

'There, you see. We're both playing against impossible odds.' I picked up the small recording machine. 'Is this what you used to record the children?' It was about as thick as a cigarette packet but a few inches longer.

'Yes. Isn't it ridiculous? It's the dictaphone we use in the office. It's high time we got some decent equipment.'

'Don't worry,' I said, as I gave it back to her. 'Everything that can be done for Oriana will be done.'

The dining hall was almost empty at breakfast time, but I heard a call of 'Rumpole! Come and join us.' So I reluctantly went to sit down with Graham Banks, the solicitor, and his wife. I abolished all thoughts of bacon and eggs and tucked into a low-calorie papaya biscuit. I rejected the yak's milk on this occasion in favour of a pale and milkless tea.

'She wants you to represent her,' Banks began.

'That's what she told me.'

'So I'll be sending you a brief, Rumpole. But of course she's in a hopeless situation.'

I might have said, 'She wouldn't be in such a hopeless situation if you hadn't handed over quite so much evidence to help the police in their conviction of your client's guilt.' But I restrained myself and only said, 'You feel sure she's the one who did it?'

'Of course. She was due to inherit all Airlie's money. Who else had a motive?'

'I can't think of anyone at the moment.'

'If she's found guilty of murdering Airlie she won't be able to inherit the money anyway. That's the law, isn't it?'

'Certainly.'

'I'll have to tell her that. Then there'd be no hope of the health farm getting the money either. Tom Minchingham's father made the contract with her personally.'

'Then you've got a bundle of good news for her.' I dug into what was left of my papaya biscuit.

'There is another matter.' Banks looked stern. 'I'll also have to tell her that the prosecution will probably oppose bail because of the seriousness of the offence.'

'More good news,' I said, but this time the solicitor ignored me and continued to look determinedly grave and hopeless. At this point Mrs Banks announced that they were going straight back to London. 'This place is now too horrible to stay in for a moment longer.'

'Are you going back to London this morning, Rumpole?' Banks asked me.

'Not this morning. I might stay a little while longer. I might have a chat with some of the other people who were with us at the table with Airlie.'

'Whatever for?'

'Oh, they might have heard something helpful.'

'Can you imagine what?'

'Not at the moment.'

'Anyway,' Graham Banks gave me a look of the utmost severity, 'it's the solicitor's job to go around collecting the evidence. You won't find any other barrister doing it!'

'Oh, yes, I know.' I did my best to say this politely. 'But then I'm not any other barrister, am I?'

It turned out that She Who Must Be Obeyed was of one mind with Mrs Banks. 'I want to get out of here as quickly as possible,' she said. 'The whole Christmas has been a complete disaster. I shall never forget the way that horrible woman killed that poor man.'

'So you're giving up on health farms?'

'As soon as possible.'

'So I can keep on being fat?'

'You may be fat, Rumpole, but you're alive! At least that can be said for you.'

I asked Hilda for her recollection of the dinner-table conversation, which differed only slightly from my own memory and that of Banks and his wife. There was another, slim, young couple at our table, Jeremy and Anna, who were so engrossed in each other that they had little recall of what else had been going on. The only other person present was Tom Minchingham.

I obtained his number from Shelagh and I rang him. I told

him what I wanted and suggested we discuss it over a bottle of wine in the dining hall.

'Wine? Where do you think you're going to find that at the health farm?'

'I took the precaution of placing a bottle in my hand luggage. It's vintage Château Thames Embankment. I feel sure you'd like it.'

He told me that it would have to be in the afternoon, so I said that would suit me well.

After lunch was over and the table had been cleared I set out the bottle and two glasses. I also moved a large and well-covered potted plant nearer to where we were going to sit.

Then I made a brief call to Shelagh and received a satisfactory answer to the question I should have asked earlier. I felt a strange buzz of excitement at the almost too late understanding of a piece of the evidence in Oriana's case which should have been obvious to me. Then I uncorked the bottle and waited as calmly as I could for the arrival of the present Lord Minchingham.

He arrived, not more than twenty minutes late, in a politely smiling mood. 'I'm delighted to have a farewell drink with you, Rumpole,' he said. 'But I'm afraid I can't help you with this ghastly affair.'

'Yes,' I said. 'It's very ghastly.'

'It's terrible to think of such a beautiful woman facing trial for murder.'

'It's terrible to think of anyone facing trial for murder.'

'You know, something about Oriana has the distinct look of my ancestor Henrietta Ballantyne, as she was before she became Countess Minchingham. There she is, over the fireplace.'

I turned to see the portrait of a tall, beautiful woman dressed in grey silk, with a small spaniel at her feet. She had none of Oriana's features except for a look of undisputed authority.

'She married the fourth earl in the reign of James the Second. It was well known that she took lovers, and they all died in mysterious circumstances. One poisoned, another stabbed in the dark on his way home from a ball. Another drowned in a mill stream.'

'What was the evidence against her?'

'Everyone was sure she was guilty.'

'Perhaps her husband did it.'

'He was certainly capable of it. He is said to have strangled a stable lad with his bare hands because his favourite mare went lame. But the countess certainly planned the deaths of her lovers. You're not going to defend her as well, are you, Rumpole? It's a little late in the day to prove my dangerous ancestor innocent.'

'What happened to her?'

'She lived to the age of eighty. An extraordinary attainment in those days. Her last three years were spent as a nun.'

'As you say, a considerable attainment,' I agreed. 'Shall we drink to her memory?'

I filled our glasses with Château Thames Embankment. His Lordship drank and pulled a face. 'I say, this is a pretty poor vintage, isn't it?'

'Terrible,' I told him. 'There is some impoverished area of France, a vineyard perhaps, situated between the pissoir and the barren mountain slopes, where the Château Thames Embankment grape struggles for existence. Its advantages are that it is cheap and it can reconcile you to the troubles of life and even, in desperate times, make you moderately drunk. Can I give you a refill?'

In spite of his denigration of the vintage Lord Minchingham took another glass. 'Are you well known for taking on hopeless cases, Rumpole?' he asked me, when his glass was empty.

'Some people might say that of me.'

'And I should think they may be damned right. First of all you want to defend my ancestor, who's dead, and now I hear you've taken on the beautiful Oriana, who is clearly guilty.'

'You think that, do you?'

'Well, isn't it obvious?'

I poured myself another glass and changed the subject. 'You're devoted to this house, aren't you?'

'Well, it does mean a lot to me. It's the home of my ancestors. Their portraits are on the walls around us. If they could speak to us, God knows what they would say about the present occupants.'

'You don't think that the health farm should be here?'

'You want me to be honest, Rumpole?'

'Yes,' I said. 'I'd like you to be that.'

'This house has been in my family since Queen Elizabeth made one of her young courtiers the first Earl of Minchingham, probably because she rather fancied him. I don't say that my ancestors had any particular virtues, Rumpole, but they have been part of British history. We fought for the King in the Civil War. We led a regiment at Waterloo. We went out and ruled bits of the British Empire. One was a young brigadier killed on the Somme. I suppose most of them would have fancied Oriana, but not as a marriage proposition. But as for the rest of the people here, I don't think there's a chance that any one of them would have received an invitation to dinner.'

'Do you think they would have invited me to dinner?'

There was a pause and then he said, 'If you want me to be completely honest, Rumpole, no.'

'Didn't they need lawyers?'

'Oh, yes. They needed them in the way they needed game-keepers and carpenters and butlers and cooks. But they didn't invite them to dinner.'

I considered this and refilled our glasses. 'I suppose you think your old father did the wrong thing, then?'

'Of course he did. I suppose he became obsessed with Oriana.'

'Did you argue with him about it?'

'I was away in the army at the time. He sent me a letter, after the event. I just couldn't believe what he'd done.'

'How did he meet Oriana?'

'Oh, she had some sort of health club in London. A friend recommended it to him. I think she cured his arthritis. It couldn't have been very bad arthritis, could it?'

I couldn't help him about his father's arthritis, so I said nothing.

'I imagine he fell in love with her. So he gave her this – all our history.'

'But she must have been paying for it. In rent.'

'Peanuts. He must have been too besotted when he signed the contract.'

We had got to a stage in the conversation where I wanted

to light a small cigar. Lord Minchingham told me that I was breaking all the rules.

'I feel the heart has been taken out of the health farm,' I told him.

'Good for you. I hope it has.'

'I can understand how you must feel. Where do you live now?'

'My father also sold the Dower House. He did that years ago, when my grandmother died. I live in one of the cottages in the village. It's perfectly all right but it's not Minchingham Hall.'

'I can see what you mean.'

'Can you? Can you really, Rumpole?' He seemed grateful for my understanding. 'I'm afraid I haven't been much help to you.'

'Don't worry. You've been an enormous help.'

'We all heard what Airlie said at dinner. That he was leaving his fortune to Oriana.'

'Yes,' I agreed. 'We all heard that.'

'So I suppose that's why she did it.'

'That's the generally held opinion,' I told him. 'The only problem is, of course, that she didn't do it.'

'Is that what she's going to say in court?'

'Yes.'

'No one will believe her.'

'On the contrary. Everyone will believe she didn't do it.'

'Why?' Lord Minchingham laughed, a small, mirthless laugh, mocking me.

'Shelagh told me what she found. The steam turned up

from the outside and a chair leg stuck through the door handle to stop it opening from the inside.'

'So that's how Oriana did the murder.'

'Do you really think that if she'd been the murderer she'd have left the chair leg stuck in the handle? Do you think she'd have left the steam turned up? Oriana may have her faults but she's not stupid. If she'd done it she'd have removed the chair leg and turned down the steam. That would have made it look like an accident. The person who did it wanted it to look like murder.'

'Aren't you forgetting something?'

'What am I forgetting?'

'No one else would want to kill Airlie.'

'Oh, Airlie wasn't considered important by whoever did this. Airlie was just a tool, like the chair leg in the door handle and the steam switch on the outside. If you want to know which victim this murderer was after, it wasn't Airlie, it was Oriana.'

'Then who could it possibly be?'

'Someone who wanted Oriana to be arrested, and tried for murder. Someone who would be delighted if she got a life sentence. Someone who thought the health farm wouldn't exist without her. I haven't seen the contract she signed with your father. Did his lawyer put in some clause forbidding indecent or illegal conduct on the premises? In fact, Lord Minchingham, someone who desperately wanted his family home back.'

The effect of this was extraordinary. As he sat at the table in front of me Tom Minchingham was no longer a cheerful, half-amused aristocrat. His hand gripped his glass and his face was contorted with rage. He seemed to have turned, before my eyes, into his ancestor who had strangled a stable lad with his bare hands.

'She deserved it,' he said. 'She had it coming! She cheated my father and stole my house from me!'

'I knew it was you,' I told him, 'when we met in the pub. You talked about the chair leg in the door handle. When Shelagh rang you, she never said anything about a chair leg. She told me that. I suppose you've still got a key to the house. Anyway, you got in after everyone had gone to bed. Airlie told us at dinner about his late-night steam baths. You found him in there, enjoying the steam. Then you jammed the door and left him to die. Now Oriana's in an overnight police cell, I suppose you think your plan has been an uncommon success.'

In the silence that followed Tom Minchingham relaxed. The murderous ancestor disappeared, the smiling aristocrat returned. 'You can't prove any of it,' he said.

'Don't be so sure.'

'You can invent all the most ridiculous defences in the world, Mr Rumpole. I'm sure you're very good at that. But they won't save Oriana because you won't be able to prove anything. You're wasting my time and yours. I have to go now. I won't thank you for the indifferent claret and I don't suppose we will ever meet again.'

He left then. When he had gone I retrieved, from the foliage of the potted plant on the table, the small dictaphone I had borrowed from Shelagh. I felt as I always did when I sat down after a successful cross-examination.

Going home on the train, Hilda said, 'You look remark-ably pleased with yourself, Rumpole.'

'I am,' I said, 'a little cheered.'

'And yet you haven't lost an ounce.'

'I may not have lost an ounce but I've gained a defence brief. I think, in the case of the Queen versus Oriana, we might be able to defeat the dear old Queen.'

Credits

'The Queen's Square' by Dorothy L. Sayers, first published in *Hangman's Holiday*, Victor Gollancz, 1933, reprinted by permission of David Higham Associates

'Sister Bessie' by Cyril Hare, first collected in *Best Detective Stories*, 1959, permission of United Agents LLP on behalf of Sophia Jane Holroyd

'Paintbox Place' by Ruth Rendell from the collection *The Fever Tree and Other Stories* © Kingsmarkham Enterprises Ltd, 1982, is reprinted with permission from Penguin Random House

'The Pro and the Con' by Margery Allingham reprinted by permission of Peters Fraser & Dunlop (www.petersfraserdunlop.com) on behalf of Rights Limited

'The Man from Nowhere' by Edward D. Hoch originally appeared in *Famous Detective Stories*, June 1956; reprinted